Guardians Of The Round Table 7
Treasure Seeker

Guardians Of The Round Table 7 Treasure Seeker

Avril Sabine, Storm Petersen and Rhys Petersen

Cracked Acorn Productions
Australia

Guardians Of The Round Table 7: Treasure Seeker

Published by

Cracked Acorn Productions

PO Box 1365

Gympie, Queensland 4570

Australia

978-1-925941-27-2 (Kindle)

978-1-925941-28-9 (EPUB)

978-1-925941-29-6 (Print)

Genre: Young Adult Fantasy LitRPG

Copyright 2019 © Avril Sabine, Storm & Rhys Petersen

Cover design by Caitlyn Petersen

For anyone who has ever wondered what it'd be like to find a way to enter their favourite game.

There are so many things Mallory wants to do. Places she wants to explore and quests she'd love to complete. Yet there never seems to be enough time to get everything done. Will she need to set some things aside or can she figure out how to do all she wants as well as continue to level up and keep her and her party from losing their limited amount of revives?

*

This story was written by Australian authors using Australian spelling.

Foreword

Opening stats, Mallory's notebook entries recapping the previous adventures and other details can be found at:

www.avrilsabine.com/series/gotrt

The notebook entries will contain spoilers if you haven't read the book they refer to.

Name Pronunciation

Like many names there is more than one way to pronounce the following ones. These are the pronunciations used in this story.

Characters
Arnnik (arn-nick)
Dalan (dal-ann)
Danae (da-nay)
Darwil (darr-will)
Deneg (den-eg)
Drohgolrik (dro-gol-rick)
Emica (em-e-cah)
Esben (es-ben)
Galna (gall-nuh)
Goswin (goz-win)
Henell (hen-nel)

Hisoki (hiss-oh-key)

Jefnas (jeff-nass)

Jenet (jen-et)

Jofren Flintah (joff-wren flin-taa)

Jorgen (jaw-gen)

Kruth (kr-uth)

Kyla (kie-lah)

Loral (lor-ral)

Milos (me-los)

Ninette (nin-et)

Relmir (rel-mer)

Remora (reh-more-uh)

Rodina (row-dean-uh)

Sarnla (sarn-la)

Segdragorn (sege-dra-gone)

Sege (rhymes with hedge)

Sidree (sid-ree)

Places

Buckneth (buck-neth)

Coastview (coast-view)

Donris Island (don-riss)

Eridell (air-a-dell)

Estwater (est-water)

Fairiron (fair-iron)

Hethgar (heth-garr)

Inadon (in-ah-don)

Lilica (lil-e-cah)

Longmeadow (long-meadow)

Merrow (mare-row)

Ransted (ran-stead)

Shadhurst (shad-hurst)

Simria (sim-re-ah)

Surith (soo-rith)

Ursen (ur-sen)

Velkden (velk-den)

Wildebay (wild-bay)

General

Lobic (lob-ick)

Shulken (shull-ken)

Vilen (vil-len)

Chapter One

Mallory shifted on the stone bench seat, trying to get comfortable. It was impossible. Her gaze was once again drawn around the demonic bank and she frowned as it stopped on her brother who paced back and forth in front of her, Ryan, Callum and Danae. His demonic armour slid across his body as his hand closed around his sheathed dagger, encasing it in red leather rogue armour, receding as he let it go. Fang followed at his heels, her tail wagging.

Ryan chuckled, leaning in closer to Mallory. "Better hope it doesn't have a limited use with the amount of times he's done that since we arrived."

Callum, who was sitting on one of the chests of treasure they'd stacked along the wall near the seat, flatpack furniture behind it, laughed. He patted Smudge when the river otter raised his head above the edge of the makeshift sling to look around. "I don't think that'd stop him."

Danae smiled, her gaze remaining on Brodie, who once again activated the armour. "It's impossible to wear it out like that. Only constant use in battle and damage from attacks will eventually wear it out."

"Pity," Ryan said. "That is going to get old pretty quick." He nodded towards Brodie.

Callum glanced at Brodie before turning to Danae. "I thought rogues can't wear enchanted leather armour until they're level five. How can Brodie wear his?"

Danae laughed softly. "Demons like to try and figure out ways around rules. Brodie's armour is actually considered a mask, not armour, so it can even be worn by level one rogues."

While Callum asked Danae more questions, Mallory leaned against Ryan, smiling up at him when he slipped an arm around her shoulders. "We should have gone home when we arrived. It's been ages since we've been home." Not that she wanted to go home. She much preferred Inadon.

"There's no rush. It was good to have a break for a bit," Ryan said.

Mallory nodded in agreement. They'd reached Longmeadow two evenings ago, dropping Deneg, along with his chest and coffin, at the local tavern, promising to stick around until something could be done about selling the treasure from the demonic dungeon. At Emica's suggestion, they'd travelled a bit over half a kilometre north to set up camp on the banks of Lake Shadhurst. It was partway along the Shadhurst River, which eventually reached the ocean beside Shadhurst, the capital of Ruby Isle. Smudge had been happy with staying at the lake while they waited to hear what Deneg could organise for the sale of the treasure. And Mallory supposed it had been good to have an entire day to rest after all they'd done and to do some hunting and gather vegetables to replenish their food supplies. As well as sell vegetables to traders along with some of their other gear.

They'd sold all the herbs they'd gathered before reaching Longmeadow, most of the ones they'd gathered since arriving, the sixteen shrivelled hearts, two goblin boots, a chisel, six large spider fangs, fourteen large spider eyes, six large demonic dog canines, a clay pot, a cure disease potion, two of the canvas tents, two mage robes, two short bows, four slings, a wooden shield, a short sword and two wandering soul branches. Brodie had argued against selling the knotwood, wanting them to keep it for a golem. Although he had been tempted to sell it when told they'd make four thousand gold pieces for it. If it hadn't been for a group of traders going through Longmeadow on their way to the capital, they wouldn't have been able to sell all of their more expensive items, as the shops in Longmeadow couldn't have afforded everything.

They'd used some of the money to buy crafting ability books on alchemy and glassblowing, which had been read by those who'd needed to read them, and also bought the spells slow target, nightfall and spellbound shield from the mage they'd rescued from bandits. Brodie had complained the entire time that the mage was ripping them off. Mallory had put them in her belt pouch and hadn't yet learnt them. After their purchases, they'd made eight thousand and fifteen gold, one silver and six copper pieces, which they'd immediately put into their bank account rather than keep it on them when the rest of their party declined a share of the money, saying they'd be happy with a share of the treasure. Their bank account now contained nine thousand nine hundred and ninety-two gold, nine silver and six copper pieces and Brodie was already making plans as to what they'd spend it on when they reached the mainland.

They'd also managed to gain experience points between the location experience for Shadhurst Lake, fishing, cooking, gathering resources and trading. Much to Brodie's disappointment, nothing had attacked them and they'd spent a peaceful day at the lake. He'd been disappointed that he'd gained very few experience points. When Fang had discovered someone's hiding place in a hollow log by the lake, and it had ended up being a vial of experience points, he'd been thrilled. They'd all agreed it should be given to Fang since she'd found it and after drinking it she'd gained a hundred and seventy-nine experience points. Brodie had scoured the edge of the lake for hours, with Fang, in the hope he'd find another vial of experience points. He'd been sadly disappointed when they hadn't found another one.

Mallory, Emica and Esben had gained a CAS point while Brodie and Jorgen had been the only ones who hadn't gained one. The rest had gained two CAS points each. Even Smudge had gained a level due to how many experience points Callum had earned and now had an increased ability to forage or hunt for food. Mallory smiled at the memory of how annoyed her brother had been that Fang hadn't levelled up, even with the extra experience points. That was until Callum had pointed out that Fang now had more experience points than Smudge even though Smudge had been added to their party first.

Ninette, Emica, Jorgen and Esben waited for them back at the lake where they'd returned with the wagon and livestock once they'd dropped the treasure at the bank. Ninette had offered to make lunch with some of the fish they'd caught and vegetables they'd gathered, but Brodie had said they'd be back before then and he'd make lunch since she'd burnt breakfast. Callum had pointed out that they'd planned to ask around to see if anyone knew who Remora was before they returned to their camp, but Brodie had been adamant he was cooking.

Spike, the wandering soul travelling with them, had remained at their camp while they'd taken the treasure to the bank, asking them once again when they wished to be shown to the treasure on the path between places. Brodie had wanted to go after lunch, while Ryan had said they'd wait and see how long it took them to sell the treasure.

Mallory's gaze was again drawn to the treasure chests. She didn't regret freeing Jenet Grayrock from being a statue, but she did hope that didn't mean there wouldn't be enough money to rescue Deneg's brother from the dark forces. Or give everyone else a share since they were expecting one.

Ryan's arm momentarily tightened around Mallory. "Stop worrying."

"I can't help it. What if-" She broke off when six demons appeared behind the bank counter, all of them wearing sheathed swords at their sides. They ranged in colour from red to black, one of them the rusty colour of dried blood. She automatically rested her hand on her wand.

The demon behind the counter talked softly to the newcomers, glancing in Mallory's direction several times before nodding and returning to his spot at the counter. The six demons came around the counter, a section at the far end lifting to allow them to exit, and stopped in front of Mallory.

The rusty coloured one stepped forward. "No weapons are allowed in the vaults. You will need to leave them with the clerk. He'll ensure their safety while you're gone."

Brodie had stopped pacing the moment the demons had appeared. He came over to stand beside his sister. "Where are we going?"

"To the vault of the Inadon International Bank," the same demon said.

"How do we get there?" Brodie asked.

"We'll use a demonic portal gateway to reach it," Danae said.

Callum rose to his feet, his gaze fixed on the point

where the six demons had appeared. "We'll get to see how a gateway portal works?"

Danae nodded.

"Hell yeah." Brodie victory punched the air, his exclamation causing Fang to bark twice in excitement.

Mallory remained seated. "Is it safe?"

The demon inclined his head. "Our portal system is completely safe. None have ever come to harm."

"Not unless the portal at the other end is destroyed during the portalling process," one of the other demons said.

Chapter Two

Mallory's gaze was drawn to the spot where they'd appeared and she swallowed hard. "Does that happen often?"

The first demon glared at the one that had spoken before returning his attention to Mallory. "The Inadon International Bank has never experienced that problem. Our banks and vaults are the safest locations on Inadon."

"Can't guarantee the portal you'll return to will be safe though," the other demon spoke again. "Only that the bank vault portals will always remain standing." He shrugged when the first demon sent a look in his direction.

Ryan rose from the seat, drawing Mallory up with him. "Where do we leave our weapons?"

"On the counter." The demon glanced at the clerk as he spoke.

It didn't take them long to leave their weapons behind and the six demons brushed them aside when they would have approached the treasure, collecting it and heading behind the counter with it.

Reaching the other side of the counter, Mallory stared at the floor. There was a compass rose in the middle of a circle with tiles of demonic runes curving around the outside. "How does it work?"

"Each portal has an address on it." Danae pointed to the runes at the top of the circle and the word that the north of the compass rose pointed to. "And the address you wish to travel to is put there. It has to match the destination address exactly." She pointed to the rune tiles around the bottom of the circle. "The rune tiles are carved on demonic stone and the portal gate is enchanted by a demon with the power and knowledge to create portals."

"Everyone stand on the portal." The demon placed the chest he'd carried on the floor beside the portal. "We'll follow you through with the goods you wish to trade."

Mallory stepped onto the middle of the compass, her gaze on the space as it was filled with her party. It was just large enough for all of them to fit when they crowded in close. Before she could ask what they needed to do next, the world went black, all sound, smells and sensations vanishing, only herself and her party visible. The familiarity of it was reassuring. It was the same sensation of travelling between their world and Inadon.

The portal took them to a large room filled with people, a mixture of races with everyone seeming to be focused on their own tasks. Some of those who arrived were led from the large room by demons who escorted them down one of the numerous corridors leading away from the room. The walls were made of stone blocks, the floor of large, worn marble tiles and glass orbs hung from chains attached to the ceiling. They gave off enough light that even the far corners of the room were well-lit.

"Move off the portal," a demon snapped. "You're not the only one who needs to use it."

"Sorry." Mallory shifted across so she was no longer standing on the compass rose. The moment all of them had moved off it, the demons and their treasure began appearing, more arriving as the portal was cleared.

In amongst the arrival of their treasure, another group arrived. They were heavily armed and headed down one of the corridors. Brodie watched them leave. "Where is everyone going? And why do they get to have weapons and we don't?"

"To a vault," Danae said. "And they would have special permission and a high reputation."

"What vault?" Brodie asked.

Danae shrugged. "Theirs or someone else's."

Callum did a slow turn. "Each of these corridors leads to bank vaults?"

Danae nodded.

"How many are there?"

"Only those demons who run the demonic bank would know," Danae said.

"How big are the vaults?" Callum asked.

"From small locked boxes in a wall to spacious rooms," Danae said.

Ryan studied the portal. "How does anyone ever leave here when there are so many people using the portal to arrive?"

One of the demons, who carried their treasure, stepped forward. "There is more than one portal." He glanced at a corridor across from them. "If you will follow me."

Mallory hurried after the demon, her gaze drawn in every direction as she crossed the room. Some of the arrivals brought all types of companion animals with them, from the ordinary to the bizarre. It wasn't until they were walking down the corridor that Mallory realised there was a journal notification in the corner of her vision. Not surprised she'd missed it with all there'd been to see in the main room, she opened her journal and saw it was a notification that they'd gained experience points from visiting a rare location.

The demon in the lead stopped in front of a closed door and placed the chest he carried on the floor before knocking on the solid timber door. The door swung open and another demon ushered them into the spacious vault. Like the rest of the place, it was lit by glowing glass globes. They hung from the twelve foot high ceiling by decorative chains.

A man sat behind a desk on the right as they entered, making notes in a large leather-bound book. His head was bald, making his pointed ears more noticeable. He wore numerous rings on his fingers and had several jewelled armbands on both the lower and upper parts of his arms. His well-made tunic was sleeveless to show them off. The rest of the vault was separated from the entrance and the section on the right by bars and a locked door. Behind the bars, the area was filled with shelves and chests, every space looking like it was packed. Behind the man the wall was covered by bookcases, most of the shelves lined with books similar to the one the man wrote in. A nephilim shelved an armful of books, reaching the highest shelves with the help of his wings.

"It reminds me of a warehouse, not a bank vault," Callum said.

The man looked up from his desk, his lips curving into a friendly smile. "Welcome. I'm Goswin." His gaze went to Callum. "I had a shop many years ago in Fairiron, but by working out of my vault, I can be a treasure broker to all of Inadon rather than one single country. I still have the original shop as I'm only allowed to sell items of significance here. All common items must be sold elsewhere. The bank vault isn't a place for ordinary shops otherwise it'd be overrun by traders. They have given me special permission to sell spells as well since our main trade is in rare items."

Brodie gestured towards the area behind the bars. "That's treasures from all over Inadon?"

"Indeed, it is." Goswin rose to his feet, glancing at the treasure the demons had brought in and piled up in the empty area past the desk. "Now if you would like to look at one of my catalogues, ask my assistant while I calculate how much I can offer you for what you've brought in." He gestured towards the nephilim who'd shelved the last of the books he'd carried.

Brodie turned to the assistant who'd glided over to them when Goswin had gestured towards him. "What's in the catalogues?"

"That would depend on which ones you wished to peruse. Shall I fetch you the ones with rogue armour and weapons? Or perhaps general merchandise that contains many enchanted items useful to adventurers."

"Are there enchanted stilettos in the rogue weapon catalogue?" Brodie asked.

"Most certainly," the assistant said.

"Maybe we should wait until we find out how much we'll earn from the treasure," Mallory suggested.

The assistant turned to Mallory. "Surely it can't hurt to see what you might like to buy while you wait. How about I fetch you one of the spell catalogues? We have a fine selection including battle, healing and utility. What level mage are you?"

"She's level two," Brodie said. "You should get her the healing catalogue. And what are utility spells?"

"Ones such as light, shrink and mend," the assistant explained before glancing at all of them. "And what catalogues would the rest of you like to peruse? Ones suited to your classes? Or maybe ones suited to your crafting abilities."

Brodie glanced at Mallory. "What about surgical instruments?"

"Certainly. There is a fine selection of surgical

instruments, all with beneficial enchantments. We have a range of individual instruments as well as complete sets." The assistant made his way to the bookcase as he spoke, needing to fly up to the second highest shelf.

"Brodie-" Mallory started to protest, her brother interrupting her before she could say more than his name.

"You need them. You said so yourself."

Ryan chuckled. "I believe she said she could have healed another if she'd had them."

"There you go. See," Brodie said.

Chapter Three

Mallory slowly shook her head rather than waste her breath arguing with her brother. Just because she glanced through the catalogue, that didn't mean she had to buy anything from it. She smiled in thanks when the assistant held a leather-bound book out to her. Propping it on the edge of the desk, she looked through the pages, her mouth dropping open at some of the prices. None of the items in the catalogue were in their price range. Not even the individual instruments. She closed the book. "I think we need to do our shopping somewhere else."

Ryan looked up from the leather-bound book he held. "From the prices of these warrior weapons, I'd have to agree. Goswin wasn't kidding when he said he traded in rare items. Going by these prices, some of these items must be extremely rare."

Brodie took the book from Mallory, opening up

to a random page. "We need to find more demonic dungeons to raid."

"Did you wish to look at our catalogue of maps?" the assistant asked.

Before any of them could reply, Goswin opened another one of the chests and the cat jumped out, causing him to stumble out of the way. "There was a cat in the dungeon?"

Ryan put the book he held on the desk and scooped up the cat. "This is Kitty. I don't know how he managed to get in there."

Goswin strode over to Ryan, slipping on a pair of glasses before he examined the cat. "It's enchanted or under a spell." He glanced at his assistant before taking the cat from Ryan. "Bring me the amulet of animal speak."

The assistant waited for one of the demons guarding the barred door to unlock it before entering the area behind the bars and heading along the narrow space between two of the shelves running the length of the area.

Goswin placed Kitty on the desk, still examining him. "Let's see if there's anything of interest about you. None of the queries I've received have been about cats. There've been requests for various horses, drakes and even a unicorn. But none for cats."

"Someone wants a unicorn?" Mallory blurted out.

"Yes. Terribly difficult to find them, let alone catch them. The interested party has a menagerie and it's a creature he's wanted for it for well over a year now." Goswin took the amulet his assistant brought him, slipping it over his head. "Now what do you have to tell me, Kitty?"

Kitty miaowed, a long drawn out sound that seemed to be a lengthy complaint. When Goswin nodded and murmured in agreement, the cat miaowed again.

"What's he saying?" Brodie asked.

Goswin again nodded, his gaze on Kitty. "At least it's only an enchantment. Could have been worse. Might have been a curse instead."

Once again Kitty miaowed, once again sounding like he was complaining.

"Well, yes, I can help you. I have a potion that breaks spells and enchantments. It's a bargain at only six thousand five hundred gold pieces." Goswin shook his head when Kitty replied. "I'm afraid I can't go lower than that. You'll have to come up with that other fifteen hundred. Or maybe you have items worth trading."

Kitty miaowed.

"I'm sorry to hear that," Goswin said. "But you

must understand I have a business to run. I can't go giving extremely large discounts to everyone who comes along with a story of misfortune. I'd be bankrupt within the week."

"What is he saying?" Brodie asked again.

Mallory didn't blame him for being impatient. She wanted to know what was going on too.

Goswin turned to them. "Maybe you might be interested in helping your friend here." He nodded towards the cat. "It seems he was in the habit of using an amulet with a transformation enchantment on it so he could get in and out of areas unnoticed when visiting some of his patients who lived well outside his village. There was an attack and the amulet was broken while he was wearing it and he became stuck in this form."

"Who is he?" Callum asked. "When he's not a cat."

"The Velkden apothecary," Goswin said.

"But he's dead," Brodie blurted out.

Kitty faced Brodie and miaowed, his tone clearly filled with annoyance.

Goswin chuckled. "It would seem that when no one could find him after the attack, they assumed he was one of the early victims."

"Why didn't anyone know he regularly turned into

a cat?" Mallory asked. "Everyone thought this was his cat. Not that he turned into one."

Kitty looked away, turning his back on them.

"Bet it was so he could get up to no good," Brodie muttered.

"And you'd know all about that." Ryan grinned.

"I would not," Brodie protested.

"That isn't the issue here," Goswin said. "What is the problem, is that the Velkden apothecary has five thousand gold pieces in his bank account and no other goods he can use for trade since the attack on the village. He needs fifteen hundred gold pieces."

When a journal notification appeared in the corner of her vision, Mallory checked it, smiling when her brother complained about the quest. *Trapped In An Enchantment: The Velkden apothecary needs one thousand five hundred gold pieces so he can afford a potion to break the enchantment he is under.*

"We're not touching the money in our bank accounts," Brodie stated. "That's for moving to Merrow. And we don't even know how much we've earned from the treasure." He gestured towards the bookshelves. "With how much everything costs, it's probably not going to be anywhere near enough to get us decent gear."

"If you give me a few minutes, I can finish

calculating what I can offer you for the treasure." Goswin strode over to the chest Kitty had come out of, returning to the task the cat had interrupted him from.

"I wonder how he got in there." Callum looked from the chest to the cat, who met his gaze unblinkingly.

"I want to know why he came with us," Mallory said.

"Do you think we could use the amulet of animal speak?" Callum asked the assistant.

"I'm afraid not. It's a terribly valuable item," the assistant said. "I can look up the price for you if you're interested in purchasing it."

Mallory spoke before her brother, who'd opened his mouth, could. She was worried he might want it. "We're fine, thank you. There are other things we need before buying unnecessary things like that."

"It'd come in handy." Brodie turned to Callum. "Wouldn't you like to know what Smudge is thinking?"

Smudge looked over the edge of the makeshift sling at the sound of his name, chattering softly.

Callum patted the river otter on the head. "I would, but Mallory is right. There are other things we need first."

Goswin returned to them, glancing at a piece of paper he held that was covered in notes and columns of numbers. "After the costs of transporting all of you here are taken from it, I can round the offer up to nine thousand gold pieces. I'll even throw the cost of the apothecary's return portal in for free if you help pay for the potion for him."

"That's it?" Brodie exclaimed. "Only nine thousand?"

"We did keep things out of it. Like your mask." Mallory didn't mention Jenet Grayrock or Scorch since she certainly wasn't about to sell a person and they planned to keep the horse.

"Are you interested in selling the demonic armour?" Goswin asked Brodie. "I have several people interested in it."

Brodie took a step back from him. "Hell no."

Ryan grinned. "That comment seems appropriate considering who once owned it."

"After Deneg's money is taken out of it, we'll all earn five hundred gold pieces each," Callum said. "Or if we give Kitty fifteen hundred gold pieces, we'll each get three hundred and twelve gold and five silver pieces."

"That wouldn't be fair to everyone else," Mallory

said. "We can't spend their share. It'd have to come from ours only."

"You can't spend my share either," Brodie protested. "Five hundred gold isn't going to buy me any of the enchanted stilettos in the catalogue."

"There's still Spike's treasure," Ryan suggested.

Brodie sighed heavily. "Fifteen hundred is so much to lose."

Chapter Four

"We wouldn't be losing the money," Mallory told her brother. "We'd be helping the Velkden apothecary."

"Are you treasure seekers?" Goswin asked. "If this other treasure you're going after is of the same quality as this one, I'd be interested in making you an offer for it. Ask at any demonic bank for an appointment to see me. The price of your portal here can be taken from the value of the treasure."

"How much is a portal here?" Callum asked.

"As account holders, it's twenty gold pieces each individual, no matter which country you're in. There's a higher fee though if you choose to go to a different destination to the one you came from," Goswin said. "Companion animals and pets are included in your fee."

"You also can't go to a destination that doesn't have a demonic bank," Danae said.

"That could be useful," Ryan said.

"Where are you based?" Goswin asked.

"Uhm, I guess that'd be Buckneth on Ruby Isle," Mallory said.

Goswin turned to his assistant. "Bring me the book for Ruby Isle." When his assistant headed to the bookshelves, he turned back to Mallory. "There are requests for treasures that were last seen in your area. Maybe you would be interested in seeking them out. My brokerage fee is ten percent of the reward they're offering."

The assistant placed a leather-bound book on the desk, turning the pages until he came to one titled 'Ruby Isle.' He stepped back from the desk to allow Goswin to come closer.

Goswin flicked forward several pages. "Ah, yes. Here we go. False Hope Goblet. Last known location was Bard's Hollow near Buckneth. Offering five thousand gold pieces." He pointed to a drawing of a rather plain looking silver goblet, demonic runes engraved in a band around the middle.

"What does it do?" Callum asked.

"The contents are deadly poisonous once the liquid in it reaches halfway. No matter what liquid is added to it," Goswin said. "Are you interested in seeking it out?"

"Five thousand gold pieces," Brodie said.

"Four thousand five hundred after the fee is taken out," Callum said.

"Still sounds good to me," Brodie said.

Goswin took a black tile out of his desk drawer and placed it down. "If the leader of your party will place their hand on the tile, it will activate the quest for you."

Mallory did as Goswin said, surprised that she instantly gained a journal notification. *Treasure Seeker I: The treasure broker Goswin will pay four thousand and five hundred gold pieces for the False Hope Goblet. The last known location was Bard's Hollow near Buckneth.*

"Now that's what I call a quest," Brodie exclaimed. "We need more like that."

Goswin returned the black tile to his desk drawer. "If you successfully bring the goblet to me, there are other treasures in the area that you may wish to seek out for a generous reward."

Brodie turned the page, quickly turning to the next one when it was a request for Scorch. The next page was the Staff Of Imp's Fury. "There's that sunken staff we want to go after. This lot are offering a mix of potions, gold and other stuff."

"There are several people interested in that staff." Goswin turned several pages, all of them offers for the staff. "But this is the one you might be most interested in." He pointed to the offer on the page he stopped on. "Property near Merrow in Eridell."

"I keep telling you we should go after that staff," Brodie said.

"How about we focus on the goblet first," Mallory suggested.

Goswin closed the leather-bound book and handed it to his assistant before glancing at each of them. "Now, about the treasure. Are you happy with the price?"

Mallory glanced around the group. Everyone except Brodie nodded.

He sighed heavily. "I suppose so."

"Do you wish to pay for the Velkden apothecary's potion out of the price?"

Kitty miaowed.

Goswin inclined his head. "The fifteen hundred that he doesn't have."

"We should pay for it and also buy a shrink reversal spell since we don't know for certain the mage north of Longmeadow has one for sale," Ryan said.

Brodie argued for a minute, eventually agreeing with a glare at Kitty, who gave him a haughty look.

Goswin sat at his desk. "I'll write a note to the bank for the amount of six thousand and five hundred gold pieces to be drawn from my funds and paid to you." He wrote the note as he spoke, finishing it with a flourishing signature and a seal dipped in red wax. Folding the letter, he held it out to Mallory.

As soon as she took the letter, a journal notification appeared in the corner of Mallory's vision. Before she could check the notification, the assistant held out the shrink reversal spell to her and Goswin administered the potion to Kitty.

The Velkden apothecary tumbled off the edge of the desk as he became human, landing on his back to stare up at them from the floor.

Brodie grinned down at him. "You'd think after how long you were stuck as a cat you would have landed on your feet."

"It doesn't work like that." The Velkden apothecary scrambled to his feet. "You can't imagine what a relief it is to finally be human again. I tried to find someone who could speak to animals at every location you travelled to." He straightened his black tunic and dusted his hands against the sides of his brown trousers before brushing his dark hair out of his eyes. "I was starting to hope you'd get a message to bring Emica to the capital so I could find someone who could understand me."

Goswin held a black tile out to him. "If you will

place your hand on this and state that five thousand gold pieces are to be paid into my account, that will cover the rest of the cost of the potion."

The Velkden apothecary did as was directed, brushing his hands against the sides of his trousers as soon as he was done.

Goswin gestured towards the door. "If you have no further business, I have another client due any minute."

There was a knock on the door at his words and one of the demons swung it open. A warrior strode in, followed by two demons carrying chests. When he spotted Brodie, he grinned at him. "I was wondering when I was finally going to meet you in this world."

"I know you?" Brodie asked.

The man chuckled. "Not yet you don't. Now when you do meet me, make sure you tell me to stock up on toilet paper. It's confusing how it all works, but I'm ahead of you in the timeline back home, so believe me when I say there are a lot of problems ahead. Oh, and make sure you stock up on it for yourself too."

"What problems?" Brodie demanded.

The man shook his head. "Can't tell you that, mate. It's not allowed. But I reckon a little hint like that can't hurt. Especially with how bleak things are looking."

"How does Brodie meet you?" Callum asked. "Or where does he meet you?"

"I'm a guardian." The man stepped out of the doorway. "Anyway, don't let me keep you and good luck with everything coming. Trust me when I say you're going to want to stock up on timeless potions so you can spend large amounts of time here. You're going to want plenty of breaks from everything that's going on back home. Or at least back home in your future."

Mallory couldn't resist glancing over her shoulder as one of the demons led them from the vault. The guardian was talking to Goswin, not even looking up as they left. She moved closer to Ryan as they headed back to the room the portal had brought them to. "Do you think whatever is coming is bad?"

Ryan shrugged. "I guess we'll find out eventually." He grinned. "And in the meantime, we grab a few large packs of toilet paper just in case he's right and we'll need them."

"I suppose." Mallory again glanced over her shoulder, even though she knew it wasn't possible to see the guardian. His words had been unsettling. She didn't know if it was because of the whole time thing or his cryptic warning.

The demon led them to a different portal, the Velkden apothecary also returning to Longmeadow with them. As soon as they arrived, the clerk returned their weapons and Mallory handed over the letter from Goswin.

"What did you wish to do with the funds?" the clerk asked.

"You don't need to give me any of it," Danae said to Mallory. "Not after having to take so much out of it."

"Same here," Callum said.

"I'm all good too," Ryan said.

"I suppose you can keep mine too," Brodie muttered.

Ryan grinned. "That sounded like it hurt really badly."

"We still have Spike's treasure," Danae reassured Brodie.

Chapter Five

Mallory looked from the clerk to her party who stood around her, the Velkden apothecary having gone to stand in the doorway to look outside. "I should have asked everyone else what they wanted done with their money."

Callum took a piece of paper out of his belt pouch. "I asked them. They each want the money put into their bank accounts and gave me the details I'd need for it to be deposited correctly."

"Three hundred and seventy-five gold pieces to each of them and five thousand to Deneg," Ryan said. "We'll split Spike's treasure between all of us once we find it and sell it since we had to use so much of this treasure to help the apothecary."

"I guess we at least got some XP out of it," Brodie said. "But it probably would have been cheaper to buy vials of XP."

Callum smiled. "One thousand one hundred and fifty gold pieces cheaper."

"We could have got a tonne of XP with that money," Brodie muttered.

At the reminder of the completed quest, Mallory checked her notification, surprised to find there were three completed quests.

Brother Enslaved: You helped Deneg earn five thousand gold pieces. You also earned five experience points each.

Treasure Hunt: You escorted Deneg to the nearest village and sold the treasure gained from the dungeon, earning nine thousand gold pieces for Deneg and your party. You also earned fifteen experience points each.

Trapped In An Enchantment: You paid Goswin the treasure broker the one thousand five hundred gold pieces for the potion to break the Velkden apothecary's enchantment. You also earned ten experience points each.

While the clerk dealt with the money, Mallory turned to Ryan. "We need to find out who Remora is before we go back to the camp."

"That'll make lunch really late if we do that," Brodie protested. "As it is, it'll be after midday by the time it's cooked."

"You should have let Ninette cook it then," Ryan said.

"Lord Dalan has a daughter called Remora," the clerk said.

Mallory turned towards him. "Does Lord Dalan live here in Longmeadow?"

"On the outskirts," the clerk said. "Along the road that heads north east towards Eastvale. About ten minutes. What sort of business do you have with his daughter?"

Not sure what the clerk might tell Remora's father, Mallory decided it was best to keep the actual details to herself. "We believe we found something she lost."

"Then I suggest going to the back door. Lord Dalan wouldn't appreciate you coming to the front door," the clerk said. "Only friends and family are welcome to use the front door."

"Thank you," Mallory said.

The clerk nodded. "All the funds have been banked. Is there anything else I can assist you with?"

Mallory shook her head, following her party outside after she'd thanked the clerk again. She turned when the Velkden apothecary called her name, waiting for him to speak.

"It would be just as easy for you to return to Buckneth through Eastvale as to return the way you've come and I have family there while there's nothing left for me in Velkden."

"They're without an apothecary," Mallory pointed out.

The apothecary shrugged. "I can't help them. Maybe one day I'll be able to return, but for now, I wish to be near my family."

"If we went that way, we could go around the north coast of Ruby Isle and I can call in and see my father and let him know what I'm doing," Danae suggested. "Then I wouldn't need to travel home again before going to Merrow. I could keep travelling with all of you."

"We'd get location XP from Eastvale," Brodie said.

"We'd have to talk it over with everyone else," Mallory said. "After we speak to Remora."

"And have lunch," Brodie added.

The apothecary nodded. "I'm afraid I wouldn't be able to pay you."

"That doesn't surprise me," Brodie muttered.

"I'd assumed that." Mallory hadn't expected him to be able to pay since they'd had to pay part of the money to Goswin for the potion. "It won't make a difference in our decision." She glanced at her brother. "At least not for most of us."

"Are we going to find Remora so we can get back to camp or you planning on making me wait all afternoon for lunch?" Brodie demanded.

"I was thinking of calling into the tavern to say goodbye to Deneg. I can meet you back at camp," Callum said. "I don't think he'd mind me waking him. Especially since I'll have the news that he has enough money to pay for his brother to be freed."

Mallory wanted to protest. She'd prefer Callum to stay well away from Deneg after the way he'd snuck away from them when they'd first met him. "You can't go on your own. A lone traveller would be a target for any bandits in the area."

"I can keep you company," Danae offered.

"So can I," Brodie hurriedly added.

After some discussion, it was decided that Mallory and Ryan would take Bug and ride out to Lord Dalan's home while the rest remained in town and returned to the camp with Callum. Which would give Brodie a chance to start lunch sooner rather than later.

It didn't take Mallory and Ryan long to reach Lord Dalan's home, the dwelling was the fanciest one they'd seen as yet with its high stone wall surrounding it and well-kept gardens. Remembering the clerk's suggestion, they went to the back door, which was answered by an older woman wearing an apron that she dried her hands on.

"Can I help you?" She looked them up and down.

"We have a message for Remora," Mallory said.

"It better not be from Milos. That young man has caused her enough problems already," the woman said.

"Can we speak to her?" Ryan asked. "We won't keep her long."

The woman sighed heavily. "Wait there. I'll see if she's available." She closed the door on them.

"What do we do if we can't see her?" Mallory's fingers brushed across her belt pouch that contained the letter and ring.

Ryan grinned. "Don't take no for an answer?"

Before Mallory could reply, the door swung open and a young woman stepped out, closing the door behind her. "Do you have news of Milos?" She kept her voice low.

Mallory handed over the letter and ring, explaining where they'd found them.

After checking the letter, Remora pressed it and the ring to her chest. "I wasn't sure he received my letter. Could you take me to him?"

"We never saw him," Mallory said. "Like I already explained–"

Remora interrupted her. "He has several revives. They're location based. He'll be in Ransted."

"We don't know if we're going that way," Mallory said.

"Please. I can pay you to escort me there. Thirty gold pieces," Remora offered.

Mallory checked the journal notification even though she was fairly certain it would be a quest. She was right. *Reunite Separated Lovers: Remora has offered thirty gold pieces to be escorted to Milos in Ransted.*

"We'll talk it over with the rest of our group and let you know this afternoon," Ryan said.

"I haven't more gold, but I can give you jewellery if that isn't enough," Remora offered.

"It's more than enough," Mallory said. "But we don't know if we're going that way."

"When will you know?" Remora persisted. "What time this afternoon?"

Ryan shrugged. "Depends on how long it takes us to get back to our camp and if everyone is there when we return."

"Can I go with you to ask them?" Remora asked.

Worried it would take them even longer to get everything organised and their next step planned, Mallory shook her head. "We will let you know as soon as our group decides."

Remora sighed, looking downwards. She frowned. "Why are there purple streaks on your boots?"

Ryan chuckled. "An unfortunate incident with some dye in the dark."

Remora's frown remained in place. "Dye? In the dark? Why would you be dyeing something in the dark?"

Not wanting to get into the long explanation of rescuing people from Cutthroat Harbour, Mallory again shook her head. "It doesn't matter." She took a step back from Remora. "We'll let you know as soon as possible."

"There's a good chance the answer will be yes," Ryan said. "If it is, would you be ready to go late this afternoon?"

"Oh, yes, absolutely," Remora said.

"Then we'll see you this afternoon to let you know what the answer is." Ryan took a step back so he was standing beside Mallory.

"Make sure you come to the back door," Remora said. "You'll be turned away if you come to the front one."

"We will," Mallory assured her.

Ryan mounted Bug first, holding out a hand to Mallory to help her mount behind him. "See you later this arve." He nodded towards Remora, urging Bug into a walk as soon as Mallory was mounted.

Chapter Six

Mallory waited until they were on their way to the camp before she spoke. "Do you think everyone else will agree to escort Remora to Ransted?"

"Callum won't mind, Ninette is happy with whatever we choose, Brodie will agree with Danae and it's on the way to where she needs to go," Ryan said. "So there's a pretty good chance we'll escort her to Milos. And the apothecary to Eastvale."

Mallory thought of all the quests they needed to complete. "We could probably get a few of our quests and other things done before we head towards a bank and hand in the goblet. That's if we manage to get it."

"You're thinking about the drake eggs and the staff," Ryan said.

"Yeah. Wouldn't it be amazing if we could exchange the staff for a house in Merrow? Then we wouldn't have to spend any of our money on buying a place."

Ryan chuckled. "That'd make Brodie happy."

Mallory couldn't help smiling at that comment. It certainly would make her brother happy. "Do you think we'll be able to get more quests from the treasure broker if we complete this one?"

"Can't see why not."

"Good. Quests like that, ones with high rewards, would be good. Especially with how much money everything costs."

"A few quests like that might also lead us to places where we can get decent gear. Look at what we ended up with from the demonic dungeon. A horse and rogue armour for Brodie," Ryan pointed out.

"That's true." Mallory scanned the area. The road they followed towards the lake was empty. No one travelled along it and no creatures seemed to be amongst the trees lining it. As useful as earning experience points was, she'd prefer their journey to remain uneventful so they could return to the camp and decide their next move.

When they reached the camp, it was to find Brodie cooking fish and complaining he needed more recipes so he could make better meals. He also wanted a compact cabin so he'd have a proper kitchen to work in. Ninette stood across the fire from him, offering to help him cook when he paused for breath and Fang sat beside him, her gaze focused on the food.

Callum was sitting by the lake fishing, Smudge frolicking in the water in front of him while the rest of their party were scattered around the camp. They all joined Brodie by the fire when Mallory and Ryan let them know they had things to talk about. The apothecary, who'd returned to camp with Callum, remained in front of one of the canvas tents that had been set up, reading a crafting ability book. Callum brought with him enough fish for their dinner, including enough for Smudge and Fang.

Ryan went over the details of Remora and Milos, also mentioning the apothecary wanted to be escorted to Eastvale and that Danae wished to visit her father in Simria and collect her gear before she travelled to Merrow.

"I wouldn't mind calling in and seeing my brothers," Ninette said. "Other than that, I don't mind which direction we take to get to Buckneth."

"We might have to send you in to Buckneth to let the hunter know we want the information on where to find the drake eggs since Rass has people there waiting for us," Callum said.

"The more port towns we have the chance to visit, the better," Jorgen said. "We need to learn where The Nelly went."

Callum took the map of Ruby Isle from his belt pouch. "We could visit Eastvale and Estwater before we reach Ransted and then head out to Coastview before going through Lilica to Simria. There's also Ursen, Wildebay and Surith we can go through on our way to Buckneth."

"We might be able to visit Kruth since his guard job takes him between Surith and Lilica," Brodie said.

Mallory turned to Emica. "What do you think?"

The kitsune shrugged, her ears currently fox ears rather than human ones. "I don't mind where we travel. It's not like I can go home yet." Emica faced Brodie. "Are there any messages from my father, goblin boy?"

Brodie glared at her, muttering under his breath as he checked the duplication paper. "Nothing." He put the paper away before checking the fish. "Lunch is ready if everyone wants to grab a plate."

Mallory rose to her feet when everyone else did. "So we're going north? And escorting the apothecary and Remora."

There were nods and murmurs of agreement as

everyone grabbed plates, Brodie calling out to the apothecary to grab a plate too if he wanted to be fed.

While she ate, Mallory checked her journal notification. It was a quest. *Journey Back Home: The Velkden apothecary wishes to be escorted to his family in Eastvale.* She supposed that at least they'd gain some experience points for helping him return to his family. Although she doubted even that would impress Brodie with how much they'd spent helping the apothecary.

As soon as lunch was over, they all pitched in to help pack the camp, Mallory working beside Callum. "Did you see Deneg?"

Callum nodded, folding up a canvas tent. "I let him know the money was in his account. He said he'd find someone who was travelling to Shadhurst and get a lift with them."

Mallory tried to think of something to say. "I'm sorry."

Callum smiled briefly. "At least he had a good reason to ditch me." He glanced towards Ryan. "I'd do anything to save my brother too."

Mallory nodded. She knew exactly what he meant. "Same." She grinned. "Not just my brother. But you and Ryan too."

The camp was packed and they were ready to head

to Lord Dalan's home at two, Ryan consulting the pocket watch when Brodie asked him what the time was.

Spike joined them by the wagon, having been wandering along the edge of the lake. "Treasure now?"

"We need to collect Remora," Mallory said.

"Treasure when?" Spike asked.

"Where is the treasure?" Brodie asked.

"On the path between places." Spike pointed out a direction with the branch that was where an arm would normally be for a human. "Many of your steps that way."

"It'd be easier to figure it out if you could tell us in time rather than steps," Callum said.

"Many time?" Spike sounded more like he asked a question than giving an answer.

Mallory sighed. "We'll get Remora first and then go after the treasure. I'm sure she'd rather come with us since she wanted to know as soon as possible if we could escort her."

"It looks like it's in the direction of Eastvale," Callum said. "Collecting Remora first would probably be the best plan."

Brodie swung onto Scorch's back. "Then let's get going. I want to find out what the treasure is." He turned to Mallory. "And you need to learn your new spells."

Mallory didn't bother replying to her brother's order, instead clambering in the back of the wagon to sit next to Ryan, who grinned at her, the apothecary on the other side of him. "I'll learn them when I'm ready," she told Ryan. It was more a case that there always seemed to be other things to do. But she should probably learn them. Before she could open her belt pouch, Ninette who sat across from them, spoke as the wagon started forward.

"Is anyone gathering resources on the way to collect Remora?"

Danae, who sat on the front seat of the wagon with Emica and Jorgen, glanced over her shoulder. "I doubt there'll be anything to gather. We've gathered most of what was near the lake and close to the village is likely to be just as empty from the villagers gathering things."

Esben, who sat between Ninette and Callum, said, "Whose turn is it when there are resources to be collected?"

Jorgen handed the reins to Danae and turned on the seat to face his cousin. "It won't be us. Not until everyone else catches up to you. Emica and Ninette are still level two. It should be them."

Emica shook her head. "Not me. You don't need to worry about levelling me up."

Brodie rode beside the wagon, level with the front seat, Fang keeping pace with him. "Why not?"

"Because I have two thousand XP at home that I haven't used," Emica said.

"Why wouldn't you have used it as soon as you got it?" Brodie demanded. "You could go up over a level with that amount of XP."

"It'll take her up to level four with how close she currently is to level three," Callum said.

"See," Brodie said. "Over a level."

Emica glared at Brodie. "Not that it's any of your business, goblin boy, but I don't like the person who gave the vials to me. She was trying to make a good impression with my father and thought giving them to me would help."

"So?" Brodie shook his head. "Who cares. You should have had them anyway. You'd have been able to use a longsword by now if you had."

Emica shrugged. "I'll probably have them when I go home. So you don't need to worry about levelling me up."

"We'll work on getting Ninette to level three then," Mallory said.

"Then we'll get all of us to level four?" Brodie asked.

Jorgen chuckled. "Sounds like it'll be awhile before we focus on levelling you up, Esben."

Chapter Seven

"Everyone should gain some XP," Mallory said. "In between focusing on whoever we're currently levelling up. We'll keep taking turns since one person can't do all the levelling without ending up exhausted." She certainly knew that from experience.

Ninette, Brodie and Esben all spoke at once. Ninette protested that they didn't need to level her up and Brodie and Esben both talked about getting the chance to level up more. By the time Mallory had finished reassuring Ninette that she should level up more, and shushed her brother when he said Ninette didn't need to level up if she didn't want to, they were approaching the gate of Lord Dalan's home. She glanced at the apothecary, who was reading another one of the crafting books, having thankfully kept out of the discussion.

Remora dashed out towards them, Danae drawing

the wagon to a stop at the sight of the young woman who kept glancing over her shoulder. "What did you decide? Can I travel with you? Oh, please say I can."

"We can escort you to Ransted for thirty gold," Brodie said.

"I hid my things behind the shrubs in the hope the answer would be yes. Well, I had the servants hide my things there." Remora gestured towards the neatly trimmed shrubs that lined the tall fence around the grounds of Lord Dalan's home. "I was worried my father would lock me in my room so I couldn't go with you."

"How old are you?" Mallory asked.

"Eighteen," Remora said.

Relief washed over Mallory. For a moment she'd been worried Remora was a lot younger than she'd thought.

"He sounds worse than our dad," Brodie muttered.

Jorgen jumped down off the wagon seat. "I'll collect your things for you."

"There are a couple of chests," Remora warned him.

Ryan hopped out of the wagon, Callum following him. "I'll give you a hand."

Mallory stared at the two large chests that were put in the back of the wagon. She managed to keep a sigh from escaping. She'd been enjoying not being so cramped now they no longer had the coffin and treasure chests in the wagon.

Callum helped Remora into the back of the wagon where she sat on one of her chests, there being very little other space to sit. "Thank you ever so much for this. There was no way I could have travelled all that distance on my own and Milos would be in the same situation. Desperately waiting for a group to travel with. Ransted is such a little place that they don't get many groups travelling through there."

"What if he travels here while you're travelling there?" Callum asked.

"We'd see him along the way," Remora said.

Spike, who was following behind the wagon, moved closer to it as they headed in the direction of Eastvale. "Treasure now?"

"Come up front so you can show us which way to go," Brodie called back, once again riding level with the wagon seat.

"Can we stay on the road all the way to where it is?" Danae asked. "Wagons do better on roads."

"We follow the path between places." Spike hurried ahead of them, his leaves rustling in the gentle breeze.

Esben clambered out of the back of the moving

wagon, glancing at Ninette as he did so. "Grab some hessian bags and I'll help you gather herbs and veggies to level up."

"I'll help you too." Emica hopped off the front seat of the wagon, following Ninette when she jumped down to the ground with two hessian bags.

Remora glanced around at those still in the wagon, her gaze coming to a rest on Mallory. "Your party is very different. I don't think I've ever heard of a more diverse group. Or heard of one that has a wandering soul. Or travellers. They usually keep to themselves."

Mallory smiled, thoughts of their many adventures filling her mind. "Every adventure has brought new friends."

Remora glanced around again. "You've had many adventures?"

Ryan grinned. "You could say that."

The Velkden apothecary looked up from the crafting ability book he was reading. "You can trust them to do right and escort you safely to Ransted. When I was a cat, they took me in and looked after me and helped pay for the potion I needed to return to my human form. They also helped others during the time I was with them."

"You plan to stay with them?" Remora asked.

The apothecary shook his head. "They're escorting

me to my family in Eastvale. I have a daughter there. I'll stay with my daughter, her husband and their two children until I'm back on my feet." He glanced at Brodie, who continued to ride level with the wagon seat. "My daughter is an alchemist."

"What level alchemist is she?" Callum asked.

While Callum and the apothecary talked about levels and abilities, Mallory took the shrink reversal spell out of her belt pouch. She read over the details. *Shrink reversal returns an object, living creature or sentient being, that has been shrunk, back to normal size.* She'd no sooner finished reading it than the paper shrank down in on itself and vanished. Checking her journal, she found that the spell took twenty-five mana and had a thirty second cooldown. She also could only do the spell on unenchanted objects and creatures up to level ten. Obviously it was a spell that would need to be levelled up if it was to be more useful. Or she'd need to look into a higher level version of it.

"About time," Brodie said. "I was beginning to think you'd never learn that spell. Now what about the other ones?"

As much as she hated the thought that her brother probably believed she was learning them because he'd told her to, Mallory learned the other three spells in case she needed them. Slow target, nightfall and spellbound shield. The first spell faded until the paper vanished, the second darkened then flaked away to nothing and the last one thinned until it had vanished. Before she could read over the details about the spells, Spike spoke.

"Need to go on small path between places." Spike gestured towards a narrow track off to their right.

Danae slowed. "Maybe we should walk from here in case there's nowhere to turn the wagon around when we're ready to come back to the main road."

"I can stay with the wagon," Jorgen offered.

"I'll stay with it too," the apothecary said.

"Will you need to walk far?" Remora asked.

Danae pulled over onto the grassy stretch beside the road, just before the track, barely enough room between the road and the trees for her to park. "I'll let Ninette, Esben and Emica know what we're doing."

"I'll go with you." Brodie swung down to the ground, walking beside Danae and leading Scorch, Fang running ahead of them.

"We need more horses for times like this." Callum looked from Bug and Augusta, who pulled the wagon, to the riding horse tied at the back of the wagon with their donkey, Bobbi. They still needed to name the riding horse. "We could probably unhitch Bug and Augusta, but then if we need to leave in a hurry, we'd be slowed down hitching them up again. Or if whoever stays with the wagon needs to move it, they wouldn't be able to."

"We can walk." Mallory studied the narrow track. "Surely it can't be too far."

Spike, who stood near Bug, facing the wagon, gestured towards the track. "Some paces that way, adventurer."

Mallory smiled at him. "It's okay. We'll find out how far soon enough."

Brodie and Danae returned to the wagon and Brodie tied Scorch up beside the riding horse, patting him on the neck when he snorted, steam rising from his nostrils. Brodie looked in the back of the wagon to where Mallory was. "They'll stay around the wagon and gather resources while we're gone."

Chapter Eight

Mallory jumped out of the wagon ahead of Callum, who had Smudge in his makeshift sling, and Ryan. She glanced around. "Where's Fang?"

"She's chasing rabbits," Brodie said. "She won't go far.

As if the mention of her name called her, Fang came out of the undergrowth, tongue hanging out of her open mouth and looking pleased with herself.

"Did you catch anything?" Brodie patted her on the head when she sat beside him, laughing when she yipped and licked his hand. "I guess not."

"Go now, adventurers?" Spike asked.

"Yeah, we'll go now," Brodie said.

"Lead the way," Ryan said.

Spike ambled along the narrow path.

Mallory followed him, Ryan at her side with Callum, Danae and Brodie following. Two could barely fit abreast on the track and at times they brushed against shrubs that pressed in close to the track. Just when Mallory was about to ask how much further, they came out into a clearing.

Brodie stepped around Mallory. "What happened here?"

"Long time," Spike said.

Mallory took several steps forward, her gaze on the scattered remains of a burnt out wagon, vines growing across most of it so that only bits and pieces were visible. "Did anyone survive?"

Danae hurried forward. "That's ash creeper. It grows really well in the ashes of campfires." She crouched beside the vine, lifting large oval leaves to peer under them.

"What are you looking for?" Callum asked.

"Seeds. Ash creeper seeds are used in potions." Danae picked a reddish-brown pod off the plant, holding it up. "When they're completely brown, they're no good. You have to pick them just before they fully ripen."

"What about the treasure?" Brodie asked. "Surely it isn't seeds."

"Deep under," Spike said. "Under the box of things and people."

Callum joined Danae, checking under the leaves. "Are they very rare?"

"A little." Danae found another seed pod.

"What is the box of things and people?" Brodie asked.

Mallory scanned the clearing. There was only one thing that could be considered a box. "I think he's talking about the wagon." She moved closer to Spike. "Where exactly? The wagon seems to be fairly spread around."

Spike moved forward, stopping near what had once been a wheel, only the outer metal rim and metal hub left. He sank his root into the ground. "Here, adventurer. Open here."

Brodie knelt on the ground, pushing away the wheel and vine that clung to it. "We should have bought a shovel while we were in Longmeadow."

Mallory knelt beside him, digging at the rich, loamy dirt. "It's fairly soft."

"We should buy a shovel in Eastvale in case we find more buried treasure." Brodie scooped up a handful of soil and tipped it to the side. He looked over his shoulder at Ryan, who stood at the edge of the clearing. "Are you going to help us?"

"Someone needs to stand on guard," Ryan said.

"Oh, yeah. I didn't think of that." Brodie scooped up more dirt.

Mallory sank her fingers into the dirt, the hole growing larger. She felt something hard against her fingertips. "I found something." She brushed the dirt out of the hole, pushing her brother's hands out of the way when he tried to take over. "Keep digging where you were. This might be nothing important." She uncovered rotted fabric. It tore as she tugged at it, the dirt laden threads easily giving way.

"That doesn't look like nothing to me." Brodie scooped dirt away from where Mallory worked. "I think I found something." He scooped the object out of the dirt, dusting it off. "It's a ring."

Mallory kept digging in the dirt. "There's more than a ring in here. I think this was once a bag of jewellery."

By the time they'd finished digging out the treasure, they had four gold necklaces, each with a jewel set in a fancy pendant hanging from them, two plain gold rings and three with gems set in them, six gold bracelets dotted with small gemstones along the wide bands at even intervals and a set of gold hoop earrings.

Danae and Callum joined them to stare at the dirty jewellery Brodie and Mallory had made an attempt at cleaning, Danae having gathered eight seed pods and Callum only seven. Ryan also came closer, spending more time glancing at the jewellery than scanning the area.

"I wonder what it's all worth." Brodie stared at the jewellery piled up in his hands. He started to shove it in his satchel.

"That one looks pretty." Danae pointed at a bracelet, the gemstones set in it having caught the sunlight.

Brodie stopped in mid-motion so Danae could examine the bracelet.

"They might be enchanted." Callum turned to Spike. "Do you know anything about the treasure?"

"They were here long time," Spike said.

Mallory couldn't resist smiling. Spike's judgement of time wasn't anything they could count on. "We should return to the wagon."

"Who are you and what are you doing here?"

They all spun to face a man who stood at the edge of a clearing, a short bow pointed at them. Mallory stepped in front of her brother, who continued to hold the pile of jewellery. "We were just leaving."

The man's gaze had focused on the jewellery until Mallory had stepped in the way. He met her gaze.

"I don't think so. This is my forest. Anything found here belongs to me. Hand over that jewellery."

Brodie shoved the jewellery into his satchel before stepping around Mallory and drawing his stiletto. The rogue armour covered his body. "There's only one of you."

The man grinned at him. "That's what you think." He glanced over his shoulder and seven people stepped forward, all armed with short bows.

"Hide now?" Spike asked. "They seek well."

"I'm afraid this isn't a game," Ryan said.

"Throw the jewellery onto the ground and the lot of you back away from it," the man ordered.

"I reckon we can take them," Brodie said. "A pity we don't have Scorch with us."

"Make a move to do anything other than throw the jewellery down and we will shoot you," the man warned.

"I don't think they're going to give it to us," one of his group said.

Mallory looked at each of the archers. They could fire before any of them had a chance to move. It was a pity there was such a long cooldown for nightfall. Casting it on only one archer wouldn't be enough. "Let me talk to my brother," she called out. "I really don't want any of us shot."

"You're not going to give them our treasure," Brodie protested. "Not after we spent so much money helping Kitty."

She angled herself so her brother could see her face, yet the archers wouldn't be able to. "What choice do we have?" She rested her hand on her wand as she winked at him and mouthed, 'make the most of this'. She cast vanish I on him, then quickly cast it on Danae as she began to move towards the edge of the clearing. "Run." She broke into a run as she said the word. She was tempted to use the essence crystals in her satchel to get enough mana to cast vanish I another two times. But she really didn't want to use them unless she had to. They were for an emergency and she wasn't sure if this counted yet.

Reaching the forest edge, she hid behind a tree, Callum joining her to peer around the tree trunk, his bow in hand. "If this takes too long, we won't reach Eastvale before dark." He took an arrow from his quiver. "Jorgen and Esben might not be able to find anyone to ask about The Nelly if it's too late in the day." He fired at one of the archers, taking him out. "He must have had less than twenty-eight health."

Mallory peered around the other side of the tree, casting fireballs at two of the archers, noticing that two of them were sprawled out on the ground. "I was worried eight might be too many for us."

Callum shot one of those Mallory had attacked, the second one dropping to the ground, impaled by Danae's arrow. "I was worried about that too. But they don't seem much worse than goblins." He shot another one.

Mallory attacked one of the archers that had been shot by two arrows. Considering he was still standing, she assumed it had been Ryan who'd attacked. The archer vanished and she hoped it was because of a revive and not an invisibility potion.

Callum lowered his bow. "I think that's all of them." He took a single step forward, scanning the area.

Chapter Nine

Mallory followed Callum into the clearing, keeping her wand ready. "I can see seven bodies. I guess only one of them had a revive."

Brodie joined them, grinning, Fang at his side. "You should have seen me move. I attacked nearly all of them at least once."

"You were meant to be taking them out, not working on gaining XP," Mallory said. "No wonder I don't usually turn you invisible."

"Aww, come on, Mal. It's not like they had much health. Callum and Danni were taking them out in a single shot, so there wasn't any problem. Besides, it gave me a CAS point."

Spike ambled out from amongst the trees. "Hide over now?"

Ryan grinned as he joined them. "Yeah, hide over now, Spike." He patted the wandering soul on the area that would have been a shoulder on a human. "I'm glad none of the archers shot you this time."

"Archer hurts." A ripple went through Spike's leaves. "Big hurt." The leaves rippled again.

Callum crouched by one of the bodies, searching it. "Anyone want to help me with this? If we take too long, we won't reach Eastvale before dark."

"I wonder if they have a trader there who'll be able to tell us if any of the jewellery is enchanted." Brodie strode to the closest body.

It didn't take the five of them long to search the bodies and Ryan, Callum and Danae were able to replace the arrows they'd used and gain fourteen spares which Callum put with the rest of the spares. They also found a short bow, steel longsword, wand, three silver and nine copper pieces, a silver bracelet and a pair of leather boots.

Ryan held up the longsword and wand. "Looks like we weren't the only ones they attacked. I found these with the coins. Probably loot from some poor unfortunates they outnumbered."

Mallory glanced around at the bodies. "Hopefully the one who respawned will have to find another way to make a living now he doesn't have his party to help him prey on others."

"People like that rarely mend their ways," Ryan said.

Mallory wanted to argue his statement, but she couldn't exactly deny the truth of it as much as she wished she could.

It was nearly a quarter past three when they arrived back at the wagon. Ninette, Emica and Esben hurried over to the wagon, Esben asking them if they'd found their treasure.

While Brodie and Esben talked about treasure and possible values of the jewellery Brodie showed Esben, Mallory turned to Ninette. "How did you go? Did you manage to gain any CAS points?"

"Two. And I'm not that far off a third CAS point, which will take me to level three. But I wasn't the only one who gained XP. Esben earned forty-four and Emica earned forty-five. She only needs another seventy-six to gain a CAS point. We were talking about how far we all were from levelling up as we gathered resources."

"Do you need help gathering more resources on the way to Eastvale?" Mallory asked.

Ninette nodded. "Then someone else can have a turn when I reach level three."

Mallory smiled, not bothering to argue. Ninette needed more experience than that if she continued to guard their wagon. She doubted Jorgen and Esben would remain with them forever. They had their own people to search for.

The rest of the journey to Eastvale was uneventful. Ninette found she had to go further off the road to find resources and Remora also helped her for a bit, wanting to contribute when everyone else took a turn helping, including the apothecary who Brodie kept calling Kitty. Which wasn't impressing the apothecary in the least with how his expression became more annoyed each time Brodie called him that.

Ninette put a hessian bag in the wagon, the last to clamber in as they entered Eastvale. She'd not only reached level three, but was two CAS points into the next level, still keeping her points for when she could use a longsword at warrior level four. She'd also put her class point into warrior and was now level three and when Callum had asked, she'd told them she'd put one point in wisdom and two each in strength and constitution, which brought her health up to forty-five, her stamina to seventy-five and her mana to twenty-five.

Mallory was determined to get Ninette's level to four so she could use a longsword like she was working towards. Surely that would help when she was left to guard the wagon.

Brodie, who rode beside the wagon on Scorch, glanced over his shoulder. "Bet you're glad to be home, Kitty."

The apothecary's lips thinned and he didn't answer immediately. "It's been quite a few months since I've seen my daughter and her family."

"It's a pity we weren't attacked by anything along the way. Some more XP would have been good," Brodie said.

"The Duke's soldiers patrol the south east corner of Ruby Isle and frequently come this far up the coast," Emica said. "So you get less bandits and aggressive creatures."

"Pity," Brodie said. "Hey, Kitty, do you think any of the shops will still be open in Eastvale so we can sell all the herbs and stuff? And the jewellery."

Once again, the apothecary's lips thinned. "You'll want to visit the jeweller. He'll tell you the value and if they have any enchantments for five copper pieces an item."

"Five copper pieces!" Brodie exclaimed.

"You might be able to talk him down with how many items you have to value." The apothecary shrugged. "If he's feeling generous. Some days he's not."

Spike ambled beside the wagon, looking in every direction. "Spike explore out there." He gestured towards the forest. "Will join you when you leave people place." He ambled back towards the forest before any of them had the chance to tell him goodbye.

Mallory glanced around the town they entered, surprised the streets were still so busy when it was almost five. Ahead of them the docks, at the end of the street, were just as busy, sailors unloading a ship at the end of a wharf while another was being loaded with crates.

Danae, who was again driving the wagon, glanced over her shoulder. "Where does your daughter live?"

While Jorgen and Esben clambered out of the wagon, saying they'd meet up out the front of the tavern on the waterfront, the apothecary joined Danae on the wagon seat to direct her through the streets.

"That's not fair," Brodie complained. "What if we wanted to do that quest?"

Frowning, Mallory checked her journal notification, having ignored it since she'd assumed it was location experience points from reaching

Eastvale. *The quest Grave Robbers has expired and is no longer available. It may have been completed by another party or individual.* "We probably wouldn't have been in that area for ages anyway."

"I suppose." Brodie still didn't look happy. "I wonder how many more quests we'll lose. We're taking too long to complete them."

Ryan grinned. "There'll be more. The treasure broker has entire books full of them."

Brodie's expression brightened. "He does. I wonder how many of them he'll let us do."

Before anyone could answer him, the apothecary pointed to a timber cottage two along the street from them, on the left. "My daughter lives there."

Danae pulled up in front of the cottage, a herb garden out the front and a metre high timber fence separating it from the street.

Remora shifted towards the back of the wagon. "I'll find the jewellers so I can sell my jewellery. Shall I meet you at the waterfront tavern too?"

Emica hopped out of the wagon to join Remora at the back of it. "I'll go with you. This region might be safer than some, but that doesn't mean there aren't any pickpockets about." She looked Remora up and down. "And with the way you're dressed and not carrying any weapons, you look like a prime target."

"I don't know how to use any weapons. My father never let me unlock a combat class," Remora said.

"Come on," Emica started along the road. "Let's get your jewellery sold and get you off the streets."

"I'll help you." Ninette turned to Mallory. "That's if you don't need me."

"It's okay. You can go with them," Mallory said.

Brodie watched the three of them leave. "I wonder how much jewellery Remora has. You don't think the jeweller will run out of money before we get there, do you?"

Callum chuckled. "We can sell it at another town. At least we'll know the value of it and they won't be able to undercut us."

Brodie's expression brightened. "Yeah. They won't be able to rip us off."

Chapter Ten

Mallory eyed the apothecary who hadn't moved and continued to stare at the cottage. "Did you want one of us to knock on the door for you?"

The apothecary shook his head. "It's hard to believe I made it here. There were so many times I thought I wouldn't."

Danae jumped down off the wagon, looking up at the apothecary. "I'll walk you to the door." She smiled at him.

Before any of them could move, a young woman came running out of the cottage to stop at the wagon and stare up at the apothecary. "I thought they must be mistaken. One of the children said you were out here. I couldn't believe it possible. They said you perished in the attack on Velkden."

The apothecary joined his daughter on the ground, wrapping his arms around her and resting his chin on the top of her head. "There were times I thought I might perish."

After a moment, the apothecary's daughter drew back to look up at him. "How did you manage to survive?"

"I'll tell you everything later." The apothecary glanced around at Mallory and her party, who were now standing beside the wagon. "But if it wasn't for these people, I wouldn't be here. They rescued me, fed me and spent their own money on breaking an enchantment that was on me. It seems wrong to only be able to thank them and not reward them after all they've done."

A man strode towards them along the street, stopping several metres from them when he caught sight of the apothecary. His lips curved into a smile and he continued towards them, clapping the apothecary on the back. "I can't believe you're here. We were told you died. Told by some of the survivors who came here rather than stay around Velkden."

The apothecary's daughter turned to the man. "We need to reward these people. They rescued my father." She glanced around the group. "How much did you spend on breaking my father's enchantment?"

"Fifteen hundred gold pieces," Brodie said.

The woman's mouth opened, a soft sound escaping.

Mallory hurriedly spoke. "It's okay. We don't expect you to repay the full amount. It wasn't like we could leave him stuck like that." She glanced at the doorway of the cottage where two young children peered outside. "We wouldn't want to run you short of money."

"There must be something we can give you in thanks," the man said.

"Are my old surgical instruments still here?" the apothecary asked. "Mallory is an apothecary and as yet hasn't any of her own."

The apothecary's daughter nodded. "They're in your chest of things you left behind when you moved to Velkden. Along with the old clothes you left and a handful of other things. But that hardly comes close to covering what we owe."

"Brodie likes to cook, Callum enjoys collecting books, Ryan looks out for everyone and Danae is an alchemist." The apothecary glanced around the group, his gaze resting on each person he mentioned.

"We have a spare frypan and some spices we can give Brodie. I could also write up some of the recipes we know," the apothecary's son-in-law suggested.

"I'm afraid we have no books to give Callum. The few we do have the children enjoy having read to them of an evening before they go to sleep."

The apothecary's daughter turned to her husband. "What about my compact alchemist station? I don't use it anymore. Not since we had the children and stopped travelling. Nor are we likely to do any travelling until they're a lot older."

"In that case, Brodie might as well have the lightweight grill too," the apothecary's son-in-law said.

The two of them turned to Mallory, the apothecary's daughter the one to speak. "Would you be happy with those items in thanks for all you've done for my father?"

"What is a compact alchemist's station?" Brodie asked.

"I'll fetch it for you." The apothecary's son-in-law strode inside before anyone had a chance to comment.

"I'm sure all of that will be fine," Mallory said. "It's more than we expected."

The son-in-law returned, carrying a timber box by the handle that was on the top of the latched lid. The box was twenty centimetres square and made from reddish brown timber. He set it on the ground and unlatched the box, opening it to take out what looked like a small closed cupboard that was made from the same timber. Placing the cupboard on the ground, well away from the wagon, he placed his hand on the front of it, stepping back when the cupboard rapidly grew in size until it was two metres square.

"That's cool. What's inside of it?" Brodie hurried forward to stop in front of it.

The apothecary's daughter opened the doors, which folded back on either side. "It's an alchemist's station. It has stability enchantments for both stabilising on uneven ground and so that potions can brew while it's shrunk and not be interrupted by the jolts of travelling. All the apparatuses on these shelves are fixed in place and the cupboards beneath the bench can store items that will shrink down when it's compact. Same with the cupboards on the walls. There are even racks in one of the cupboards to store vials so they aren't broken in transit."

"Hell yeah." Brodie opened one of the cupboards. "This is so cool."

The apothecary's daughter smiled at his enthusiasm. "You're happy with this then?"

"I'd love to have a compact alchemist's station to work from while we're travelling," Danae said. "Not that I know many potion recipes. Nor am I a high enough level to make potions yet."

"I can give you a recipe too," the apothecary's daughter offered. "Boneset. The ingredients can be used to make herbal tea, tinctures or potions."

"This seems like too much." Mallory stared at the 'U' shaped bench that went along the three sides of the alchemist's station, cupboards beneath it and a mixture of shelves and cupboards on the walls above it. "We can't take this."

"Why not?" Brodie demanded.

The apothecary's daughter smiled again. "You brought my father home. This seems like too little in comparison. I knew he had a location revive for here and no others so when he never appeared, we thought him truly dead. That someone had siphoned his revive from him."

Brodie turned to Mallory. "See. It isn't too much. We can keep it. And think of all the potions Danni can make while we're travelling around. Once she's a high enough level."

"I guess we-" Mallory started to say.

Danae interrupted Mallory, throwing her arms around her. "Thank you. This is more than I ever imagined."

"Hell yeah." Brodie victory punched the air.

"Surgical instruments and a compact alchemist's station."

Mallory returned Danae's hug. "You do know he's going to be trying to get you to make potions to sell when you reach that level."

Danae laughed softly as she let Mallory go. "I know, but I'll also have to learn some recipes too."

"You accept our offer?" the apothecary's daughter asked.

Chapter Eleven

Mallory nodded. "We accept your offer." She smiled as a journal notification appeared in the corner of her vision. "And we were more than happy to help your father." She glanced at her brother before returning her attention to the apothecary's daughter. "All of us were."

The apothecary's daughter smiled. "I'll write out four cooking recipes for you and the one for boneset." She interrupted her husband when he tried to say he could write out the cooking recipes. "You stay here and show them how to use the station. I won't be long." She hurried inside, her husband staying with them to show Danae how the compact alchemist's station worked, answering Brodie's many questions about it.

Mallory checked the journal notification, surprised to find there were two completed quests. Considering

Brodie hadn't said anything, she assumed he was too fascinated by the compact alchemist's station to have checked his notifications.

Journey Back Home: You escorted the Velkden apothecary to his family in Eastvale and were rewarded with surgical instruments, a compact alchemist's station, a frypan, spices, four cooking recipes, an alchemist recipe and a lightweight grill for your party. You also earned twenty experience points each.

Widow Needs Closure: The emissary you sent discovered the fate of the man who was lost at sea the previous year, returning his bones to his family on your behalf. Your emissary declined the reward of a gold wedding ring on your behalf. You also earned two experience points each.

"Since when do we have an emissary?" Callum asked.

Brodie looked up from the compact alchemist's station that was once again in its compact form. "What are you talking about?" He frowned. "We sent an emissary to do our quests? Can we do that? And who did we send?"

Before anyone could answer him, the apothecary's daughter came outside carrying two cloth bags, a grill and a frypan. They took the items from her and the apothecary gave them directions to the jeweller when Callum asked.

Danae read over the boneset recipe before putting it in her satchel. "As a strong herbal tea, it'll increase healing of bones by ten percent."

"That will be useful." Mallory couldn't resist glancing at her brother as she said the words.

He gave her a glare before he mounted Scorch, looking down at the apothecary. "See you, Kitty."

"Kitty?" the apothecary's daughter turned to her father with a frown.

He shook his head. "I'll tell you later."

"Try and land on your feet in future." Brodie turned Scorch in the direction they needed to go.

Callum smiled. "I think he did. When he chose to join us." He sat beside Danae on the wagon seat, waving as she urged Bug and Augusta forward.

Ryan chuckled when Brodie muttered about fifteen hundred gold pieces, waiting until they were partway down the street before he spoke. "At least we ended up with a compact alchemist's station. With the prices of the compact cabins, surely it'd have to be worth what we spent, or more."

Mallory decided it was best to stay out of the discussion. She let the others point out all the benefits. She cast magelight since the sun had set and the lanterns hanging on street corners and at the front of some of the houses didn't cast that much light.

"We also gained one rep for here," Callum said. "I'm assuming that was because we helped the apothecary."

"I guess," Brodie muttered. "And I have four new recipes too."

"What ones did she give you?" Danae asked.

"Apple pie which is a level eight recipe, fish fritters which is only level four, venison pie which is level ten and hunter's potluck stew which is also level ten." Brodie kept Scorch alongside the wagon so he could talk to Danae, slowing the horse when he tried to go ahead. "The potluck stew looks good. Looks like it only includes the meat, vegetables and herbs that we've been getting while travelling. Next time we have both bear and venison I'll be able to make it." Brodie paused a moment. "Maybe I should put more points in cooking rather than add them to barter."

"If you keep putting them into barter, you'll eventually be able to assess the value of general goods," Callum said.

"I've only got six CAS points." Brodie was silent a moment, frowning. "I just don't have enough. How can I level up both barter and cooking? What if I get a really good recipe that I'm too low a level to make?"

"You hoarding points?" Callum smiled. He laughed when Brodie glared at him.

"Not like you can talk," Brodie muttered. "You've still got twenty-nine points to use."

Danae pulled up in front of the jewellers. "We better get inside before it gets much later." She glanced at the star-studded sky. "It's probably close to time for him to close."

Brodie dismounted and tied Scorch to the rear of the wagon, entering the shop before anyone else had the chance, Fang at his heels.

Callum took out the sword the merfolk had given them. "I'm surprised he forgot about wanting this valued. Or at least wanting to know what enchantments are on it."

"I'm sure he would have remembered before we were finished here." Mallory headed inside, pausing just inside, surprised at the many pieces of jewellery on display in glass fronted timber cabinets.

Danae stepped around Mallory. "Is something wrong?"

Mallory slowly shook her head. "I didn't expect this." Her gaze travelled across all the jewellery again, barely sparing a glance for the man with the thinning hair who studied the jewellery Brodie had put on the counter. "There must be a small fortune in here."

Danae laughed softly. "There is. But Eastvale isn't that far from Shadhurst so there's plenty of travel between the two places. You'll find all the towns around Shadhurst have a lot more variety and far more wealth than the rest of the places on Ruby Isle. Even more than Ursen, Simria and Lilica all of which are fairly large towns themselves."

Mallory glanced around again. "I was expecting to find Remora, Emica and Ninette here. But I suppose we did take a while to drop the apothecary at his daughter's place."

Ryan and Callum entered, Smudge peering over the edge of the makeshift sling. When he caught sight of all the jewellery, he stretched out his paws, making soft chattering sounds.

Callum smiled down at Smudge, patting him on the head. "Unless there's something for a gold piece, I'm afraid you're out of luck."

The jeweller looked up at Callum's comment. "I have a fine selection of jewellery suited to companion animals that size. If you give me a moment, I'll be happy to show them to you. Including a few cheaper pieces that are close to your budget."

Smudge chattered excitedly, looking pleadingly up at Callum who smiled down at him with a nod.

"After we've sorted out the rest of what we need to

do." Callum laughed when Smudge threw himself at his chest. He wrapped an arm around the river otter, patting him with his other hand. "I'm not making any promises. Everything might be well out of my budget."

"What is it that you'd like to sort out first?" the jeweller asked.

Chapter Twelve

Mallory stepped forward, holding out the sword. "Can you tell us about this weapon? What the jewel is and if there are any enchantments on it?"

The jeweller took the weapon with a nod, placing it on the counter and studying it. "Hmm." He ran his hands over the blade, turning it over and examining the back of it. "It's a common mistake."

"What is?" Brodie asked.

"Don't feel bad. People often mistake channelling crystals with jewels. Especially the coloured crystals like this one."

"It's a sword for a mage?" Callum asked.

The jeweller nodded. "A warrior mage."

Mallory grinned. "Guess it's a sword for me then."

Ryan chuckled. "It looks that way."

"You need to be a level ten mage to use a channelling crystal," the jeweller said.

"Oh." Mallory stared at the weapon. She was a long way from being able to use it.

"There's nothing preventing you from using it as a longsword once you meet the requirements of being able to wield an enchanted steel longsword," the jeweller explained. "Level seven warrior."

Ryan slipped an arm around Mallory's waist. "You'll have a good weapon to use when you level up your warrior class and will be able to use it for your magic when you reach level ten mage."

"So it has enchantments," Brodie said.

The jeweller nodded. "First enchantment is bleed effect which upon hitting your target causes a loss of two hit points a second for a duration of five seconds. The second enchantment is sea warrior. It gives you a bonus five damage when the sword is wielded in the ocean."

"That makes sense since we got it off mermaids," Brodie said.

"Merfolk," Callum corrected him.

Brodie answered with a shrug, returning his attention to the jeweller. "What about all the jewellery I brought in? Do any of them have enchantments?"

"Did you want a full evaluation on the longsword? It's three copper pieces for the information I've given you or a total of five copper pieces if you want to learn the monetary value of the item too. If you choose to sell the item to me, the valuation fee is waived," the jeweller explained.

"Nah, no point spending money to find out what it's worth when we're not selling it." Brodie turned to Mallory. "Unless you wanted to sell it."

Mallory laughed at her brother's hopeful expression. "No. We're not selling it." She wasn't about to let her brother be the only one with decent gear.

Brodie turned back to the jeweller. "Does the jewellery have any enchantments? You know, like mana regen ones or something."

The jeweller slowly shook his head. "I'm afraid not. There isn't a single one here that does. But that's not to say they're not valuable. Some of these jewels are well sort after. Are you interested in a monetary value as well?"

"We're interested in selling them. They aren't any good to us without enchantments," Brodie said.

"Individual prices or a total price?" the jeweller asked.

"Total," Brodie said. "We plan to sell the lot of them."

The jeweller nodded, turning to Callum. "I'll show

you where the companion animal jewellery is that you might be interested in." He glanced at Brodie before returning his attention to Callum. "This could take a while."

Mallory smiled. The jeweller was probably right. Brodie did like to haggle. She joined Smudge and Callum at the display case the jeweller had directed him to, having told him there was nothing over five gold pieces in the case, while Brodie and the jeweller began the back and forth process of agreeing on a price.

Ryan joined them, chuckling as Smudge chattered excitedly over his many options. "He's like a kid in a lolly shop."

Danae joined them in time to hear his comment. "What's a lolly shop?"

"A shop that sells confectionery of all kinds," Ryan said.

"You have entire shops dedicated to selling only sweets?" Danae asked.

"Yeah. I-" Ryan broke off as Smudge's chatter became higher pitched and louder.

He clutched a small bracelet in his paws, tiny colourful jewels creating a bright band that glinted as it caught the lamplight.

"I guess he's found what he wants," Ryan said.

"Let's see if it fits." Callum unclipped the bracelet and wrapped it around Smudge's forelimb. "It's not too loose that it'll fall off and it has enough space that it shouldn't be too tight when he's fully grown."

Smudge turned his paw back and forth, causing the tiny jewels to sparkle, making soft contented sounds.

"I guess we should see how much it costs," Callum said.

"Even if it costs five gold pieces, we'll still buy it for him," Mallory said. "There's no way I could take it from him with how much he loves it."

Ryan chuckled. "I can't wait to hear what Brodie has to say about that."

"He better not say anything," Mallory stated. "Not after how Smudge let us sell his pearl when we needed money at the beginning of our time here."

They reached the counter as Brodie and the jeweller settled on a price, the cost of assessing the sword included in the figure of five thousand and four hundred gold pieces.

"If you prefer, instead of the gold, you can trade me for some of the jewellery I have that increases mana regen," the jeweller suggested.

Mallory wished she could say yes. "The money needs to be split between a group of us. I won't get much of that at all."

"Six hundred of it is yours," Callum said. "You can have most of my share other than what I need to pay for Smudge's bracelet."

"It won't hurt to find out the cost. You might be able to afford one with your share," Ryan said. "You can also have mine too."

"You can have my share of the treasure if you need it," Danae said. "You do use your magic for the benefit of all of us."

Brodie looked like he was in pain as he looked from Danae to Mallory. "I suppose you can have mine too. But you better make sure you heal us when we're getting low during a fight."

"Don't I always?" Mallory asked.

"Shall I bring out my selection of mana regen jewellery?" the jeweller asked.

"Before you do that, how much is this?" Callum gestured towards the bracelet Smudge wore. The river otter was still causing it to catch the light, making flashes of colour race across the floor in front of Fang who batted at them in fascination.

"Five gold pieces," the jeweller said.

Callum smiled fleetingly. "I suppose I shouldn't be surprised that he has expensive tastes. Not after he found the pearl."

"You'll take it then?" the jeweller asked.

Callum nodded. "It can come out of my share of the money." He turned to Mallory. "The rest can go to mana regen jewellery if you need it."

"How much is mana regen jewellery?" Mallory asked. "It doesn't need to be decorative, just useful."

"In that case, I have a few outdated pieces that no one seems interested in. Give me a moment to fetch them." The jeweller stepped out through a narrow door at the rear of the shop, returning within minutes with three black, velvet bags. He tipped the contents onto the counter. There were two gold rings, both with jewels set in them, the setting bulky and unbalanced, and a narrow silver bracelet. It had a single jewel set in it, the pattern engraved into the metal half worn away.

Chapter Thirteen

Mallory picked up one of the rings, checking to see if it fit. "How much mana do they regen?"

"Both rings regen five mana a minute while the bracelet regens ten a minute," the jeweller said.

Mallory wanted to say she'd take them. Twenty extra mana a minute would make a big difference. "What is the price?"

"Like I said, no one has been interested in them and they've been sitting around for almost a year," the jeweller said. "But I can't give them away, mind you. That's no way to run a business."

"They're taking up space," Brodie pointed out.

"Very little space," the jeweller said. "I can offer the three of them to you for five thousand gold pieces."

"That's way overpriced," Brodie protested. "They're barely worth three grand."

"Three!" the jeweller exclaimed. "You're trying to swindle me. I can come down to four eight."

"You call that coming down in price? How about three and a half?" Brodie offered.

Mallory smiled as they traded prices back and forth, throwing in the occasional mild insult. As the price Brodie offered increased, her smile faded and she began to worry about how they would pay for the jewellery. She started to speak when Brodie held out his hand to the jeweller.

"Done. Four thousand and one hundred gold pieces for the mana regen jewellery and Smudge's bracelet."

The jeweller shook Brodie's hand. "Agreed."

Mallory momentarily closed her eyes. What had Brodie been thinking? That was well over their budget.

"Even with the five of us putting in our share, we're still going to need to take eleven hundred gold pieces out of the group funds to pay the others their share of the treasure," Callum said.

"She's always running out of mana," Brodie said. "We need them."

Mallory slowly shook her head. Of course he would have to focus on it being for all of them. "I don't think we should–"

Brodie interrupted her. "We can pay for it out of the treasure money and take money out of the bank to pay the rest of our group."

Before Mallory could again attempt to speak, Ryan spoke, turning to her as he did. "This is something you need. Something that will make a big difference in what you'll be able to do."

"I suppose. But it's a lot of money." Mallory hated to think of how long it'd take them to earn that amount of money.

Ryan chuckled. "Not with how we've been earning it lately."

It took her a few seconds to realise he was replying to her comment of it being a lot of money. She'd thought for a moment that she'd spoken her thoughts aloud. "I guess." She thought of the book the treasure broker had. It had looked like there were quite a few treasures to be found on Ruby Isle. And they were going after the drake eggs soon. "I'm sure none of them will mind waiting until we visit the bank to get their share."

"Ninette probably won't even want her share when she hears what you spent it on," Brodie said.

"I'll give you a note for the bank telling them to pay the bearer one thousand and three hundred gold pieces." The jeweller took out a piece of thick parchment, writing out the details of the transaction and signing it before handing it to Brodie.

Brodie stared at the parchment. "It's like an old-fashioned cheque."

Ryan took the parchment from Brodie, handing it to Mallory. "We need to see if there's still a trader open and find out what time the bank closes."

"The bank will be open until quite late." The jeweller took out a gold pocket watch, checking the time on it. "But if you wish to buy anything from the trader, you'd best go now. She shuts in a quarter of an hour. She will stay open later though if she has paying customers in the shop."

Mallory took the jewellery that the jeweller slid towards her on the counter. "Thank you." She slipped on the rings and bracelet. They were going to make a big difference. With the help of all her jewellery, and her mage armour, her mana regen was now fifty-four a minute. Another six and she'd be able to have her entire mana pool regen every minute. But that would have to wait. They couldn't keep spending money or they'd have none left for when they travelled to Eridell.

"Where is the trader's shop?" Danae asked.

"Along the waterfront," the jeweller said before explaining the directions in more detail.

It didn't take them long to drive to the traders, leaving the wagon directly out the front. Brodie was first in the shop, taking with him many of the herbs and vegetables Ninette had gathered. The rest of them followed him inside, taking the herbs and vegetables he hadn't been able to carry.

Callum had barely placed the ones he carried onto the counter when he was speaking to the trader. "I don't suppose you sell coffee."

"You're the first person who's asked me. I heard rumours about it last time I was in Shadhurst. They were saying it's worth more than gold," the trader said.

Callum stared at her for a moment. "You've heard of it?"

The trader nodded. "It's a beverage, isn't it?"

"It is. How expensive exactly is it?"

The trader shrugged. "Depends on which rumours you listen to. Some said it was worth ten gold pieces a cup while others put it at a much higher price." She gestured to all the items on the counter. "Is this all you have for sale? I was mostly cleared out recently by a party of eight adventurers."

"That's it for herbs and veggies, but we've got other things if you're interested," Brodie said.

Mallory checked the journal notification, surprised

it was a quest update. *In Search Of Beans: You discovered coffee can be purchased in Shadhurst, but it is very expensive.* At the prices the trader had mentioned, she hoped they found another way for Callum to get his coffee. Catching sight of a book on a table against the wall, the word 'spells' written on the leather-bound cover, she wandered over to flick through the book while Brodie listed some of the things they didn't need. Not only did the book contain a list of spells available, but also details of what each level gained for the spells. Some of the ones she had were in the book, as well as higher level versions of most of them.

It didn't take her long to realise that it'd work out better to replace her low level spells with higher level ones rather than use CAS points to level them up. Especially with how long it took to earn points. Improving her spells would have to wait. Especially after how much money had been spent on mana regen jewellery.

Danae joined her. "Are you going to buy some?"

Mallory shook her head. "We really can't afford them. Not after all we spent today." She kept her voice low, not wanting Brodie to comment on the money they'd spent helping the apothecary. Although it had worked out well in the end since they'd been given the compact alchemist's station. She glanced at her brother when he dashed outside.

Ryan, who'd joined them as Brodie had left, chuckled. "He's gone to get all the other things we don't need. He was muttering something about not wanting to take money out of the bank and that maybe we'd get enough from selling all our unnecessary things."

Mallory stared at the doorway. "Should one of us go with him? What if he brings in things we want to keep?"

"I'll help him." Callum strode outside, Smudge in the makeshift sling still playing with his new bracelet.

It took them nearly an hour to sort out what they wanted to sell and for Brodie to haggle over the price. As well as all the herbs and vegetables they'd initially brought in, they also sold the plain silver bracelet from the archer, leather boots, full leather leg armour, studded leather vambraces, two dark brown trousers, a pair of navy trousers, the hatchet and second axe since Brodie didn't think they needed it and two axes, two tree leech mist, a hunting knife, a short bow, two slings and the fifteen ash creeper seeds. When they were offered five gold pieces for each one, Brodie wanted to return to where they'd found them and search for more. Ryan interrupted him, reminding him they had other plans and Brodie finally finished haggling and accepted two hundred and fifteen gold pieces for their items, giving the money to his sister.

Chapter Fourteen

Mallory was glad when they could leave, all of them clambering into the wagon that Danae drove to the tavern that was further along the road. She'd needed to argue with Brodie about several of the things he'd wanted to sell and she thought they should keep. Callum suggesting they should sell Scorch to the treasure broker had ended some of Brodie's arguments.

When they pulled up, a young man approached them. "I've been paid by Remora to watch your wagon so you can all have dinner."

Mallory smiled at him. "Thank you."

The man brushed aside her thanks. "It's my job."

They all headed inside the tavern, including the companion animals. Mallory paused just inside the door, surprised at how busy the place was. It took her a moment to spot their friends where they sat at two tables on the far side of the tavern, extra chairs set aside for the rest of them. As they crossed the room, Mallory smiled as Ninette fiercely defended one of the extra chairs when an orc tried to take it. He backed away, hands raised and looking rather apologetic.

Ninette sat back down as they arrived, turning to Mallory. "Did you get everything done?"

"We still have to take a note to the bank to cash it in. The jeweller doesn't keep large amounts of money at his shop." Mallory turned to Remora. "And thank you for paying someone to look after the wagon." When Remora nodded, Mallory glanced at the plates of food on the table, her mouth watering.

Catching her gaze, Emica gestured towards the array of food. "Help yourself. Remora paid for dinner. She also wanted to arrange for a room for the night, but we told her you might have other ideas."

"Surely you'll want to stay here for the evening," Remora said.

Mallory shook her head. "We'll travel onto Estwater tonight."

"It's dangerous to travel of an evening," Remora protested.

"There are enough of us to take on any bandits we might encounter," Ryan said.

"And Mal has magelight so we don't have to wait for day." Brodie helped himself to more of the food, having grabbed some when Emica had first told them it was for everyone.

Mallory smiled reassuringly at Remora. "We'll get you safely to Ransted." She helped herself to the food, guessing she better eat something before her brother had more than his share. She glanced around the tables once Remora nodded. "We also need to get money out of the bank to pay everyone for their share of the treasure." She explained what they'd done and also mentioned the two hundred and fifteen gold pieces from the trader.

"Why don't we make it three fifty each," Jorgen suggested. "It's more than we expected the treasure would sell for." He nudged his cousin when he started to protest.

Emica shrugged. "I don't mind either way. It's not like I've needed to spend any money while I've been travelling with you."

"You don't need to give me any. Not after all you've done," Ninette said.

Brodie reached for more food. "Done. We'll go to the bank before we leave and pay you three hundred and fifty gold pieces each."

"It can go in the bank," Jorgen said. "It's best not to wander around with that kind of money."

"I'll keep five gold pieces out," Esben said.

Remora's hand went to her belt pouch. "I wonder if I should visit the bank too."

Finished eating, Mallory leaned back in her chair, looking to Jorgen. "Did you have any luck finding out about The Nelly?"

He shook his head. "Not a word. No one here has heard of her."

"They might know about her in Estwater," Danae said.

"Maybe." Jorgen didn't look like he believed her.

"Isn't Lilica bigger?" Brodie asked. "And the other two towns up that end of Ruby Isle? The Nelly might have been to one of them."

Callum took out the map and the conversation remained on discussing likely towns and villages while they finished eating, Brodie being the last to be done.

They stepped outside the tavern, Brodie several paces ahead of them. "Can you smell that?" He took a few more steps forward. "It's sweet. I wonder what it is." Spotting a group of people, he hurried forward, Fang as usual at his heel.

Mallory shook her head. "How can he even think of food after all he ate?"

"Hey. What's–" Brodie's words broke off as he and the group of people vanished.

Mallory's mouth dropped open as she stared at the place where her brother had been. "What happened? Where is he?" She did a slow turn as she searched the area, even casting magelight to help her see better.

"He could be anywhere," Emica said. "Even in one of the other countries of Inadon."

Mallory turned to the kitsune. "What do you mean?"

"He was caught up in a portal that was likely an area of effect one rather than a group or individual one," Emica explained.

"How are we meant to find him?" Mallory didn't know what to think. The thought of her brother stuck in another country with very little money made dread pool in her stomach. What if she could never find him again? Inadon might not be as big as Earth, but it wasn't exactly small either.

Ryan chuckled. "It's ironic that it was food that got him into this mess."

Mallory turned to Ryan. "It's not at all funny."

Ryan continued to grin. "Yeah, it is. And when we find him again, you'll think it is too."

"How are we meant to find him?" Mallory demanded.

Ryan took a step towards Mallory, reaching for her.

She stepped away from him, glaring. "Well?"

He took another step towards her, resting his hands on her shoulders. "Look at his stats. He's gained enough XP it was probably for a new location and his health is full. You'll know if he's okay or not. And we will find him. We'll figure it out."

She breathed out slowly, looking at her brother's stats. A weak smile formed. "He's probably happy he earned XP."

Callum joined them, resting a hand on Mallory's back. "I bet there are spells we can buy that will help us find him."

The dread in her stomach eased a little. "We should go to the bank and sort out the money." She wanted to be ready to leave the moment they found out what had happened to Brodie.

Ryan grinned. "I bet he's busy having fun and not even thinking about how worried you might be."

Mallory sighed heavily. Ryan was probably right. She kept hold of his hand as they walked to the wagon, thanking the young man who'd been watching it. Danae drove them to the bank the moment all of them were on the wagon.

Mallory was the first off the wagon and striding inside before the others had a chance to move. A glance around the interior showed the place was almost identical to the one at Longmeadow.

The bank clerk looked from Mallory to a piece of paper he held as she entered, about to put it down when everyone entered, except Remora who waited in the wagon. He looked from the paper to the group, his gaze resting on Smudge. He spoke when they approached the counter. "What are your names?"

Mallory frowned. "Our names?"

Emica stepped forward, rattling off all their names.

"And the river otter?" the clerk asked.

"Smudge," Callum said.

He picked up a folded piece of paper from the counter, still holding the first piece of paper. "I have a letter here from a Brodie Owens of Brisbane. He was certain you'll be willing to pay the ten gold pieces for delivery."

"Brodie sent a letter to us?" Mallory stared at the folded piece of paper.

The clerk inclined his head. "Yes. And someone needs to pay the ten gold pieces delivery fee."

"What happens if we don't pay it?" Callum asked.

"Then the sender will be expected to pay the fee either in gold or items of value," the clerk said. "If they're not capable of paying, they'll be expected to work off the value of the fee. It would not be pleasant. Do I send a message back that you've declined to pay the fee?"

Callum shook his head. "I was just curious."

Chapter Fifteen

Mallory fumbled around for the money in her satchel, where she'd put the coins from the trader, and handed over ten gold pieces. She took the folded piece of paper from the clerk when he held it out, having first put the money away before he did. She stepped away from the counter as she glanced over the letter, looking up to see that everyone watched her. "He's in Estwater. The group he's with is making their way north, a short distance at a time, and they've offered to let him go with them to Lilica."

"He's going north without us?" Emica demanded.

Mallory shook her head. "He wants to know what he should do. If we want him to meet us in Lilica or want him to wait there."

"Is that all he said?" Danae asked. "There seems to be an awful lot of writing to say so little."

Mallory smiled. "They let him have some of their

food. There's an entire paragraph on what it tasted like."

Danae laughed softly. "That sounds like Brodie."

"So what are you going to tell goblin boy?" Emica asked.

"To wait, of course." Mallory dreaded to think how much mischief her brother could get into if left on his own too long.

Jorgen nodded. "That's probably the sensible decision. Especially with the trouble he ends up in. Someone should suggest to him that he needs to put a lot of points in luck. I think that would be a beneficial stat for him to increase."

Ryan chuckled. "Probably. Especially with how he tends to act first and think later."

"I think you're giving him too much credit," Emica said dryly. "Does he think later?"

Mallory felt like she should protest Emica's comment, but it was a little hard to argue with the truth. Her brother didn't always think later. Or at all. "I better let him know to stay there before he gets bored and goes with the other group."

Emica followed Mallory to the counter. "You know, he could have accessed your group bank account and used that to pay to send the letter."

Callum smiled. "Weren't you the one who said he doesn't think?"

"Point taken," Emica said.

Mallory tucked the letter from her brother into her belt pouch, waiting for the clerk to look at her before she spoke. "How do I send a reply?"

"Ten gold pieces includes the paper, the use of the writing implements and the cost of sending it to the bank of your choice," the clerk said.

Mallory took out another ten gold pieces. It was always Brodie who seemed to cost them money. If she hadn't been worried he might head to Lilica, she wouldn't have spent so much money on sending him a reply. She would have made him wait for their arrival. She thanked the clerk when he handed her a piece of paper and put ink and a nib pen on the counter for her. It didn't take long to write a letter to her brother, telling him to stay in Estwater and to try and stay out of trouble. She folded the letter and handed it over to the clerk.

The clerk took another piece of paper, holding the pen poised over it. "And who do you wish to send this to?"

"Brodie." Remembering what the clerk had said earlier, she corrected herself. "Brodie Owens of

Brisbane and Fang the wolf cub. Currently in Estwater."

Once the clerk had finish writing, he wrapped his piece of paper around the letter from Mallory. "I'll be one moment." He made his way to the compass rose on the floor and placed the letter in the middle of it. He changed the location tiles before sending a letter and returning to the counter. "Is there anything else I can help you with?"

Mallory took out the note from the jeweller, handing it over along with what was left of the money from the trader, except for five gold pieces that she gave to Esben. She explained how they wanted to split it up and everyone stepped forward to place a hand on the black tile the clerk put on the counter. Three hundred and fifty gold pieces was put in each of Ninette's, Emica's and Jorgen's bank accounts while ninety-five gold pieces were put in the group bank account and three hundred and forty-five gold pieces were put in Esben's.

"Can I help you with anything else?" the clerk asked.

Mallory shook her head. They'd already spent too much money and couldn't afford any more of his help. Not that he could help her with her problems. What she really needed was her brother not to go running into danger all the time. "No, that was all, thanks."

When they returned to the wagon, Remora waited until they were settled before she spoke. "You were much longer than I had expected you to be."

Callum gave some of the fish they'd planned to have for dinner to Smudge, glancing at Remora as he did so. "We ended up finding out where Brodie went."

"How?" Remora asked.

Mallory cast magelight and while Danae drove out of town, she told Remora what had happened, answering her many questions. She also mentioned that she'd thought Remora might want to use the bank. The young woman had shaken her head, pointing out that most villages were too small for a bank so she'd decided it was best not to.

Spike joined them before they'd gone far, peering inside the wagon then looking at Scorch who was tied to the back of it. "Lost one?"

"Not quite," Mallory said. "We'll meet him in Estwater."

"How did you know when to meet up with us?" Callum asked.

"Sound of you," Spike said.

"You could hear us speaking as we left town?" Callum asked.

"No. Tap, tap." He gestured towards the horses. "Rumble, rumble. Tap, tap." This time he gestured towards the wagon wheels before gesturing to the horses again. "Feel it." He pointed to the ground.

"You feel the vibrations through the ground?" Callum asked.

"Vibrations." Spike spoke the word like he was savouring an extremely delicious meal. "Vibrations." He said it firmly this time. "Know sound of you."

"That's pretty cool," Callum said.

Ryan turned to Spike. "Can you hear others coming?"

"Many noises. Many, many noises. Small noises, big noises, in between noises." Spike gestured vaguely around them, his leaves rustling with his movements. "All noises. All everywhere."

"Guess you can't let us know if something is approaching then," Ryan said.

"Most noises hurry away," Spike said. "Not like our noise."

Ryan chuckled. "Guess that makes sense." He turned to Callum. "How far away is Estwater?"

Callum took out the map, waiting for Mallory to recast magelight before he calculated the distance. "If nothing holds us up, it'll take a bit over an hour and a half. We'll be there before eleven tonight."

"Are we going to gather resources along the way?" Esben asked.

"We should." Mallory checked her brother's stats as she answered Esben. "Ninette needs more XP."

"Who will work on their XP when she's taking a break?" Esben asked.

Ryan grinned. "I'm sure you'll get a chance to have a go."

It took them a few minutes to arrange who was doing what and while Emica took a turn driving the wagon, Ryan, Callum, Danae, Jorgen and Esben helped Ninette gather resources. Remora gratefully accepted the use of a couple of blankets and stretched out to sleep, now most of them were out of the wagon.

Mallory joined them after she wrote in her notebook, worried she wouldn't have time when they reached Estwater. Who knew what trouble her brother might have found. They were halfway there when a journal notification appeared in the corner of Mallory's vision. She frowned as she read over the quest. *Mage In Need Of An Escort: A mage needs an escort from Estwater to Coastview and offers the spell tracking magelight in payment.*

Chapter Sixteen

Mallory turned to Danae who helped her find the next lot of resources for Ninette. "How did we get a quest?"

"It's because we're all sharing information," Danae said. "And tracking magelight is a good spell. I wonder why the mage is offering such a valuable item."

Jorgen joined them, holding a hessian bag for Ninette. "It's probably because the quest isn't as simple as it sounds."

Mallory dreaded to think what trouble her brother was mixed up in. And going to get them mixed up in.

Once Ninette picked the herbs Mallory and Danae had found, Danae swapped places with Emica, taking a turn driving so the kitsune could gather a few resources too. Like the last journey, they found that there weren't as many resources in the area and they had to go further off the road to find them. This meant they weren't able to gather as many and Mallory was a little disappointed in how many experience points everyone gained. She was also surprised they encountered no creatures or bandits.

Emica grinned at her comment. "Don't get used to it. After Estwater, the roads aren't as safe. The Duke's soldiers rarely go much further north than that. Unless they're on an actual mission."

"What's Coastview like?" Mallory couldn't help worry it was another dark forces village since the Duke's soldiers rarely went that far north.

Emica shrugged. "Small."

"Do dark forces live there?"

Emica shook her head, pointing out a herb to Ninette as she approached them. "Mostly fisherman. There isn't much there. I don't know why anyone would want to go there, let alone a mage."

Mallory sighed. She supposed she'd find out soon enough. And find out why the quest would give them such a valuable reward.

As they drew near Estwater, they all returned to the wagon, disturbing Remora who sat up, blinking at the brightness of the magelight. "Are we there?" Remora blinked sleepily, rubbing at her eyes.

"Nearly." Mallory turned to Ninette. "How did you do? Level up much?"

Ninette nodded. "I'm halfway through this level."

"I gained a CAS point," Esben said. "One more CAS point until I reach level five."

"I gained a CAS point too," Callum said.

"So did I." Danae, who was driving, glanced over her shoulder as she spoke.

Mallory smiled. "I guess we did better than expected considering how much harder it was to find resources in the area." She was also pleased with how close Ninette was to level four. Soon the young warrior would be able to use a longsword. They had one from the orc mage that Ryan could use when he reached level four so Ninette could have the one from the archers. None of them would be able to use the one from the merfolk until they reached level seven since it had enchantments, but hopefully before she reached warrior level four they'd gain another one or might be able to buy one.

"Ninette could have been further along if you hadn't insisted I take a turn," Jorgen pointed out. "I'm well ahead of the rest of you. It isn't necessary."

"It was fair." Mallory looked ahead of them through the arch of canvas, watching the town as they approached. It was quiet and there were very few lights. Most of the noise seemed to come from the direction of the waterfront. Seeing a notification in the corner of her vision, she checked that it was only the location experience points. Before she could comment on the experience points, Spike ambled away, telling them he'd meet them when they were leaving.

"I gained a CAS point from the location XP," Ryan said once Spike had moved away.

Mallory checked how close she was to gaining a CAS point. Another ten experience points and she'd gain one. Only one more after that and she'd reach level six.

"Where do you want me to take us?" Danae again glanced over her shoulder. "Did Brodie say where he'd wait?"

"No," Mallory said. "Take us to the bank since that was the last location where we know he was."

Emica directed Danae to the bank since she'd been to the town before and had a bit of an idea where they could find locations.

They found the bank closed and no one nearby. Mallory clambered down out of the wagon so she could check the area more closely.

Ryan joined her. "I don't think he's here."

Mallory returned to the wagon with one last glance

at the bank. "He could be anywhere." She was certainly going to have words with her brother when she found him. He could have said where he would wait.

Emica gestured towards the waterfront and the tavern that was well-lit up. "Goblin boy is probably there. A place with food. With how much he eats, it makes sense."

Mallory's gaze was drawn to the tavern that was barely visible from where she stood. "It's worth a try." If he wasn't there, she didn't know where to look for him. She climbed into the back of the wagon, moving towards the front so she'd have a better view of where they were going. As they travelled through the streets, she scanned the quiet buildings, her gaze frequently drawn back to the waterfront.

Danae parked the wagon several buildings away from the tavern, other wagons parked along the sides of the road. "Are we all going in?"

"Shouldn't someone wait with the wagon?" Callum nodded towards the tents, bedrolls, basket and chest, hessian bags of herbs and vegetables stored amongst them. "What if there are thieves in the area?"

"I can wait with the wagon," Ninette offered.

Remora yawned. "I'd rather not go in the tavern. I can stay out here too."

"We'll go in, if you don't mind," Jorgen said. "I'd like to ask around about The Nelly."

Ryan jumped down to the ground, walking around to the front of the wagon. "If there's more trouble than you can handle, make a lot of noise and we'll come out and check on you."

Ninette nodded. "I'm sure having the two of us wait with the wagon will be enough to discourage anyone from stealing your things."

Emica led the way into the tavern, stopping not far inside to gesture at a table across the room. "There he is." She strode towards Brodie who was at a table with two other people, talking and laughing with them. A man and a woman, both a couple of decades older than him.

Brodie glanced up as they approached, rising to his feet to wave them over, grinning at them when they reached the table. "I have a new recipe."

"What did you think you were doing ending up getting caught in the portal area of effect?" Mallory demanded.

"Aww, come on, Mal. How was I meant to know?" Brodie demanded. "Besides, I wouldn't have got the recipe if I hadn't ended up being brought here with them. And they asked me to go with them." He turned to Callum. "And what's with all the XP you're all earning? You're getting so many CAS points and you're not even using them."

"I'll make a decision when we've found all the crafting ability books and I can learn all about them," Callum said.

"Then I guess we better find them in a hurry so you can do something useful with them." Brodie turned to Ryan. "Is that what you're waiting for too? All the crafting ability books."

Ryan shook his head. "I'm thinking of keeping them for when I can use a longsword. Like Ninette is doing."

"That's not a bad idea." Brodie glanced at Callum before returning his attention to Ryan. "A better idea than some people have."

Jorgen indicated the bar. "We'll ask about The Nelly." He turned to the man and woman. "Unless either of you know of a ship by that name."

The man and woman rose to their feet, shaking their heads. "Sorry," the man said.

Jorgen inclined his head before heading to the bar, Esben following him.

The woman glanced towards a set of stairs over near the bar. "I guess these are the people you were waiting for, Brodie. We'll retire for the night since we have an early start in the morning."

The man nodded at the woman's words. "Don't forget you're welcome to join us if you want. Our last cook decided he wanted a less eventful life and gave up adventuring."

Brodie grinned. "Don't know why. I've earned heaps of XP adventuring. Hardly any from cooking."

Chapter Seventeen

Mallory waited until the man and woman had left before she spoke to her brother. "Where's the mage you agreed to help?"

"I didn't exactly agree," Brodie said. "Told him I had to wait and see if you lot wanted to help."

"Where is he then?" Emica asked.

Brodie lowered his voice. "Hiding. I'll take you to see him later. First though, I've organised selling all the herbs and resources to a trader. He's waiting for us." Brodie half turned away, his gaze on Fang who was asleep on the floor beside his chair. "Come on, girl. Time to go."

Fang trotted behind Brodie as he led the way to the tavern door, Jorgen and Esben joining them before they stepped outside.

"Any luck?" Mallory asked.

Jorgen shook his head.

"This way." Brodie led them several buildings along in the other direction to where the wagon was. He knocked on the door, which was opened by a man rubbing sleep from his eyes.

He looked from Brodie to those with him. "I'd begun to think they'd encountered trouble. The roads are fairly quiet, but we have the occasional bandit prey on those who think to travel of an evening. Where's the resources?"

"I'll bring the wagon closer." Danae hurried away before anyone had the chance to comment.

The trader held the door open wide. "Come on in then. For such a small town, we've been doing quite a brisk trade lately in all types of resources. Makes me wonder if something is going on that I haven't heard about. Ships have been docking daily and cleaning out the shops."

"Where are they coming from?" Emica asked.

The trader shrugged.

"Has The Nelly docked here?" Jorgen asked.

Again the trader shrugged. "I really couldn't say."

Danae returned with the wagon, interrupting the conversation, and the trader was kept busy going through the resources and making them an offer of ten gold pieces. As they left the shop, after Callum had asked about coffee, Mallory couldn't help thinking about how much more profitable it was to do demonic dungeons.

When they were all in the wagon, Brodie glanced around. "Where's Spike?"

"He'll join us again when we leave town," Callum said. "I don't think he likes people places."

"Where are we going?" Danae sat on the driver's seat, gathering up the reins.

"We can't meet up with him tonight. That's unless none of you agree to escort him, and then he wants to talk to you. You should see how he gets to where he's staying. It's like this puddle you step into. It doesn't matter whether it's against a wall or on the floor. You still enter it at the same point. He was telling me all about it. And about his rooms. There's even an oven in them. How awesome is that?" Brodie paused a moment. "I wonder if you could enter the portal if it was on a ceiling."

"We can't sit here all night," Danae said. "So where are we going?"

"The better question is, are we going to escort him to Coastview?" Ryan asked.

"What's the catch, goblin boy?" Emica asked.

"He wants to travel during the day," Brodie said. "He's meeting up with his party in Coastview. They hunt down the dark forces."

"Then why is he here and not with his party?" Callum asked.

"He has family here," Brodie said. "One of them was sick so he came to visit. Wanted to make sure they were on the mend."

"Why did he want to travel during the day," Jorgen asked.

"I was telling him how we level up by gathering resources between destinations," Brodie said.

"So he expects us to help him level up?" Esben demanded.

"He said we can keep the resources. He just wants the XP," Brodie assured them.

"And that's the only reason he wants to travel during the day," Ryan said.

"It's safer during the day. Especially going north." Brodie barely paused for breath before he added, "He said there's a shortcut along the coastline. He can show us the way. We can get a wagon along the track."

"He's being hunted by dark forces," Jorgen stated.

"There's the catch," Emica said. "Don't you think we have enough of our own problems, goblin boy?"

"It's not like we haven't faced the dark forces before," Brodie protested.

Mallory sighed softly when Emica and Brodie

argued the matter between them. "We'll escort him to Coastview."

Emica stopped mid-sentence to face Mallory. "Don't we normally vote on it?"

"Normally-" Before Mallory could finish her explanation, Ryan interrupted.

"Mallory is right. He needs our help. Anyone taking on the dark forces needs all the help they can get."

"I'm in," Callum said.

"I'm not saying I don't want to help," Emica said. "I was just wondering why we didn't call for a vote."

"Because it's the right thing to do," Mallory said.

"Of course it is," Brodie said.

Ryan chuckled. "And it had nothing to do with getting an expensive spell that would be beneficial to you?"

"It's not like I'm a mage," Brodie protested. "It'd be for Mal."

Danae smiled. "She has a magelight spell. A tracking magelight spell is one a mage can cast to follow someone else."

Taking pity on her brother, Mallory asked, "Where are we meeting the mage?"

Brodie directed Danae and they set up camp on the beach just north of Estwater where he'd agreed to meet the mage the following morning at daylight. It was nearly midnight when they settled down to sleep, having given Smudge and Fang the rest of the fish to eat.

They were woken by Fang, who gave two sharp barks as light began to fill the sky. A young man entered their camp, wearing mage armour, a wand in a leather loop that hung on his belt. He smiled at them in greeting as they all sat up, Brodie jumping to his feet to hurry forward.

"They agreed," Brodie said. "We can escort you to Coastview and help you gain some XP along the way."

The mage's smile broadened. "Lovely. Absolutely lovely. You can't imagine how much I appreciate your help. Normally it wouldn't be a problem. But my party and I are in the middle of a quest. If our guild was larger, I could have called on the help of one of our members."

"Your guild?" Callum asked.

The mage nodded. "Yes, I'm afraid the Adventurers Guild has fallen into a bit of a decline these days. Everyone wants to specialise. No one is interested in random quests that might one day be an escort mission or another day be searching out a certain location or finding missing objects. We've even let it be known to other guilds that we're willing to take on their unwanted quests. We thought it might bring ourselves to the attention of more people. It hasn't helped. With how membership has declined in the past decade, we'll be lucky if there's still an Adventurers Guild around a few years from now."

"Fighting quests too?" Ryan asked.

The mage sighed. "Everyone wants to do fighting quests. Hack and slash. Get in, cause maximum destruction, grab everything in sight and get out again. There are no true adventurers left."

Ryan grinned. "I didn't say that was all I liked to do. I was just asking if they were amongst the quests the Adventurers Guild takes on."

"At the moment, my group has taken on a contract to hunt down a dozen dark forces. They must be north of Shadhurst. Any place on Ruby Isle that is situated above Shadhurst."

Chapter Eighteen

Mallory shared a look with Ryan before she faced the mage. "There's a member of the dark forces waiting in Buckneth for us. Or at least that's what we've been told."

The mage took a step towards her. "You don't want to take them on yourself?"

"We're fine," Ryan said. "Plenty of other things we plan to do."

The mage turned towards Ryan, grabbing his hand in both of his and shaking it enthusiastically. "Thank you so much. We only have another three to find. There are so many quests that need doing. We haven't enough members to get through all of them."

"What do you get for taking out twelve members of the dark forces?" Brodie asked.

"Brodie!" Mallory shook her head, about to turn to the mage and apologise for her brother's question.

"No, no. It's perfectly fine. I don't mind telling since I'm sure you've probably guessed by now that I am trying to encourage everyone I meet to join the Adventurers Guild," the mage said. "Well, that is people who I think would be suitable for our guild."

"Really?" Ryan asked dryly. "I hadn't really noticed."

The mage looked confused. "You hadn't-"

Trying to hide a smile, Mallory interrupted him. "Ryan is teasing."

"Oh, yes. Of course. Well, it isn't one of the better paying quests, but the party will earn fifty gold pieces."

Brodie stared at him for a moment, his mouth open. "From a quest. From a single quest. Fifty gold pieces."

"Yes, I'm afraid that's all. I wish I could say it was more. Especially with how large your party is."

"They're not all in our party. Or they aren't always in our party," Brodie said. "What are the other quests worth? The ones you said are more than fifty gold pieces a quest. Are they much harder than hunting down dark forces?"

"I could take you to the guild house if you want to learn more about us. Although technically it's a sentient demonic castle, not a house as such," the mage said.

"Is it far from here?" Callum asked.

"It's on the demonic line on an island in Middle Ocean, far from any other lands," the mage said. "A place called Donris Island."

Mallory stared at him, trying to recall what the map of Inadon looked like. She was pretty certain that was a long way from them. "Don't you need to join your party?"

"Yes, but it won't take long," the mage assured them. He smiled, holding out his hand. "I'm Darwil." When everyone had introduced themselves, he spoke again. "I know for certain that Jofren Flintah, our guild master, would like to meet you. He's always encouraging us to recruit more members. In fact, one of the bounties is to bring in more members or groups to the guild."

"Bounties?" Callum asked.

Darwil nodded enthusiastically. "Yes. There aren't many bounties. Clear the island, clear the castle grounds, feed the castle, castle repairs and new guild members. For a group, my group would earn two points. We're not far off the next reward level, which would give us another room in our suite."

"The place your portal takes you to was given to you by your guild?" Brodie asked.

"Not exactly given to us," Darwil said. "We earned it. Me and the other three members of my group. We each have our own personal portal to it."

Brodie turned to Mallory, moving close enough to grab hold of her arm. "Can we join them, Mal? We'd get an oven."

"Not until level six," Darwil corrected.

"Level six doesn't sound like much," Brodie said. "Come on, Mal."

"Depends on what you need to do to reach level six," Callum said.

"It wouldn't hurt to visit the Adventurers Guild," Danae said. "I've never seen a sentient demonic castle before. I've heard they live on mana and can change their shape and form."

"They can. It's amazing what they can do." Darwil took out what looked like a piece of black fabric that seemed to have an appearance of depth to it. "I can take all of you there now."

Jorgen took a step back. "Not us. Travellers don't join guilds." He glanced at his cousin as he spoke.

"We can keep an eye on the camp," Esben offered.

"You don't have to agree to join just because you travel there," Mallory pointed out.

Jorgen shrugged. "No, but then it'd feel like we were going there under false pretences. Besides, you need someone to stay behind to keep an eye on things."

It didn't take them long to sort out who was going and who was staying. Remora also stayed behind with the travellers and Darwil put the portal on the sand and gestured for them to step through.

Mallory was the second one to step into the portal, Brodie having rushed ahead of her. It felt like every other portal she'd used, even though it was a different method of portalling. She glanced around the simple room that she'd stepped into, drawn to the single window. When a fireball struck the glass, she stumbled away from it, glaring at her brother when he laughed at her.

"What was that?" Callum gestured towards the window, turning to Darwil.

"Ah, well, we have a bit of a pest problem on the island. No one dares venture outside." Darwil opened the door. "Should I take you to meet Jofren now?"

Mallory checked the journal notification that was in the corner of her vision. She'd gained twenty experience points for a location. With that many points, sentient castles must be rare locations. The experience points were enough to gain her another

CAS point. One more point and she'd reach level six. She glanced at everyone's stats to see if any of them had gained a CAS point. She frowned. "Why do none of us have any mana and why isn't mine regenerating?"

"It takes the castle a hundred mana to bring each person here. Going through the portal temporarily links you to him so he can draw on your mana and refill what he used to get you here," Darwil explained.

Mallory watched her mana until it started to come back. "What about when we leave?"

"It's similar, except he can only take what mana you actually have, not continue to draw on it after you leave. You also can't leave until the castle has drawn a hundred mana from you to pay for your portal here." Darwil gestured towards the corridor. "Are you ready for me to take you to Jofren now?"

They followed him through a maze of corridors, needing to go down several flights of stairs. Darwil tapped lightly on a solid timber door that led off what appeared to be an entrance hall, the doors firmly closed with large timber bars keeping them shut.

Callum slowly turned around as they waited for someone to answer the door. "It's like we're in a medieval castle. One with very little furnishings and no people."

"There's a person." Brodie pointed to a man wearing a mask who came from a door that led to the rear of the castle. A broom went ahead of him, sweeping the floor. "Your servant is a mage?"

The mage stopped, hands going to his hips. "You think I'm a servant?"

"You do have a broom," Brodie said.

The mage crossed the distance between him and Brodie, Fang's hackles rising at how close he stood to Brodie. "You think that's all it takes to be a servant? Do you think I should live in the dust and dirt that being on this island creates? It wasn't always like this. It was an oasis before the guild diminished and the towers of warding were no longer maintained and the demonic creatures took over the island again."

"How was I meant to know?" Brodie muttered.

Mallory stepped forward, drawing her brother back from the mage. "Sorry about that. My brother tends to speak before thinking." She glanced at the broom that had continued its task. "Is that a very high level spell? It seems rather useful."

"Level six." The mage strode away, going up the stairs they'd used to reach the entrance hall.

Chapter Nineteen

Mallory stared after the mage. "I was going to ask what the spell is."

"Animate objects," Darwil said. "If you're not careful, it can lead to disastrous results. The animated object can only do that which it was designed for and will keep going until it's stopped."

"Could you animate a kitchen knife to cut up vegetables?" Brodie asked.

"You could, but it isn't clever enough to know what size to cut them into," Darwil said.

"I see you've met, Sege."

They all spun to see a man, who looked to be in his thirties, standing in the now open doorway. Darwil hurried forward, a smile forming. "Jofren, I've brought a group interested in learning more about the Adventurers Guild and possibly joining us."

Jofren looked them up and down. "And what makes you think you'll be suited to this guild?"

Mallory spoke before her brother could, worried he might offend the guild master. "I like the idea of not having the same type of quests over and over again."

Ryan nodded. "Yeah, a mixture of quests sounds good. And hearing that you're against the dark forces is also good. I wouldn't want to join a guild that would go against what the guardians believe in."

"You're guardians?" Jofren asked.

"Hoping to be one day," Callum said. "At least the four of us are." He indicated himself, Ryan, Mallory and Brodie. Behind them stood Emica who studied the castle and Ninette who was silent, her eyes wide open.

Danae stood next to Ryan. She took a step towards the guild master before she spoke. "I've been thinking about joining them too."

Smudge popped his head up over the edge of the makeshift sling, chattering excitedly.

Callum laughed. "And Smudge too." When Fang gave a soft bark, he added, "And Fang."

Jofren studied them for a moment. "If you're interested, come and meet Drohgolrik."

"Who?" Brodie asked.

"The castle." Jofren led the way to the room

opposite his on the other side of the entrance hall. "Everyone place your hand in the font."

"The bird bath?" Brodie asked.

Mallory wanted to hit her brother. With comments like that, she wouldn't be surprised if the guild rejected them even though they were low on members. "They have them in churches, Brodie. For things like baptisms." She hurried forward to place her hand in the deep stone dish of the font that had to be a metre in diameter. The pedestal part was of intricately carved stone, vines with woodland creatures peering out from amongst them. A shiver went through her when her hand came in contact with the warm stone. It felt like it breathed in long, slow pulses. Around her the rest of them placed their hands against the stone.

Brodie drew his hand back quickly, eyeing the font. "What is that?"

"It's where we feed Drohgolrik, but it's more than that," Jofren said.

"You're feeding us to him?" Brodie demanded.

Mallory had been about to remove her hand from against the stone when Jofren shook his head and Darwil chuckled. "What are you doing then?" She'd tried to ask the question politely, but she noticed there was a slight accusatory tone to her words.

A glow emanated from the font before anyone could answer Mallory, and Jofren smiled. "You can take your hands from the font. Drohgolrik approves of you."

Brodie continued to eye the font suspiciously. "I don't know if we should join the guild. It's weird here. There's people who talk to castles and others who wear masks and animate brooms."

Ryan chuckled. "Not like you can talk. You're always wearing a mask."

Brodie glared at him. "That's different. It's part of my face. Like it's moulded to it. The mask Sege wore is a proper mask."

"He's wanted by the dark forces. Alive. If no one can see his face, then no one will know who he is. Ten thousand gold pieces can be rather tempting to some people," Jofren said.

"Ten thousand," Brodie exclaimed. "What did he do?"

"He's killed thousands of them over the decades. They'd like him to endure an eternity of pain in repayment." Jofren headed for the doorway. "I'll give you a copy of the guild handbook to take with you and a single use portal so you can return with your answer. I wouldn't expect you to make a decision about joining before you knew all the details."

It was Callum who stepped forward and took the slim book from Jofren when they reached his study, his gaze fixed on the bookshelves behind the solid timber desk. "Do you own a copy of all the crafting ability books?"

Jofren smiled. "I see, a man after my own heart. There's much knowledge to be gained from books." He turned to gaze up at his bookshelves. "I'm afraid I don't, but then I wasn't all that interested in learning about all the crafting abilities. I knew from a young age what I wished to do with my life." He turned to face them again. "I'll let Darwil return you to where you've come from and hopefully I'll hear back from you in the not too distant future."

Darwil led them back to his suite and Mallory couldn't resist taking one more look out the window. She drew in a sharp breath at how high up they were, the red, dusty ground at least five storeys below them. They were along one side of the castle and there was an outer wall keeping most of the demonic creatures at bay, although some of them had made it onto the castle grounds.

"No one goes out there," Darwil said. "My group has done a few clear the castle grounds bounties, but it's usually easier to do quests. They're all at least level five on the island."

Ryan joined Mallory at the window. "Wouldn't it make sense to clear the grounds so they can be used?"

Darwil shook his head. "Not with the state Drohgolrik is in. There aren't enough of us to supply the mana he needs to maintain more than the castle and to some extent the grounds in a minor way." He gestured to the book Callum carried. "Read the guild handbook and if you have more questions, come back and ask them of Jofren. He's been here for over a hundred years."

Mallory stared at Darwil at that news. "The guild master is over a hundred?"

Darwil nodded. "Are you ready to return to Ruby Isle? I should get back to my party and although I can show you a shortcut, it still takes more than a few minutes to travel it." He gestured towards a portal on the wall near the exit door. "If you're ready."

Mallory took one last look out the window before stepping through the portal, feeling the same familiar sensation of other portals. She stepped out onto the beach, Jorgen and Esben having packed the camp, the two of them hitching Augusta and Bug to the wagon the moment Mallory appeared on the beach.

Callum was out second last, turning to Darwil when he joined them. "What happens if someone discovers the portal when you're using it?" He watched Darwil pick the object up and put it away.

"They can't," Darwil said. "As soon as I enter, the portal vanishes. That's why I let all of you go through first."

"He's right," Jorgen said. "None of us could see it as soon as he went through."

"Cool," Brodie said. "Will we get one if we join?"

Darwil's gaze was momentarily drawn to the book Callum held. "Read the handbook. It'll answer all your basic questions and a few more." He glanced around the group. "Are we ready to go now? I can show you the shortcut and I'd really like to get started on earning some XP if you're still happy to assist me with that."

Once they were all ready to leave, which didn't take long, Darwil showed them to a shortcut a little way along the beach. It cut through the trees that were set back from the beach, a narrow track barely big enough for a wagon to travel along. Spike joined them before they'd gone far along the rough track, ambling behind them, talking to Brodie who was riding Scorch.

Mallory organised everyone into groups to help Darwil gain experience points. Callum remained in the wagon to read the handbook in case there was information they needed to ask Darwil before they left him in Coastview and Jorgen drove the wagon. Remora joined them, saying she'd be interested in learning more about how they helped someone level up. Particularly someone who wasn't in their group.

Chapter Twenty

They were about three quarters of an hour into the journey, and Mallory was beginning to think the escort mission was going to be their simplest one yet, when a hail of arrows had them scattering and hiding behind trees.

Mallory glanced along the track, wondering if someone should run along it and let Jorgen know to stay back with the wagon until they dealt with the archers that were hiding amongst the trees. She had no idea how many there were, only that with how many arrows had been fired, there had to be at least ten.

"Hand over the mage and your party can pass unharmed," a man called out from amongst the trees.

Mallory nearly jumped when Spike spoke from beside her.

"Hide now?"

"What we need is someone to take a message to Jorgen so he doesn't end up caught in this mess," Mallory said.

"Spike take message," the wandering soul offered.

"Be careful. Don't let any of them see you."

With a rustle of leaves, Spike retreated, heading back in the direction they'd come from.

"The offer won't last forever," the man called out.

Mallory had no idea where any of her party was and what they planned to do, but she did know one thing. "You can keep your offer. We're not about to hand him over."

"You're making a very big mistake," the man warned.

"Our mistake to make," Ryan called out.

Mallory looked in the direction Ryan's voice had come from. He hadn't sounded that far away. Casting vanish I on herself, she quietly made her way towards him. She grinned at the sight of how quickly her mana came back these days. Before she could find Ryan, she spotted an archer hiding behind a tree. Moving across slightly she realised he was aiming his bow at Brodie. She recast vanish I then threw a fireball at the archer.

He spun to face her, firing in her direction. "They're attacking."

Mallory barely had time to move to avoid the arrow when a sound behind her had her spinning to find out what approached. It was Spike. Facing the archer again, she backed away when she couldn't see him. Nor could she see Brodie or Ryan. A quick check of their stats showed that only Ryan had lost any health. Four of them. Not that it made her feel any better. She would have preferred to see for herself that they were both okay.

Spike reached her side. "Jorgen said safe back there. Said thank you for message."

Mallory looked down at herself, having expected to be visible again. She wasn't. "How could you tell where I was?"

"Sound of you."

Before Mallory could figure out a way to use Spike's ability to their advantage, another sound caught her attention. This time it was an archer and she threw herself out of the way of his aim, quickly recasting vanish I which had worn off while she'd been talking to Spike.

Hiding behind a tree, she watched the archer scan the area, trying to figure out where she was. If she attacked him, it'd give her position away. Yet she really didn't have any other choice. Scanning her spells, she tried to figure out which would do the most damage. She guessed her best option was poison dart. She really needed to get better attack spells. With a grin, she cast lightning trap directly behind him and then cast poison dart.

The archer took a step back, activating the lightning trap. He vanished from the damage over time effect caused by the lightning trap.

Mallory glared at the spot where he'd been. It was always a worry when they had a revive. A glance around showed she was alone. Not even Spike had remained with her. She checked everyone's stats as she continued to scan the area. Fear raced through her when Ryan's health dropped by twenty-six. He'd already been missing four. With only nine health left, there was a good chance he wouldn't survive this fight. She needed to find him in a hurry so she could use a healing spell on him. That was something else she needed. A better healing spell.

She darted from tree to tree, not wanting to use her mana to recast vanish I in case she needed to heal Ryan. While she searched for her party members, she kept checking their stats in her journal. When Danae's health went to zero, she froze for a moment. She tried to remind herself that Danae had three revives. It didn't help. There was no guarantee any of them would survive the fight so that Danae could use one of her revives. She kept searching.

The soft sound of an arrow being loosed caught her attention and she silently hurried towards it, in time to cast poison dart at an archer who aimed a bow at Ryan who fought another archer up close. The archer he fought used a hunting knife, the weapon of little use against Ryan's cutlass.

Mallory cast health I at Ryan three times, frustrated by how little health that gave him. He was now at ten health, not enough to keep him alive if he ended up being attacked by the archer who'd taken so much health from him before.

The archer Mallory had attacked readied another arrow. Torn as to what to do, she cast slow target on the one Ryan attacked, then cast fireball twice at the archer who readied an arrow. Again her enemy vanished and somehow she managed not to make a sound in frustration. Instead, she threw a fireball at the archer Ryan fought. This one dropped to the ground the moment the fireball hit him.

Once more she checked everyone's stats. Callum had lost most of his health and Brodie had lost half of his. She assumed his armour was helping. Hurrying to Ryan's side, she glanced around the area. "You need a health potion." She took the vial from him before he could drink it, using her apothecary ability of weak increased healing to double the effectiveness of the potion.

Ryan took the empty vial from her and slipped it back into his belt pouch. "Thanks." He scanned the area. "We need to figure out where everyone is and find out how many archers are left."

Brodie stepped out from behind a tree. "Darwil thinks that's all of them."

Mallory frowned at her brother when she saw how many experience points he'd earned. "Will you stop trying to attack everything in sight? Finish them off."

"I wasn't," Brodie protested. "I was with Darwil and Callum. You need some attack spells like Darwil has. They were awesome. He was finishing them off after one hit from me. Sometimes after a hit from Callum too."

"Is Danae back?" Mallory did a slow turn as she scanned the area.

"What do you m-" Brodie broke off mid-word. "Danae was killed! How do we get her back?"

"I'm fine."

They all turned to see Danae standing several metres from them. Brodie hurried over to her. "I didn't even know you'd been killed."

Danae smiled weakly. "Not something I want to experience too often."

"Bet your mum's not going to be happy about it," Brodie said.

Danae laughed softly. "I'm certainly not looking forward to telling her."

While the two of them had been talking, Mallory had kept healing Ryan and Brodie, alternating between the two of them. By the time everyone else found them, she'd finished healing them and could start on Callum and Emica, wondering if Darwil had his own healing spell. "Where's Ninette?"

"I had her take Remora back to the wagon," Emica said. "I didn't think we should risk letting her get killed since we're meant to be escorting her, not putting her in danger." She glanced at Darwil. "Maybe we should have taken her to Ransted first."

"Let's search what bodies are left behind, then get back on the road." Ryan glanced towards the track with a grin. "Or back on the track."

"I know where some of them are." Brodie dashed off, Fang at his heels, before anyone could reply.

"Guess this means you've finished your kill quest." Ryan nodded to the body he searched, a tattoo on the archer's right hand indicating he was a hellion and a member of the dark forces.

Darwil shrugged. "That'll depend on if it counted for the other members in my party."

"Can't you tell?" Brodie asked.

"We've chosen not to share journal information," Darwil said. "It doesn't matter. I'll find out soon enough. It shouldn't take us long to search the bodies and then it's only about half an hour to Coastview at our current pace."

A search of the handful of bodies left behind gave them enough arrows to replace all the ones used as well as four spares, a short bow, a belt pouch they gave to Esben since he was the only one without one, three silver and eleven copper pieces that Mallory put in the chest the moment they were back at the wagon. She also put in some of the other coins in her belt pouch, not wanting to carry all of them on her. She kept five gold, ten silver and eleven copper pieces of the group money in her belt pouch along with her own nine silver and fifteen copper pieces. In total, she put twenty-four gold, eleven silver and thirty copper pieces in the chest. She immediately noticed the difference in the weight of her belt pouch.

Spike waited for them at the wagon with Jorgen, Esben, Ninette and Remora. He ambled towards them, waiting for Mallory to finish putting coins in the chest before speaking. "Message worthy of name?"

Chapter Twenty-One

Mallory hopped out of the wagon to stand in front of Spike, nodding her head. "Absolutely. Things would have been a lot worse if you hadn't taken a message to Jorgen. Remora wouldn't have had anywhere safe to stay during the fight. I don't even know if she has a revive." She glanced up at Remora who sat on the wagon seat talking softly to Jorgen, not seeming to have noticed the conversation with Spike.

"Name worthy," Spike stated.

Callum joined them. "It'd have to be. You may have saved a life again."

Mallory thought about how Danae had lost a life, but that hadn't been anything to do with what Spike had or hadn't done. That had been to do with facing overwhelming numbers. She still didn't know how many they'd been up against. From all the experience points they'd gained and considering Brodie probably hadn't taken any of them out on his own, there had to have been over fifteen. Maybe even as many as sixteen.

"Life saved?" Spike asked.

"Life saver doesn't sound like much of a name," Brodie said. "Messenger doesn't sound like much of one either."

"What about Hermes for the messenger of the gods? The Greek gods," Callum suggested.

"That sounds like an old man's name," Brodie argued.

"The messenger of the Roman gods was Mercury," Callum said.

Ryan grinned. "You suggesting we're gods, Cal?"

Callum smiled, shaking his head. "No, but they're the first messenger names that come to mind. Unless you want to go with something like herald. Or maybe even look at biblical type messengers."

Worried Callum might spend ages making suggestions, Mallory said, "Hermes and Mercury are both suitable." Hermes also seemed like the kind of name that would be found on Inadon. More so than Mercury. Before she could add that comment, Brodie spoke.

"Mercury's a bit better than the other name."

Brodie turned to Spike. "What do you think? Mercury?"

Spike closed his eyes, remaining silent for a moment. His eyes opened and he met Brodie's gaze. "All say Mercury. Some say Hermes. I am honoured to accept the name Mercury, adventurers. Your gift is precious." Spike's name now Mercury too. Have three names." Spike moved back from them so he could bow, his upper branches brushing across the ground. He straightened. "Protector Spike Mercury. Very honoured by your help to get three names. Thank you, adventurers. New family."

"We're honoured that you chose to travel with us," Mallory said.

Again Spike bowed to them before he turned away and ambled towards the trees.

"Where are you going?" Brodie hurried after him.

Spike turned to face Brodie. "Have three names now."

"You're leaving us?" Brodie asked.

Mallory had been about to ask the same as her brother.

"Three names," Spike said.

"That doesn't mean you have to go," Brodie protested. "You can stay with us as long as you like."

"Go now," Spike said. "Go to my people. My family."

"Don't you like it with us?" Brodie asked.

Mallory moved to stand beside her brother, fighting the urge to slip an arm around his shoulders at the tone of his voice. He wouldn't appreciate her doing that. "You're going, Spike?"

Spike lowered its upper branches so that the leaves brushed against Brodie. "Spike miss new family. Must return to old family now. Have three names."

Ryan rested a hand on Spike where his shoulder might be if he was human. "We're going to miss you, Protector Spike Mercury. I'm glad you got the number of names you wanted and, like Mallory said, we're honoured you chose to travel with us."

"I'm honoured most. New family make three names happen fast," Spike said.

Ryan chuckled. "I guess that's to be expected with how much danger we tend to face on a regular basis."

Mallory wasn't sure what to say to Spike. "Will we see you again?" She couldn't believe he was going. She'd expected Spike to be with them a lot longer than this.

"Will come see you if hear you. Know sound of you."

"I hope we see you again." She was tempted to hug

Spike, but wasn't sure how the wandering soul would react to that. Did people hug wandering souls or was it frowned upon?

Danae stepped forward. "Have a safe journey back to your family, Protector Spike Mercury."

"Move slow. No one see. Good at hiding."

"Yes, you are good at hiding," Danae said.

"Go now." Spike ambled away, not looking back before disappearing amongst the trees.

"I'm going to miss Spike terribly," Danae said.

Mallory nodded. "I think we all will." She managed not to glance at her brother when she said it, but she was pretty sure he was going to miss Spike the most out of all of them with how much time he'd spent talking to the wandering soul.

"We shouldn't have given Spike another name," Brodie said. "Then Spike would still be with us. I had so many more questions to ask." He patted Fang's head when she leaned against him and whined once. "You going to miss Spike too, girl? It's not fair. I didn't know that would happen. Why didn't someone say?"

"I didn't know either," Danae said. "None of us did. Wandering souls don't tend to spend a lot of time with the other sentient races, so there isn't a lot known about them."

Mallory looked towards the wagon where most of those with them waited. "We should get going before other dark forces members come after us. I want to get both Darwil and Remora to their destinations today. Without anyone else losing a life." She turned to Callum. "Did you come up with any questions for Darwil after reading the handbook?"

"Not that I could think of. The handbook has a lot of information in it. It would have been nice if the guardians had given us a handbook that was just as detailed as the one from the Adventurers Guild," Callum said. "All of us should read it. Or at least read the bits about what we'll gain by joining them." He started back to the wagon as he spoke, everyone accompanying him.

"What sort of things?" Brodie asked.

Callum didn't have the chance to answer. Esben spoke as they neared the wagon. "Are we ready to leave now? And will Spike be meeting up with us later?"

"Spike has returned to the wandering souls," Mallory said.

Ryan turned to Danae. "You can drive for now. The five of us need to go over some details. The other four can help Darwil gain XP."

Once they were again on the road, only Mallory,

Ryan, Brodie, Callum and Danae in the wagon, Callum was finally able to answer Brodie's earlier question. "They have people in the guild that provide different services as well as other benefits. The one I think is the most important, is a trader who sells valuable items at a large auction house for ten percent of the profit." He opened the handbook and held it out to Brodie. "Even you'd have to appreciate that benefit."

Brodie read over the page, pointing to one of the benefits. "You sure it isn't access to their library of myth and lore books that you're most interested in?"

Chapter Twenty-Two

Mallory took the handbook from Brodie, scanning the benefits of joining. "Did you notice they've got four recipes that were created by previous members with adventurers in mind?"

"Where?" Brodie took the handbook back from her. "They have. I wonder what they are."

His words reminded Mallory of the recipe he'd received from the party who'd accidentally portalled him. "What recipe did you get yesterday?"

"Sweet custard pastry," Brodie said. "I can't wait to make it. I wonder if I could make it back home too."

Ryan gestured towards the handbook. "What does everyone say?"

"We can join it as a group or as individuals," Callum said. "The rest of you really should read it."

"Are you sure you don't have any questions to ask Darwil after reading it?" Mallory asked.

Callum shook his head. "I might think of some in a few days, but I doubt it. The handbook is very comprehensive."

"So we don't have to make the decision immediately or worry about asking Darwil questions before we leave him in Coastview then?" Mallory asked.

"I suppose not," Callum said. "But when we do vote on it, I say yes. They've even got a list of famous past members of the Adventurers Guild. One of them is called Marcus Segdragorn. He supposedly died a decade ago, but a lot of his story sounds a lot like Sege. This Marcus destroyed an entire dark forces city all by himself. He was wanted by them before that, for killing thousands of them. They had a bounty on his head. Ten thousand gold pieces to have him brought in alive. Sound familiar?"

"Maybe that's the figure the dark forces always offer for their enemies," Ryan suggested.

Callum shrugged. "I don't know, but I'm not about to ask him. He obviously doesn't want anyone to know who he is. And if he's the one who took out an entire city, then how powerful must he be? I'm not about to annoy someone who might be that powerful."

"We could ask Darwil," Brodie said.

"Don't you dare." Mallory turned to her brother, eyes narrowed. "Some questions shouldn't be asked."

"Why not?" Brodie demanded.

"They might think we're part of the dark forces," Danae said. "Or that we'll sell the information to them."

"Why did they tell us the information and risk it?" Mallory asked.

"There are potions and spells that can wipe memories for varying lengths of time. If we'd failed Drohgolrik's test, maybe they would have wiped all memory from us of our time at the Adventurers Guild castle," Danae said.

"How would we know if they'd done that?" Brodie asked.

"We wouldn't," Danae said.

"That's not right," Brodie protested.

Ryan took the handbook from Brodie. "We'll worry about this later. For now, we'll help Darwil gain more XP." He put the handbook on the driver's seat beside Danae, checking his pocket watch. "We only have about fifteen minutes left. We did promise him some XP."

They all helped Darwil gain experience points, except for Danae who continued to drive the wagon. Mallory caught regular glimpses of the beach as they continued along the track, relieved that they reached Coastview without running into any further problems. She couldn't help worrying about Danae having lost a revive. Maybe they should be putting money into armour and better weapons rather than saving it for when they travelled to the mainland. Especially if they were going to join the Adventurers Guild. Would they really need a place of their own if they did that? Yet she still liked the idea of them having their own place, even if they did join the Adventurers Guild. Somewhere completely their own that they could do what they wished with.

Pushing aside unsettling thoughts of revives and lack of them and gear, Mallory checked her journal notification. As she'd assumed, it was location experience points. A quick check at the stats of everyone in her party showed that no one had gained a CAS point from the ten location experience points. But they would gain more experience points today. There were two quests to complete and at least one more location to visit. And depending on how much time everything took, they might have enough time to reach one more location after Ransted.

Danae pulled up in front of the shop Darwil had directed them to. He climbed down off the wagon seat, where he'd sat beside Danae. He stood by the wagon, his hand resting on it. "I'll let the trader know you'll be in. I hope all the herbs and vegetables I gathered will be as useful to you as all the XP you helped me gain."

"How many points did you get?" Brodie asked.

Mallory was tempted to sigh upon hearing her brother's question. She was beginning to think her brother would never figure out that there were just some things you shouldn't ask people. Rather than comment, she quickly added everyone except Remora to the party so they could gain experience points for completing the quest.

Darwil smiled. "I earned enough XP to gain several CAS points. It's a good way for a single person to gain XP. Not so much if you want a group to level up." He took out a parchment and handed it over to Brodie. "Maybe one day I'll see you in the Adventurers Guild."

Mallory took the parchment from Brodie, assuming it was the spell for her. Ignoring a notification in the corner of her vision, she turned to Darwil. "Thanks for introducing us to them. We're still deciding, but some of our party is definitely interested."

"That's great," Darwil exclaimed. "Do you have any questions?"

"Not about the Adventurers Guild." Mallory hadn't been able to stop thinking about how she'd felt when she couldn't find Ryan and his health had plummeted so dramatically. And how she'd felt when Brodie had disappeared. "Are there spells that can help you locate someone? Like a party member."

Darwil nodded. "I and the other mage in my party both have a locate party spell. It shows you were all your party members and their companions are on your journal map. It lasts for five minutes at a time, but you can level it up to show them for a longer amount of time."

"Now that sounds like a useful spell." Mallory glanced at Brodie.

"It wasn't my fault," Brodie muttered.

Mallory ignored her brother's comment. "What level is it?"

"The one we have is for level three." Darwil smiled at Mallory. "We have a spare one. If you join the guild, we could give it to you as a welcome gift."

Ryan chuckled. "You seem pretty keen to have us join."

"They earn points for members that join," Callum said.

"It's not only that," Darwil said. "The points are

useful, but I really want to see the guild grow and regain some of its former glory."

"Is it difficult to gain levels?" Callum asked. "How long does it take to gain them?"

"I guess it depends on how active you are." Darwil took a step back from the wagon. "Anyway, I'd best be moving. I'll let the trader know you'll be in shortly to sell some resources."

Brodie grabbed one of the hessian bags and jumped out of the wagon, Fang following him. "I'll go in there with you."

When Darwil led Brodie inside the shop, Mallory removed all the extras from their party before she checked the journal notification. *Mage In Need Of An Escort: You escorted the mage to Coastview and were rewarded with the spell tracking magelight for your party. You also earned twenty experience points each.*

Chapter Twenty-Three

Mallory put the spell in her belt pouch to learn later. This time when she checked everyone's stats, she noticed Brodie had gained a CAS point. "We should take the rest of the resources in and see if they have anything at a good price," Mallory said.

"Like more mana regen jewellery?" Ryan teased.

Mallory smiled at his comment. "I wish, but I doubt it. Regen jewellery doesn't seem like something you can pick up at a discounted price very often. Another six mana and I'd be able to regen my entire mana every minute instead of only the twelve that regens without buffs."

Brodie burst out of the shop before anyone had done more than gather the hessian bags. "The trader will take all we've got. I like these waterfront places where ships regularly call in and stock up."

It didn't take them long to gather all the resources

and for Callum to check if there was coffee or crafting ability books. There were neither and they once again said goodbye to Darwil and accepted seventeen gold pieces from the trader. Mallory put the coins in the chest where the other ones were stored, settling in the back of the wagon with the Adventurers Guild Handbook after organising who was to help Ninette level up on their way to Ransted.

It only took Ninette forty minutes to reach level four. Not quite enough time for Mallory to read the handbook. She needed another five minutes, finishing it up while Brodie and Esben were arguing over who should gain experience points next.

Mallory closed the handbook and set it down beside herself. "No one will get a chance to gain XP if you spend the rest of the trip arguing about it."

"There's still two and a quarter hours until we reach Ransted," Callum said. "They'll be doing well to argue that long."

Mallory held the handbook out to Ryan. "Well, in that case, Ryan can read the handbook then earn some XP after he's done. Jorgen can drive the wagon for a while and Danae can take turns with Emica, Brodie, Callum and Esben to gain XP." Now Ninette had reached character level four, it was time to help the rest of them reach that level too.

Mallory joined Ninette, looking for resources that the two of them could point out to Danae. "Do you mind me asking what you put your attribute points into?"

"Not at all." Ninette smiled. "I put two in strength so it's now at fifteen, one in constitution which has given me forty-eight health and eighty stamina and one each in wisdom and luck. I now have thirty mana and my general luck has been taken up to nine percent." Ninette's smile became a grin. "And I can now use a longsword and I've put thirty CAS points into it so I'll be able to do thirty percent more damage."

Mallory pointed out the resources they'd found to Danae before she walked with Ninette to the next lot. "You can have the longsword from the archers."

"Won't Ryan want it?" Ninette asked.

Mallory shook her head. "He has the one from the orc mage." Seeing that Danae had spotted the herbs they stood near, she scanned the area for the next lot of resources, heading towards them with Ninette at her side. "I'll get it out for you when we return to the wagon."

"How can I ever repay you for all you've done for me?" Ninette asked.

"We don't need you to repay us. We're glad we could help," Mallory said.

Ninette laughed softly, glancing towards Brodie who was pointing out some vegetables to Danae. "All of you?"

Mallory couldn't help smiling at the comment. "Yes. All of us. Even Brodie. No matter the comments he makes occasionally."

After Danae had gathered resources for ten minutes, Emica had a turn followed by Brodie, Callum and Esben. When Esben had finished his ten minutes, Ryan joined them and Brodie returned to the wagon, amidst grumblings, to read the handbook. There was just enough time once he'd read the handbook for him to get in a second turn at gathering resources, pointing out that it wouldn't have been fair if he hadn't had a second turn since everyone else had managed to have one. While he had his turn, Danae returned to the wagon to read the handbook.

Seeing Ransted ahead of them, they went back to the wagon and Mallory eyed all the resources taking up most of the space. Hopefully, they could sell them at Ransted, but considering it was only a village, she didn't think they'd have much luck. While she shifted resources around to get the longsword for Ninette, she checked her party's stats.

Brodie had earned a CAS point and now had a hundred and eight of the hundred and thirty-four experience points needed for another CAS point. Fang now only needed another hundred and thirteen experience points before she reached level four. Danae had managed to earn two CAS points and was now halfway through level three. Mallory was tempted to focus on levelling Danae up so she could gain another revive after having lost one recently.

Callum had also earned two CAS points and was halfway through character level three, while Smudge was still four hundred and seventy-six experience points away from level four. Ryan, like Brodie, had only earned a single CAS point and was thirteen experience points off his next CAS point, which would put him at halfway through level three.

Finding the longsword, Mallory handed it over to Ninette, who took off the short sword and stored it with the swords from the orc mage and merfolk. "What attack stats does it have for you?"

"With the thirty percent damage from my strength and thirty percent damage from level thirty longsword affinity, it has a low attack of seventeen, a normal attack of twenty, and a crit of twenty-five," Ninette said.

"What are the base attack stats?" Callum asked.

"Eleven, thirteen and sixteen," Ninette said.

Callum turned to Brodie. "Now that is why I'm hoarding CAS points. When I know the best place to put them to make the most amount of difference, then I'll use them."

Brodie set aside the handbook he was meant to be reading and eyed Ninette. "Maybe I should have become a warrior." He turned to Callum. "She does almost as much damage as you with your longbow."

Jorgen, who was still driving the wagon, glanced over his shoulder. "Done right, rogues can be more powerful than a warrior."

Brodie clambered over the back of the wagon seat to join Jorgen. "How do you do it right?"

"You need to choose what weapon you're going to focus on to start with."

Fang jumped over the back of the wagon seat to sit beside Brodie, who absently patted her as he peppered Jorgen with questions, often not giving him a chance to answer.

Emica distracted Mallory from the conversation between Brodie and Jorgen. "Thanks for letting me gather resources. I reached character level three from all that XP."

"That's okay." Mallory glanced at Jorgen when he hushed Brodie so he could ask Remora where she needed to go. She turned away so neither would see her smile, checking her journal notification. It was location experience points like she'd expected.

Remora directed them to a farmhouse north of Ransted and they waited for her to have someone come out and collect her luggage. She came hurrying back towards the wagon only minutes later, hands clasped together and a worried expression on her face.

Brodie started to climb down off the wagon. "I suppose we have to take your stuff inside for you." He remained standing on the wagon when Remora shook her head.

"Is something wrong?" Mallory asked.

"He's broken up with you?" Brodie asked. "After you came all this way."

"He isn't here," Remora said.

"Where is he?" Brodie demanded.

"In Coastview," Remora said.

"But we've just come from there," Brodie exclaimed.

"Milos left early this morning. He would have arrived before we did," Remora explained. "He leaves for Estwater this afternoon by ship. It sails at four."

Chapter Twenty-Four

Seeing a journal notification, Mallory checked what it was for. It was a quest update. *Reunite Separated Lovers: Remora has a little over two hours to return to Coastview before Milos leaves the village and sails to Estwater.* "It took us three hours to get here."

"I'll never catch him before he leaves," Remora said.

"We weren't going that fast on the way here. We could have done it at a quicker pace," Jorgen said. "Not in two hours though. You never know, we might get lucky and his ship will be held up leaving Coastview."

Brodie sighed. "So much for lunch." He looked down at Remora. "I bet Scorch could do it in less than two hours with the two of us riding him."

"He could?" Remora asked hopefully.

Brodie jumped down to the ground. "Yeah. Come on." He untied Scorch from the back of the wagon and swung into the saddle, holding his hand out to Remora. Once she was behind him, he patted the front of the saddle when Fang sat beside Scorch and looked up at him with a whimper. "Come on then, girl." He leaned down, stretching out his hands to her.

Fang tried to jump high enough, but she was still too young. Jorgen climbed down off the wagon and handed her up.

"Thanks." Brodie looked towards his sister. "I'll see you in Coastview."

Before Mallory had the chance to tell him to be careful, he raced back the way they'd come. She drew in a deep breath. What if he encountered problems along the way? "We'd best go as fast as we can. Just because the trip here was quiet, it doesn't mean it'll be the same on the way back."

The entire trip back, Mallory kept checking Brodie's stats, relieved that they didn't change. She was also relieved that they made good time and nothing slowed them down. They reached Coastview at four thirty and made their way to the tavern, since all of them were certain that was where they'd find Brodie since he'd missed lunch.

Ninette, Jorgen and Esben waited with the wagon and Mallory hurried ahead of her party, reaching the tavern first. She spotted Brodie the moment she stepped inside, an empty plate in front of him. He was raising a cup to have a drink when he saw her, lowering it to wave them over, the rest of her party having entered the door behind her.

"Milos said he'd pay for lunch for the rest of you," Brodie said when they reached the table.

Milos glanced around at all of them, smiling as he placed his hand on Remora's where it rested on the table. "How can we thank you for reuniting us?"

"By paying the thirty gold pieces you said we could have for getting you to him," Brodie said.

"Certainly." Remora reached for her belt pouch.

Mallory held up a hand. "Give me a minute first." She added Emica to the party before she dashed outside and added the other three. She returned to the table to find Danae explaining what was going on and Remora and Milos' looks of confusion fading. "I'm all sorted now."

Remora handed over the thirty gold pieces to Mallory. "Thank you for all you did in reuniting us."

Mallory took the coins, slipping them into her belt pouch with plans to put them into the chest with the other coins when she went back outside. "We were happy to help." She read over the journal notification. *Reunite Separated Lovers: You reunited Remora and*

Milos and were rewarded with thirty gold pieces for your party. You also earned twenty experience points each.

"Hell yeah. I gained a CAS point," Brodie exclaimed.

"I did too," Ryan said.

"I did as well," Emica added.

Milos cleared his throat. "We were wondering if we could trouble you to escort us back to Ransted. We'll pay you, of course."

Mallory checked the new journal notification. *Return Home: Remora and Milos are willing to pay to be escorted to Ransted.*

"But we just came from there," Brodie protested. "We don't even need to go there to get to Lilica."

"I could pay you another thirty gold pieces," Remora offered.

"Thirty isn't much," Brodie said. "We're meant to be raiding a drake nest. If we take too long someone else might find the eggs. Or they might hatch before we get there. We were only supposed to take you to Ransted to find Milos. Not to Coastview too."

Remora turned to Mallory. "I have a ring that regens eight mana a minute. More than what you're looking for. I once thought I might become a mage, but my father wouldn't allow it. The ring is yours if you escort us to Ransted."

"How much would it be worth?" Brodie asked.

"I don't know," Remora said. "I couldn't bring myself to sell it when I sold my other jewellery at Eastvale." She took a ring out of her belt pouch, holding it so they could see it. The narrow gold band had a single blue stone set in it.

Mallory wanted to offer to take Remora and Milos back to Ransted without payment. Remora appeared to be extremely reluctant to part with the ring. But that was a lot of mana to regen a minute and might make a big difference in future fights.

Brodie took the ring from Remora, examining it before handing it back. "It looks a lot better than some of that other jewellery you have." He turned to his sister as he spoke. "I reckon we should accept. You need all the mana you can get with how little your healing spell does."

"A higher level healing spell would improve on that for very little extra mana cost," Danae said.

Remora put the ring away. "Does that mean you'll escort us back to Ransted?"

Milos put an arm around Remora's waist. "If you don't wish to part with it, we can remain here until another party travels back that way."

Remora shook her head. "No. It could be weeks. I'd

rather part with the ring than wait here for weeks to start our life together."

Mallory momentarily closed her eyes, taking a deep breath before she spoke. "I vote yes to escorting Remora and Milos, but no to the ring."

"Are you insane?" Brodie demanded.

Ryan chuckled. "I guess we all know what Brodie's vote is. It'll be yes, to both the quest and the ring."

"It's a mana regen ring," Brodie said, as if his comment explained everything.

"I vote the same as Mallory," Callum said.

Ryan nodded. "Yeah. Me too."

"I don't mind what you choose," Emica said. "It's not like I have to be anywhere else." She turned to Brodie. "You haven't heard anything from my father?"

Brodie shook his head. "I check regularly. Nothing."

Remora smiled at Mallory. "That's very kind of you, but I'll have no need of the ring. Becoming a mage isn't something I wish to do anymore. Not after seeing what it's like to travel and fight. It's far different than I'd imagined. It's just hard to put aside those dreams when at times they were all that helped get me through living in my father's home." She glanced at Milos, her smiled broadening. "I'm sure life will be far better in the future. With new dreams to follow and work towards."

"If you're certain," Mallory said.

Remora nodded. "Very certain."

"Okay. We'll escort the two of you to Ransted." Before Mallory could say anything else, food was brought to the table and handed around. She looked down at the fish set on a bed of rice. "I didn't order anything." It was the same meal that had been placed in front of everyone else.

"You've gotta try it," Brodie said. "It's amazing. I don't know what herbs they use, and they refused to tell me, but it's the best meal ever."

Ryan grinned. "Until your next meal."

When the laughter died down, Brodie glaring at them as he rose to his feet. "I organised for the trader to buy all the resources we gathered. I'll get that done while you have lunch. And collect Scorch from him. He let me leave Scorch out behind his place."

"What about Ninette, Jorgen and Esben?" Mallory asked. "They'll need something to eat too."

"I ordered food sent out to them," Brodie said. "Milos said he'd pay for all of us."

"I'm surprised you didn't order dessert too," Mallory said.

With another glare for his sister, and everyone who

laughed at her comment, Brodie strode from the tavern.

Chapter Twenty-Five

Mallory tried the food as soon as her brother left, having to agree that the food was amazing. "What's it called?"

"It's a Coastview speciality," Milos said. "It's coastal barbed lobic with island rice."

"Is that a type of rice?" Mallory asked.

"No, it's the name of the herb and rice dish that is served with the fish." Milos said.

Mallory had another mouthful, savouring the food. If anyone could manage to get a hold of the recipe, she was certain it would be her brother.

Once they'd eaten, they returned to the wagon, which was now empty of all the resources they'd gathered on the way to Ransted. Scorch was also tied up at the back of the wagon and Brodie was arguing with Esben about the best types of food.

Brodie turned to them as they neared, taking a

piece of paper out of his belt pouch to hold it up triumphantly. "Look what I bought." He took out some coins and dropped them into Mallory's hand. "I also managed to get seventeen gold pieces for the resources."

Mallory put those coins, along with the thirty gold pieces, into the chest, asking as she did so, "What did you get?" She had a pretty good idea what it was with how excited her brother was.

"It cost me a gold piece so I've only got seven copper pieces left, but I bought the recipe for coastal barbed lobic with island rice."

Mallory took a gold piece out of the chest and handed it over to her brother. "You didn't need to spend your money on it. You make the food for all the party so we can't expect you to pay for recipes that we'll all eat."

"You might want to add that it doesn't count if he wants to buy ones worth a lot of money," Ryan said.

"I was about to say that should be obvious, but…" Mallory let her words trail off as she gave her brother a look to let him know her comment was about him.

"As if I'd waste too much money on a recipe," Brodie protested.

"You won't be able to cook that recipe while we're travelling," Esben pointed out.

"I can't make it yet, anyway," Brodie said. "Not until I put five CAS points into cooking. It's a level fifteen recipe." He was silent a moment. "Level fifteen gave me the ability to make inferior quality food. I can't wait to find out how much better inferior is compared to poor quality."

Jorgen gathered the reins, nodding towards Augusta and Bug who pulled the wagon. "Are we ready to go?"

Milos took a second look at Bug. "I recognise her. Your horse came off a farm out from Ransted."

"A second one would be useful," Callum said. "We don't know if Danae's father will want Augusta back."

"My cousin is married to one of the farmer's sons," Milos said. "I'm sure that with all the help you've given us, they'd be willing to give you a discount if you wanted to buy one of their horses. I'm fairly certain they have a couple for sale."

"I wouldn't mind having a look at what they have to offer, but I don't know that we'd have enough money," Callum said. "We don't carry a lot of it around with us."

As they headed out of Coastview, everyone now in the wagon along with Milos' luggage, Brodie said, "I wonder if they ever got a demonic gateway portal at the Adventurers Guild. We could use the portal they gave us to go there, give them an answer and see if we can travel to a bank so we can get money out."

"Would that work?" Mallory asked. "Or would it cost too much?"

"The bank vault has a teller where you can withdraw your money from your account," Danae said. "You wouldn't have to travel to an actual bank."

"A pity we can't get to level twenty really quick and get our own bank vault," Brodie said.

Mallory looked at each of them. "Does everyone want to join? I really like the idea of having our own bathroom. No more going behind bushes along the side of the road. I could use the personal portal, go back to our suite, when we have one, then return to whatever our current location is."

Brodie's expression brightened. "I never thought of that."

"I bet all you were thinking about was the kitchen," Ryan said.

"I wasn't just thinking about the kitchen," Brodie protested. "I was thinking about the chest we can lock stuff in too."

"I wouldn't mind joining them," Danae said. "It'd be good to have a place we can easily travel to."

"That'll eventually have a kitchen," Brodie said.

Ryan chuckled. "Are you sure that wasn't all you were thinking about?"

Brodie glared at him. "Bet you wouldn't turn down a meal cooked in it."

Mallory turned to Ninette. "Did you want to read the handbook?" She glanced at Emica. "You're all welcome to read it and join as individuals, if you want."

"Thank you," Ninette said. "I'm not sure that I'd want to join. Living in a sentient demonic castle would be strange."

"I wouldn't mind reading the handbook," Jorgen said. "I'm not interested in joining, but that doesn't mean I don't want to learn more about them."

Danae took over the driving so Jorgen could read during the journey back to Ransted. Since things were quiet, Mallory decided to get a head start on her notebook. They'd reach Ransted at eight thirty at the earliest and probably wouldn't have much time for anything before bed.

Once she finished writing in her notebook, Mallory returned it to the chest she stored it in and recast magelight. Casting it reminded her of the spell she needed to learn and sitting back down, she took it out of her belt pouch. The parchment went in a burst of light once she'd learned it. Checking her journal, she discovered she couldn't use it yet. Not until she went up a level in mage. Or put another eight points into intelligence. Luckily it wouldn't be long until she reached her next character level.

"About time you learned that spell," Brodie said.

Chapter Twenty-Six

Mallory laughed at her brother's comment. "Not that it'll help. It's a level four spell. I need another sixty-seven XP to gain my next character level."

"A pity we couldn't have spent that money on XP potions," Brodie muttered.

"Then we wouldn't have a compact alchemist's station," Callum pointed out.

"I guess." Brodie turned back to Mallory. "You should be gathering resources so you can use the spell."

"We cleaned this area out earlier," Mallory said.

"Then go further from the road," Brodie said.

Mallory slowly shook her head. "I'm not going to level up tonight. You'll just have to wait for me to be able to use the spell."

"Tracking magelight is one of the types of spells it's worth levelling up," Danae said. "It doesn't have a higher level spell for that level of brightness light. Same with magelight. Unless of course you want a light that's a lot brighter than either of those two. The only difference in the higher versions of them is that the light cast is brighter."

"No," Mallory said. "Magelight is more than bright enough to do the job." She looked over both spells, wondering if she should put CAS points in the one she could currently use. Having it last for a longer amount of time and cost less mana would be useful, but then she only had five CAS points available. What if she needed them for something else? After some back and forth over the dilemma, Mallory decided to keep the CAS points for now and worry about levelling the spells up later. They were good enough as they were and she might need the CAS points for something else. Something unexpected.

They reached the farm where Milos lived without encountering any problems, Remora having fallen asleep, as did Brodie, curled up next to Fang. The farmhouse was dark and everything silent. Milos jumped down from the wagon, helping Remora down too.

Remora blinked sleepily, fumbling at her belt pouch. "I want to thank you for bringing me back here." She held out the ring, the single blue stone glinting in the magelight.

Before Mallory shifted forward so she could take the ring, she added everyone to the party. "Thank you. This will come in handy." She ignored the journal notification, planning to check it once she'd finished talking to Remora.

Remora smiled up at her. "I'm glad. After everything you've done for us, it now seems so little." She glanced at Brodie. "After everything all of you have done."

Milos slipped an arm around Remora's waist, his gaze on Mallory. "You're welcome to camp here tonight, over by the large tree near the barn, and I can take you to see the people who bred your horse in the morning if you're interested."

"At least we can shrink them and don't need to find anywhere to keep them these days," Brodie said.

"A horse might cost more than what we carry on us." Mallory mentally calculated what was in her belt pouch and the chest. Ninety-two gold, twenty-one silver and forty-one copper pieces. Probably a lot less than what they'd need. They might have enough, since Bug had only cost them eighty gold pieces, but that wouldn't leave them much left over for any other expenses.

Milos smiled reassuringly. "As I said, I'll see if I can talk them into giving you a discount."

"We should at least find out what one would be worth," Callum suggested.

Mallory nodded. It'd also be good not to have to travel all night and to get some sleep in a relatively safe area. "Okay. We'll have a look in the morning."

Ryan and Callum helped Milos with Remora's luggage while the rest of them set up camp, including pitching the tents and putting food on.

Before Mallory helped, she removed everyone from the party then slipped the new ring on, smiling when she saw that her mana regen was now sixty-two a minute. More than her maximum mana. She should probably put more points into wisdom when she levelled up so she could gain more mana. Finished looking at her stats, Mallory checked the journal notification while she helped with one of the tents. *Return Home: You escorted Remora and Milos home and were rewarded with a ring that regens eight mana a minute for your party. You also earned twenty experience points each.*

Mallory checked her experience points. She now only needed to earn another forty-seven experience points to reach character level six. They'd done a lot in the nineteen days they'd been on Inadon. She was looking forward to seeing what they did when they reached Eridell.

Since Brodie had sold all the vegetables and herbs in Coastview and they hadn't been hunting for meat, he used up the dried rations. Callum took his plate and cup of coffee from Brodie, sitting by the fire with everyone else before he spoke. "Don't sell everything in future. Now we don't have anything in case we go through another area that's been picked clean."

Brodie glared at Callum. "It wouldn't have mattered anyway. We still didn't have any meat to make a stew or something. And there's only enough coffee left for two cups. You'll have to give me some of the coffee from your satchel if you want me to keep making it."

"All of it can go with the food supplies," Callum said. "And there would have been nothing wrong with making a vegetable stew. Or even cooking them in the coals."

"Vegetable stew is nice," Danae agreed. "You have spices you could have added."

"Food doesn't taste exactly right unless you have a recipe for it. It's odd like that here," Brodie protested.

"Then find a vegetable stew recipe," Ryan said. "Or vegetable soup. Something you can make when we don't have meat."

Mallory left Brodie and Ryan to their disagreement, focusing on her meal and thinking about the Adventurers Guild. She really needed to find out if they had a bathroom that members could use before they had one in their personal quarters. Including a shower. She'd love a shower right now after all the travelling they'd done. Would it be too late to visit them?

Going to the map in her journal, she zoomed out, surprised at the distance between the two areas they'd visited. The rest of the map was dark and unexplored. She couldn't help thinking of the first time she'd seen the map and how only the area around her icon had been visible. Now a fair bit of Ruby Isle showed on the map. Turning to Danae, she waited until she'd finished talking to Emica before she spoke. "Is there a way to unlock all of a map without actually visiting everywhere?"

"I don't know," Danae said.

Jorgen leaned towards them so he could see past his cousin. "I believe there's a mage spell that copies that knowledge from others. You could also add people to your party and share information. Sharing information doesn't always work reliably when it comes to maps though. It can take a bit for the areas to fill in. Particularly if there are a lot of differences between the areas uncovered by each person."

"Demons," Emica said. "They can do it with one of their spells. Only a really high level demon though."

"I bet it'd be expensive," Brodie said.

Jorgen shrugged. "Probably."

Chapter Twenty-Seven

Mallory again looked at her map, about to ask if it was too late to visit the Adventurers Guild. It occurred to her that the guild would be in a different time zone. "How do I figure out what hour it'd be at the Adventurers Guild?"

"Where is it?" Jorgen asked.

Callum took the map of Inadon out of his satchel, showing it to Jorgen. "Right here. Or as near as I can figure out from my journal map."

Jorgen glanced skywards. "It's about nine thirty here, so at a guess, that location would be somewhere between three and five in the morning."

"How do we figure out a more accurate time?" Ryan asked. "I'm not sure that anyone would appreciate being woken at three in the morning."

"I wouldn't," Brodie muttered.

"It was daylight when we visited there," Ninette said.

"A bit after midday at a guess," Callum said. "Maybe as much as an hour after midday."

"We could get up early in the morning and head over to Donris Island," Ryan suggested.

"I was hoping to go tonight." Mallory thought wistfully of a warm shower.

Ryan chuckled. "You're thinking of their bathroom, aren't you?"

"Maybe," Mallory said.

"Is that the only reason you want to join them?" Ninette asked.

Mallory laughed at the question. She supposed she shouldn't have been surprised to be asked since she'd mentioned it a few times. "No. I wouldn't join a guild just for that reason. It's just if we are going to join them, it'd be nice to have a shower before bed."

"Or sleep in their beds?" Emica asked. "Does that mean the rest of us would have to stay here and guard your gear?"

Mallory shook her head. "If we couldn't all travel there and stay the night, then none of us would stay overnight. It wouldn't be fair otherwise."

"We'd need chests that would allow us to shrink them and the contents," Danae said. "It's the only way we could take everyone and everything with us to stay the night."

The conversation quickly turned to items they wanted with Brodie being the one who suggested the most amounts of things. Partway through Brodie talking about a kitchen, Ryan interrupted. "Are we going there tonight?"

"No." Mallory tried to ignore her disappointment, but it was hard. "As much as I'd like to see if we do get access to a bathroom, it's probably best to go there at what we know is a reasonable time rather than risk going when it could be extremely early in the morning."

"We going there tomorrow morning?" Ryan asked.

Mallory shrugged. "I suppose we'll have to wait and see what else happens in the morning. I want to go there and activate our membership, but not when we might disturb them."

Ninette rose to her feet. "If we're all staying here, then I'll go to bed. I better get some sleep in case you want to travel there in the morning and you need someone to guard the camp."

There were murmurs of agreement, most of them heading to bed, only Callum and Brodie staying awake to clean up after cooking. Callum also put all the coffee from his satchel in with the rest of the food.

The next morning they didn't have a chance to go anywhere. Milos woke them wanting to know if they needed an escort to the horse farm. After a quick discussion with her party, Mallory faced Milos. "We'd appreciate you showing us where the farm is. We wouldn't mind looking at the horses he has for sale." They didn't want to risk being left with only Bug to pull the wagon if Danae's father wanted Augusta back.

Leaving the majority of their party behind to pack, Mallory, Ryan, Brodie, Callum and Danae, along with the two companion animals, saddled the horses and followed Milos who rode one of the farm horses.

Brodie rode between Milos and Danae, peppering Milos with questions. He was on Scorch while Danae was on Augusta, Fang darting back and forth between Brodie and the bushes along the side of the road. Behind them was Callum on the unnamed horse and Mallory and Ryan were both on Bug.

"We really need to give this horse a name." Callum patted the neck of the horse he rode.

"No point asking me to name it," Ryan said. "You never like what I come up with."

Mallory couldn't help laughing. "Can you blame him?"

"What about escape?" Ryan asked. "The horse did escape from being owned by the dark forces."

Mallory slowly shook her head. "That's a terrible name. You might as well call the horse refugee or something."

"How about Dodger?" Callum asked.

"That could work," Mallory said.

Ryan shrugged. "I don't mind what name you come up with."

Callum smiled. "That's only because any name has to be better than the ones you come up with."

Ryan grinned. "Maybe."

Before Mallory had the chance to comment, they arrived at their destination. Milos left them by the front door while he went to find the horse breeder, heading towards a barn that was behind the house. While they waited for him to come back, Callum told Brodie and Danae the name of the horse, disagreeing with Brodie when he suggested a few other names they could use instead. None of them could agree on a name.

Milos returned to the front of the house with an older man at his side, interrupting Callum and Brodie's disagreement. Milos nodded towards the man. "This is Arnnik. I told him you're interested in what horses he has for sale." Milos introduced them, mentioning each of their names.

Arnnik nodded in greeting, his gaze drawn to Bug. "I have one of her siblings available. Another mare with her temperament. I can offer her to you for a hundred and ten gold pieces."

"But Bug was only worth eighty," Brodie protested.

"Then you got her for a bargain," Arnnik said. "I'd normally sell the mare for a hundred and twenty gold pieces, but since Milos put in a good word for you, I've given you a discount."

"Do you have one that's cheaper than that?" Callum asked.

"I'm afraid not," Arnnik said. "I have three I can offer you at that price with the rest I have available being a lot more expensive."

"We don't have that much money on us." Mallory couldn't help thinking about the money in their bank account. Should they have left more of it out? Yet travelling around while carrying a lot of money wasn't a good idea. Not with the amount of bandits and dark forces members they'd encountered.

"They did help me reunite with Remora," Milos said. "Is it possible to give them a larger discount?"

Arnnik rubbed at his chin. "I do have a small quest that needs doing."

"What type of quest?" Callum asked.

At the same time, Brodie also spoke. "How much of a discount would the quest give us?"

"If you can convince my neighbour to let me use their stallion for breeding during the next year, I'll drop the price to half. But it has to be for a full year and at the previous stud fee," Arnnik said.

"That sounds easy enough," Brodie said.

Chapter Twenty-Eight

Mallory opened her journal and read over the quest. *Stud Fee Negotiations: If you can convince Arnnik's neighbour to agree to let him use his stallion for breeding during the next year at the previous stud fee Arnnik will sell you a mare at half his asking price.* Closing her journal, she studied Arnnik. He didn't seem like the sort of person who would find it difficult to negotiate on his own behalf. "What's the catch?"

Arnnik chuckled. "It's not exactly a catch. Jefnas refuses to speak to me. I've tried numerous times now. He's as irritable as a harpy. I'd quite happily avoid him, like any sane person would avoid a harpy, but his stallion has just the traits I'm looking for."

"What if he doesn't want to talk to us?" Danae asked.

Arnnik shrugged. "Then I suppose if you can't

come up with the price for the mare, you'll have to go somewhere else."

"I guess there's only one way to find out." Ryan swung into Bug's saddle, holding out a hand to Mallory. Once she was behind him, he turned towards Arnnik. "Whereabouts is your neighbour?"

Arnnik pointed in the direction opposite to where they'd come from. "Keep going down the road and take the next turnoff."

Brodie mounted Scorch. "I bet we can convince him."

"Did you need me to come with you or can you find your own way around?" Milos asked. "It's been so long since Remora and I have been together."

"We'll figure it out," Ryan said. "Arnnik's directions sound easy enough and we can find out way back to your place without a drama too."

"Then I'll leave you to your quest," Milos said.

Once Milos had left and Arnnik had returned to the stable, they rode over to his neighbour's place. It had a similar layout to Arnnik's farm and when no one answered a knock on the front door, they made their way to the closest stable, leaving their horses tied up at the rail in front of the house.

A man in his fifties met them at the stable door, a

permanent frown etched into his forehead. "What do you want?"

"Are you Jefnas?" Ryan asked.

"Who's asking?" the man demanded.

Ryan introduced each of them.

"That still doesn't tell me what you want," the man said.

"Are you Jefnas?" Callum repeated his brother's question.

"Hurry up and tell me what you want of me. I don't have all day to stand around gossiping."

"We came here on behalf of Arnnik." Before Mallory could say anything else, Jefnas interrupted her.

"Then you can go back over there and tell him he's wasting his time. If he can't help me out, I can't help him out." Jefnas started to turn away.

"Help you out with what?" Mallory asked.

"Ahh, I see. He's not told you the whole story, has he?" Jefnas demanded.

"What is the whole story?" Brodie asked.

"Why don't you go ask him?" Again Jefnas started to turn away, stopping when Danae spoke.

"Maybe it's you who's the one who needs help to deal with Arnnik and not the other way around."

Jefnas looked Danae up and down. "About the only one of you who's speaking any sense."

Mallory took a step towards him. "How can we help you?"

"You tell that Arnnik that if he wants my stallion to service his mares then I need hay to keep my herd fed."

"Okay," Mallory said. "We can do that. We'll be back as soon as we have an answer for you."

It didn't take them long to return to Arnnik's place, and they found him in the stable. Between them, they explain the situation.

"I can't sell him hay. Is he still going on about that? I thought he understood. One of my fields was burned," Arnnik said. "You go back and tell him I have no spare hay. I'll barely have enough to feed my horses until the field is ready to harvest again."

When they were on their way back to Jefnas' farm, Brodie said, "I hope they're not going to expect us to run backwards and forwards carrying messages. I don't want to be stuck here all day doing that."

"All we have to do is convince Jefnas that Arnnik has no spare hay," Mallory said. "Then talk him into the deal with Arnnik."

"Jefnas didn't strike me as a sort of person who

could be easily convinced of anything that didn't suit him," Callum said.

Reaching the house, Mallory dropped to the ground once Ryan brought Bug to a stop. "Hopefully you're wrong."

"I hope so too," Callum said.

Once again they found Jefnas in the stable and he wasn't in the slightest bit convinced that Arnnik had told the truth.

Mallory slowly let out a breath, trying not to let her annoyance enter her tone of voice. "Isn't there someone else you could buy hay from?"

"Not at the price I was getting it from Arnnik. Everyone else wants a quarter more than what he was charging," Jefnas grumbled. "I tried to buy from Galna up the road from here, but that woman was determined to bleed me dry. She knocked back my offer and refused to come down on the ridiculous price she wanted to charge."

"If we can talk her into taking your offer, would you be willing to make a deal with Arnnik?" Ryan asked.

Jefnas laughed, a short, sharp sound. "I doubt you can talk her into accepting the offer. Not with the way she carried on."

"Where does she live?" Callum asked.

Jefnas nodded in the opposite direction to Arnnik's farm. "Along that way a bit. The second turn on the right."

"I bet we can talk her into it," Brodie said.

"If you can, then I'll come to terms with Arnnik."

Mallory checked the journal notification, surprised to find it was another quest. *In Need Of Hay: If you can convince Galna to accept Jefnas' price for her hay, Jefnas will accept Arnnik's offer.* "We'll be back as soon as we've talked to her."

"Don't bother coming back unless you've got good news," Jefnas stated.

None of them spoke until they were heading down the road. "Two quests isn't all that bad," Brodie said. "Unless of course they're the stupid kind where we don't get much XP for them."

Ryan grinned. "They probably will be. But at least we'll save a lot of gold by doing them."

"I suppose," Brodie muttered.

"I was beginning to think we'd be stuck running backwards and forwards between Arnnik and Jefnas," Callum said.

"We might be stuck running between Galna, Arnnik and Jefnas," Ryan said.

"We better not be," Brodie muttered.

Mallory laughed at her brother's expression and

tone of voice. "Maybe you should put your CAS points in bartering. Getting it to twenty-one might make a difference and help you talk Galna into the trade with Jefnas."

"But I need to keep some in case I need a higher cooking level." Brodie turned to Danae. "Do you think it'd make a difference if I added one extra point?"

Danae shook her head. "Most of the time you need to put five points into bartering for it to make much of a difference."

Brodie turned to Callum. "You have thirty-two CAS points. You could put all of them into bartering."

"I'm not about to waste them like that," Callum said. "I'm keeping them until I know the details of all the crafting abilities and can decide which would be the most useful to put them into."

Chapter Twenty-Nine

Mallory interrupted her brother when he started to argue with Callum. "Looks like we've reached Galna's place." She gestured towards the dirt track that led off the road to a house with an apple orchard behind it and off to the left and hay fields out to the right. They followed the track to the house, a timber post and rail fence running along the side of the track and separating them from the orchard. A small herd of sheep grazed beneath the trees.

Before they reached the house, a woman came out to greet them, a broad brimmed straw hat shading her face. "Can I help you?"

Mallory waited until they'd all dismounted before she spoke, introducing all of them and learning that the woman was Galna before she explained why they were there.

Galna laughed, disbelief filling the sound. "He sent you to me? Are you sure he said it was me to visit?"

Mallory nodded. "Arnnik has no hay. One of his fields was burned so he can't get hay from it like he usually does."

Galna nodded slowly, her expression becoming serious. "None of us around here are likely to forget that. We were all worried the fire might spread. We were lucky to have a mage passing through who helped put the fire out."

"So what do you reckon?" Brodie asked. "Jefnas really needs hay for his horses."

"He should have thought about that, or paid me for the apples his horses ate from my orchard," Galna said. "You tell him if he pays for the apples, I'll accept the price he offered. If he doesn't pay for them, then he'll have to accept the price I offered if he wants my hay."

Mallory tried not to sigh. It was close. "We'll be back with his answer." Again she waited until they were down the road and out of hearing before she spoke. "This is starting to feel like one of those quests that send you all over the place and back and forth. The sort that takes you forever to get anywhere."

"The old woman who swallowed a spider type quest," Callum said.

Mallory nodded while Ryan chuckled.

"What does that mean?" Danae asked.

Brodie turned to Callum. "Yeah, what does that mean. It doesn't make sense. I know the kid's song, but how does that work as a quest?"

"She kept swallowing one more thing to deal with the previous thing," Mallory said. "We keep getting asked to deal with one more thing so we can deal with the previous quest."

"That song takes forever to end and then she dies. Does that mean we won't be able to finish any of the quests?" Brodie asked.

Callum shrugged. "We'll have to wait and see."

"Then how are we meant to pay for the horse?" Brodie asked. "I don't want to have to travel back to the bank. We've already wasted enough time running backwards and forwards with Remora."

Ryan pulled out the pocket watch. "It's half past eight. We'll give it till lunch to try and complete it."

"Then we better get moving." Brodie urged Scorch into a trot.

Arriving back at Jefnas' place, they found him in the barn, glaring at them as they entered. He looked at each of them, a self-satisfied smile forming. "Told you she wouldn't sell the hay at that price."

"She will if you pay for the apples your horses ate," Mallory said.

"Why should I be forced to pay for them when it's her fences that are broken?" Jefnas demanded.

"How did your horses get over to her place?" Callum asked.

"I caught bandits trying to steal them. I sent my dogs after the bandits, but they'd already broken my fence and the horses ran off. It took me all day to round them up and I found the last of them in Galna's orchard. If her fences hadn't been broken, then my horses wouldn't have been able to get into her orchard." Jefnas gestured towards Galna's place, the movement sharp. "You tell her that if she wants anyone to pay for the apples then she can track down the bandits. It wasn't like I let my horses out."

Mallory tried not to let the annoyance she felt colour her words. "We'll let her know." Again she waited until they were riding along the road before she spoke. "Maybe we won't be able to complete any of these quests."

Brodie glanced at Callum. "If one of us had higher bartering, it might make a difference."

"I don't think even a higher level in diplomacy would help," Danae said.

When they arrived back at Galna's, she again came

out to greet them, listening as they passed along the message from Jefnas. "Anyone would think I enjoy having broken fences and haven't bothered to try and get them fixed. I've been asking the carpenter for over a month and she keeps telling me she'll let me know when she has time to get around to fixing them. Yet I never hear back from her."

"What if we can get her to come out and fix your fences today?" Brodie asked.

Mallory felt like hitting her brother. How were they meant to do that? He could have suggested a longer time frame. Like a week. It was too late now. She doubted Galna would accept a different offer with the gleam in her eyes.

Galna grinned. "You manage that and I'll accept that old man's offer. Not that I really want to do business with him. Always cranky. But to get my fences fixed after waiting for so long, I'd be willing to put up with him."

"Where would we find the carpenter?" Callum asked.

"Loral is a couple of houses along from the tavern. You can't miss her place. She has a fence that's unbroken." Galna pointed in the direction of the village.

Biting back a sigh, Mallory took a step back from

Galna, ignoring the notification which she assumed was a quest. "We'll be back as soon as we've talked to Loral." She waited until they were on their way before she checked her journal notification. Like she'd assumed, it was a quest. *Broken Fence: If you can convince Loral to fix Galna's fence today, then Galna will accept Jefnas' price for her hay.* Mallory closed her journal before looking at her brother. "What were you thinking? A day? How are we meant to get the carpenter to fix the fence today? She sounds busy."

"We find out what she wants," Brodie said. "She's sure to want something."

"Why is she?" Mallory asked.

"Everyone else does," Brodie said.

Ryan chuckled. "It doesn't always work like that, Brodie."

"Or if she does want something, we might not be able to get it for her," Callum said.

"She'll want something and we'll figure out how to get it for her. Look at all we've organised so far," Brodie said. "We just have to find the person who needs something we can get."

Mallory slowly shook her head, leaving Brodie and Callum to their discussion of the topic. She looked ahead to the village they approached. Like many of the other villages they'd been in, it consisted of timber houses and dirt roads. The carpenter's house was easy to find. Loral had a sign out the front, neat words painted across it. 'Carpenter. Enquire within.' She also couldn't help taking notice of the fence. The unbroken paling fence.

Danae remained on Augusta. "Should some of us wait here and watch the horses? In case those bandits are still in the area."

"I'll wait out here with you if you want," Callum offered.

Brodie looked between the carpenter's house and Danae, obviously torn.

Laughing, Mallory dismounted. "You can wait out here too, Brodie." She didn't need him making any more unrealistic offers.

"But what if you need my bartering skills?" Brodie protested.

"Then we'll call you." Ryan dismounted and handed his reins over to Callum. "We shouldn't be long." He opened the gate and waited until Mallory stepped into the small front yard before he closed it.

Chapter Thirty

Mallory walked beside Ryan to the front door, taking a deep breath before she knocked on it. How were they ever going to convince Loral to fix Galna's fence today? Inside she heard the sounds of children arguing and wondered if her knock had been loud enough to be heard over the noise. About to knock again, the door swung open.

A little girl stood in the doorway, looking up at them, her hands behind her back. She grinned at them. "Did you want to help me hide? My brother doesn't like to share."

"Uhm." Mallory was at a loss as to what to say.

"What doesn't he like to share?" Ryan asked.

The little girl took her hands from behind her back and held out two wooden warriors. "Anything. He thinks I'll break them. But I just want to play."

Ryan squatted down in front of her. "Do they have names?"

When the little girl nodded and began to tell him all about the warriors, Ryan looked up at Mallory, glancing between her and the open doorway.

Assuming he was asking her to find the child's mother, she slipped past her and into the house. It was larger than the typical village house and the sitting room opened into a small hallway that led to a kitchen. A woman was trying to clean food off a toddler that was sitting at a table trying to grab a bowl of food while two young boys argued over a wooden horse that looked to be of a size to go with the wooden warriors.

"Hello." Mallory smiled apologetically when the noise abruptly stopped and they all turned to look at her. "Your daughter is at the front door hoping we'll help her hide." Or at least she assumed it was the woman's daughter.

The woman grabbed hold of one of the boys by his collar when he started to run towards the front door. "No you don't. The two of you wait here and watch your sister." She cut off the boy's protests. "I mean it. Stay here and keep your sister out of trouble." She looked from one boy to the other, moving away from the toddler when the two of them took over the job of trying to feed their sister. "If you're here about a carpenter job, I'm afraid I don't have any time to take on more work." She strode towards the front of the house.

"We were here to see if you could repair Galna's fence." Mallory said as Loral scooped up her daughter, ignoring her protests. "She said she's been waiting over a month to have it fixed."

Loral hushed her daughter's protests. "Thank you for keeping this one safe, but I'm afraid it'll take more than that to make it possible for me to fix Galna's fence any time soon."

"What would it take?" Ryan asked.

"A miracle," Loral said.

"What type of miracle?" Mallory asked.

"Someone who can take my mother to an apothecary and bring her home again." When her daughter tried to wriggle out of her grip, Loral put her down and pointed her in the direction of the kitchen. "Join your brothers and sister and stop taking their toys. You have plenty of your own." Loral turned back to Mallory and Ryan once her daughter had headed towards the kitchen. "As you can see, I can't very well take off and leave my children here to fend for themselves. They'd probably burn the place down."

"Who watches them when you're working?" Ryan asked.

"My mother." Loral smiled wryly. "Hence the reason why I don't have time to take on any work. It's a good thing I had some savings or we wouldn't have managed so long without me working."

"Would you like me to see if I can help your mother?" Mallory asked.

Ryan spoke before Loral could. "If Mallory can cure your mother and one of the people with us can look after your children, will you fix Galna's fences for her today?"

"I'm not about to leave my children with just anyone." Loral looked Ryan up and down. "How much experience have you had with children?"

Ryan grinned. "Very little. I was thinking of Ninette, a friend of ours who's waiting for us at Milos' place. She has younger brothers, so she's had plenty of experience with kids."

"Where is she from?" Loral asked.

"Buckneth," Mallory said. "She was raised on a sheep farm there."

"Buckneth is a good place. They're good people." Loral looked thoughtful. "Bring her back for me to meet. If I'm happy with her she can look after my children while I show you to where my mother lives and then I'll fix Galna's fence."

Mallory couldn't resist smiling when she checked the journal notification that appeared in the corner of her vision. Finally a quest they might be able to complete without the help of one of the inhabitants of Ransted and its environs. *Sickly Relative: If you can cure Loral's mother and take care of her children for the day, she will repair Galna's fence.* "We'll be back as soon as possible."

"Come right on in when you return. I can't hear anything over my children half the time." Galna remained in the doorway as they returned to the horses, waving to them as they turned towards Milos' place.

Brodie spoke before they'd barely moved a few metres away from the carpenter's house. "Who has to look after the kids? It better not be me."

"We want them to survive the experience so it definitely won't be you," Ryan said.

"Did you want me to help?" Danae asked.

"Have you had experience looking after kids before?" Mallory asked.

Danae shook her head. "How hard can it be?"

Ryan chuckled. "You don't want to know. I'll feel sorry for Ninette if she agrees."

"Let's hope she's willing to help," Mallory said.

By the time they returned to Milos' place, it was ten and Brodie started telling them to hurry now they had a chance to complete all their quests. Ninette agreed to help, even before Mallory had finished explaining the situation. She tried to assure Ninette that it wasn't compulsory.

Ninette interrupted Mallory. "I know what it's like to look after children. I'm glad I can help you even a small fraction of what you've helped me."

Jorgen looked up from the fire he sat beside, reading through one of the crafting ability books. "Did you need us to join you?" He glanced at his cousin as he spoke, most of his attention on the book he'd been reading.

Mallory shook her head. "We need you and Esben to look after the wagon. I can add you to the party and hopefully we'll be close enough you gain XP when we complete the quest."

Brodie, who'd just finished hassling Ryan to check his watch again, asked, "Does this mean we'll keep going even if we reach midday before we're done? We only have to sort out the one quest and all the rest will fall into place."

"We'll decide that after we find out what's wrong

with Loral's mum," Mallory said. "She might be too sick for me to cure."

"But you've got level fifty apothecary," Brodie protested.

"Mallory can treat all ailments and diseases, even rare ones," Danae said. "But if Loral's mother should need something like complex surgery, Mallory won't have the levels to perform it."

"Hope it's only an ailment or a disease then," Brodie said.

Mallory slowly shook her head. "That sounds terrible, Brodie. It's like you're wishing something on her."

"I wasn't," Brodie exclaimed. "I was just saying that I hope it's something you can cure."

"I've not had anything to do with youngsters, but if you need the extra help…" Emica's words trailed off and she finished her offer with a shrug.

Mallory smiled as she thought of Loral's children. They'd need more than a total noob looking after them. "That's okay. We need some of you here to guard all the gear and wagon. You can help Jorgen and Esben."

Emica grinned. "Probably best I stick with that job. I doubt their mother would appreciate me threatening them with a sword if they misbehave."

Ryan chuckled. "I think she'd do some threatening of her own if you did that."

Brodie glanced at the campfire that burned low. "Should we have something to eat before we get back to the quests?"

"Absolutely not," Mallory said firmly. "I want to be heading north before the day ends." And she wanted to have a new horse to take with them. The only way they'd manage that, without making a trip to the bank, would be to complete the quests.

Chapter Thirty-One

The trip back to Loral's house was accompanied by questions from Ninette about the children and Brodie correcting every answer Mallory gave. She sent him a look as they approached the house. "They aren't that bad."

"She'll soon see that they are," Brodie warned.

Before Mallory had a chance to reply, the door burst open and the two boys ran outside, one chasing the other with a stick. The one in the lead clutched something to his chest, a broad grin on his face as the other demanded that he return the item he stole.

Ninette swung down from behind Danae, grabbing hold of the child who was in the lead and taking the item from him. "How about we check with your ma about who this belongs to." She marched both boys inside.

"Looks like Ninette has this under control," Callum said.

"I'll see how long it'll take before Loral can leave." Mallory began to dismount, stopping when Loral came outside.

"You were certainly accurate when you said she was good with children," Loral said.

Mallory didn't bother correcting Loral. All she'd said was that Ninette had plenty of experience with kids. "Does your mum live far from here?"

"Only a couple of streets over." Laura pointed to hitching posts over at the tavern. "You can leave your horses there. No one will touch them. We all look out for each other in town."

When they'd left their horses at the tavern, Loral led the way to her mother's home. It was a similar style building to Loral's even having a paling fence around it. But where Loral's house was large, this one was small enough to be called a cottage.

Loral stopped at the front door. "I'll let her know you're here to see her. Wait here a moment." She slipped inside, closing the door behind her before any of them had the chance to speak. She returned a couple of minutes later. "Only the apothecary can come in."

Mallory took a step towards Danae. "I'll need my alchemist in case a herbal tea needs to be made."

Loral looked from one to the other a couple of times before eventually nodding. "Just keep your voices down. Everything makes her head ache. Bright light, movement, sounds. Everything."

Mallory followed Loral inside, Danae directly behind her. She glanced around at the sparse living area. There was a closed door at the far side of the space, a window on either side with curtains drawn shut and a door off to the right. This door was open and she followed Loral into the bedroom.

An elderly woman lay on the bed, the bed linens thrown back and her face flushed with fever. She opened her eyes, squinting up at them, no sound coming from her cracked lips.

Mallory hurried forward, taking the hand that was stretched out to her. She cradled it in both of hers, the heat emanating from the old woman almost unbearable. She instantly knew what was wrong. "Fire scale sickness from the bite of a pyre bug." She checked the journal notification, relieved it was only an update for their quest. *Sickly Relative: Loral's mother has fire scale sickness from the bite of a pyre bug.*

"Are you certain?" Loral asked.

Mallory nodded.

"But they're only found near the demonic line," Loral said. "My mother has never been out of Ransted."

"They sometimes get taken to other place in the gear of people who've travelled through there," Danae said. "Maybe that's what happened. We came across a group doing a quest that involved taking out members of the dark forces up this end of Ruby Isle. Who knows how long ago members of the dark forces arrived up this end of Ruby Isle and where they came from."

Loral nodded thoughtfully. "We had more travellers than usual through the village back when my mother first fell ill. We thought she might have picked up a simple ailment from one of them. But when all the potions we had access to and the cure disease potion didn't help, we had no idea what ailed her."

Mallory let go of the elderly woman's hand, placing it back on the bed. "You can give her a cure disease potion twice a day for thirty days. That will cure her. But it won't be until the last dose that she'll feel any better. Or we can make a herbal tea that is specifically designed to cure fire scale sickness. That's if we can get the ingredients."

"Why a herbal tea and not a potion?" Loral asked. "Wouldn't a potion work better?"

Mallory nodded. "Yes, but Danni can't make potions yet. And a herbal tea will work. She'll need to take it for a week, each day at the same time, but every dose will improve her health."

"What are the ingredients?" Loral asked.

The elderly woman made a sound, clutching at her head.

Mallory took a step away from her. "We'd best go into the other room. Our voices will be causing her extreme pain." She stepped forward as she spoke, not speaking again until they were all in the living area with the bedroom door nearly fully closed. "I have a list of ingredients we can use."

"I should have brought pen and paper in with me," Danae said. "Maybe I should get the notebook out of the blanket wrapped bundle of my things. It has alchemy recipes in the front and cooking recipes in the back." She smiled. "No cooking recipes that you don't already have or I would have shared them with Brodie. And I should have said alchemy recipe in the front since I only have the health tea one. I didn't think I'd need it since I'm not going to the academy yet."

"There's the spare notebook in the chest from

Rodina," Mallory suggested. "If it's too difficult getting yours out."

"No, it's fine. If I'm going back to Milos' farm, I might as well get the notebook out." Before Danae could leave, Loral put out a hand to stop her.

"It'll take you too long. Go to my house and ask my oldest for pen, ink and paper."

With a nod, Danae left the cottage, closing the door behind herself.

"Will she be able to make the herbal tea? If she's not capable of making potions, will she be able to make a herbal tea of suitable strength?" Loral asked.

"Yes, she can make double strength herbal tea. You'll see. Your mum will start feeling better after a single dose and we'll leave enough doses here to cure her. Probably a few spare doses just in case." Mallory didn't want to risk a dose being knocked over or something similar and the elderly woman being unable to finish the seven days. It would have been better if Danae could have made a potion, but then again, a potion would have taken longer to make. "Will we be able to make the herbal tea here once we have all the ingredients?"

Loral didn't have a chance to answer as Danae came back inside. "Sorry I took so long. Brodie had a lot of questions."

"Brodie always has a lot of questions," Mallory said dryly.

Danae smiled. "I like that about him. That he's not afraid to ask things." She laughed softly. "At least not afraid to ask most things."

Mallory couldn't help laughing at Danae's reference to the fact Brodie still hadn't been able to ask her out on a date. "Some things you'll need to ask yourself."

Danae sat at the small timber table that was over near the fireplace, a pot hanging above the unlit timber. "Now what are the ingredients we can use?" She placed the paper and ink on the table, dipping the nib pen in the ink as she spoke.

At a sound coming from the bedroom, Loral looked from the almost closed door to Danae seated at the table before sighing and hurrying back to the bedroom.

Chapter Thirty-Two

Once Loral was in the bedroom, Mallory leaned close to Danae. "You can do this, can't you?"

Danae nodded. "As long as a herbal tea is strong enough. Do I assume that the recovery ingredients are the same as what they are for the cure corpse rot tea?"

Mallory nodded. "Shulken, river moss, night bloom, coral puffball, crimson shelf fungi, vilen root or death tulip."

Danae scribbled the ingredients down on the open page of her notebook. "And what are the options for the two base ingredients?"

"The first lot are snowbells, russet daisies, searing poppies or golden lily bulbs." Mallory frowned. "You know, I have the feeling that there are other ingredients that could be used, but those are the ones that can be found in this region."

Danae nodded. "That would be correct." Finished writing the ingredients down, she looked up at Mallory. "What are the choices for the second base ingredients?"

"Dead man's creeper, blue ivy, red lace fern or spear leaf."

Danae wrote the next list of ingredients down. "A pity we sold all our herbs because we had russet daisies and shulken amongst what we'd gathered."

"Then we can find more of them. And something from the other list," Mallory said.

Loral came out of the bedroom in time to hear Mallory's comment. "You can find the ingredients you need?"

Danae placed the pen on the table and rose to her feet. "We're going to try."

"What ones do you need?" Loral glanced at the piece of paper Danae held out to her. After looking over the list, she handed it back. "You could talk to the hunter. I can take you to see him. He might know where some of those herbs can be found."

The three of them headed outside, Mallory hushing her brother when he peppered them with questions. "We need to gather herbs to make a herbal tea to cure fire scale sickness and Loral is going to take us to visit the local hunter who might be able to tell us where to find some of them."

"Who gets to gather the herbs?" Brodie asked.

"What if some of us gather herbs outside the village, in the opposite direction to Coastview?" Callum suggested. "We can meet back at Milos' place in an hour."

Ryan took out his pocket watch. "That'll put us at around midday."

"We're going to keep looking until we find the herbs we need to cure Loral's mum." Mallory wasn't about to leave the elderly lady in pain. "Fire scale sickness causes dehydration due to how hot it makes the body, blinding headaches, a fever that feels like the skin is being burned away and muscle weakness."

"Would health tea help?" Ryan asked.

Mallory shook her head. "Nothing will help other than a potion, tincture or herbal tea to cure fire scale sickness."

Ryan turned to Brodie and Callum. "The two of you ride back to Milos' farm and get hessian bags to put herbs in. Search the area for an hour and then we'll meet back at the farm."

"Which herbs do we need?" Callum asked.

Danae handed over the piece of paper, which he

returned to her once he and Brodie had read over the details.

"We're going to have to start keeping some of the herbs we gather," Callum said. "Instead of selling all of them." He glanced at Brodie.

"It's not like we've got heaps of space," Brodie protested.

"We could hang them in the compact alchemist's station to dry," Danae suggested. "Then store them in the cupboards once they are."

Mallory took a step back from everyone. "We need to get moving. Fire scale sickness is painful."

"I'll show you to the hunter's home," Loral said.

"We'll meet you back at the farm." Callum strode down the road with Brodie beside him, Fang trotting after them and Smudge peering over Callum's shoulder.

Smiling at Smudge, Mallory waved at him, grinning when he waved back. "He's so cute." She turned to Loral. "Where does the hunter live?"

He was only a few minutes away and Loral knocked on the door, explaining what they needed when he opened it. Instead of inviting them in, the hunter stepped outside, leaving the door open, scratching at his chin as he frowned. "About the only group of herbs you might have trouble finding are the ones from the last lot. There's a pond south of here where you can find river moss and golden lily bulbs. Or you can get russet daisies over near Galna's place. Out behind her orchard. Night bloom can often be found out behind the tavern of an evening and vilen root on the way to Ursen. That's if you wanted to travel that far."

"And the third group of herbs?" Mallory prompted.

The hunter scratched at his chin again. "Now that's where it gets tricky. About all I can think of is a cave on the way to Estwater, about ten minutes out of the village. Red lace fern grows in the depths of it. But you don't want to go in there. It's a den of leatherback bears."

"What are they?" Ryan asked.

"Angry creatures," the hunter said. "Very angry creatures. There are only a few places on their leathery hide that they're vulnerable and they're extremely aggressive. Has to be at least three of them, if not more, in those caves."

Mallory closed her eyes. How was she to ignore the plight of Loral's mum? Taking a deep breath, she opened her eyes. Obviously she couldn't. "How hard is it to find the cave?"

The hunter studied her. "You're going after them?"

"You're going to find red lace fern?" Loral asked.

Mallory turned to Loral. "We're not about to leave your mum in the state she's in."

"Are you certain that all you need me to do is fix Galna's fence? It seems so little now I know exactly what you need to do," Loral said.

"It'll be enough. Especially if you can fix it today," Mallory said.

"Will you need anything else from me?" Loral asked. "If you don't, I'll get started on that fence."

"Not unless you know where the cave is," Ryan said.

Loral shook her head. "I've heard of it. I vaguely know where it is. If only enough to know where to stay clear of the vicinity."

"They're going to cure your ma?" the hunter asked.

Loral nodded. "Mallory is an apothecary."

"Maybe when you're done, you could come and have a look at a few old injuries of mine that have been playing up," the hunter suggested.

"I can do that," Mallory said.

"Then give me a minute and I'll draw you up a map of the location." The hunter returned inside, Loral leaving at the same time, letting them know they could find her at Galna's if they needed her.

Mallory turned to Ryan. "We'll need everyone if we're going to take on the leatherback bears."

Ryan nodded before facing Danae. "Can Mallory ride with you? I'll head back to the farm and see if I can catch Callum and Brodie before they go looking for herbs." He grinned when Danae nodded and turned back to Mallory, drawing her close. "I'll see you at the farm." His lips brushed across hers.

She returned his embrace, reluctantly letting him go. By the time the hunter came back outside, Ryan was out of sight.

The hunter looked up and down the road. "Where's the other member of your party?"

"Getting everyone organised to take on the leatherback bears." Mallory took the piece of paper from him, looking at the surprisingly detailed map he'd drawn. Even to putting estimates of time and kilometres. "Thank you for this."

"No, thank you for being willing to come back and look at my old injuries," the hunter said. "We can talk prices when you return. I know how bad Loral's ma is. You'll be wanting to get her seen to as soon as you can."

Chapter Thirty-Three

Mallory tucked the map into her belt pouch. "We'll be back as soon as we can." She took a step away before turning back to the hunter. "You said their skin is tough and they have vulnerable places."

The hunter nodded. "You'll only do a quarter of the normal damage if you hit them anywhere but under the limbs." He pointed to his armpit. "Right in close there. That'll give you fifty percent of your weapon's damage."

"What about spells? Are there any they're weak to?" Mallory asked.

Again the hunter nodded. "Poison. It's the only spell that'll do full damage against them."

"Thank you," Mallory said, smiling when he nodded. "We'll be back as soon as we can."

It didn't take them long to collect Augusta, and the ride to the farm was quiet. Mallory was relieved to find Brodie and Callum there, Ryan saying that he'd caught up with them on the road after they'd left the farm. She explained what Loral had said and showed them the map from the hunter.

"A pity we don't have an oven," Brodie muttered. "I have an apple pie recipe and Galna's trees are full of apples."

Mallory thought it best to change the topic before her brother became focused on food. They only had about three quarters of an hour until it was midday and he was sure to want lunch then. "Do you think we should take the wagon and all our gear to Loral's house and ask Ninette to keep an eye on it while we're tracking down leatherback bears and red lace fern?"

"I wonder if Remora would look after our things while we're gone," Danae said. "We did help her find Milos."

"I bet she would." Brodie grabbed Danae's hand. "I'll go with you and ask her."

Mallory didn't have the chance to argue. Not that she was sure if she should argue. They had a lot of things, including a lot of money, in the wagon. She thought of the benefits of joining the Adventurers Guild, in particular access to a large storage chest that was locked with magic so that only they could access it. A storage chest that was always monitored by Drohgolrik. That sounded like a pretty safe place to store things. Such as large amounts of gold. If it wasn't so important for them to cure Loral's mum, she would have suggested visiting the Adventurers Guild first.

Brodie and Danae returned with Remora, who beamed at them. "I'm so glad I can help you. Especially after all you did for us. Milos will be over here shortly. The two of us will make sure no one comes near your gear."

"We'll leave the horses here too," Ryan said. "Just in case there are any bears outside the cave. We don't want anything to happen to them."

It didn't take them long to sort out what they were taking, which included Ryan wearing the empty leather backpack, and to head along the road towards Estwater. Brodie held up a vial. "Do you think they'd be weak against weapon poison too?"

"It's probably worth a try. Talking of potions." Mallory took a health potion out of her satchel and held it out to Ryan. "To replace the one you used yesterday."

"Thanks." Ryan slipped it into his belt pouch. "I put the empty vial in the chest Rodina gave us."

"We should probably start storing stuff like that in the compact alchemist's station," Mallory said.

Ryan shrugged. "It seemed like a lot of effort setting it up for a single vial. It can go in it next time we have it out."

Callum glanced around the area when Smudge made soft warning sounds, Fang also growling softly. "I think we're nearly at the cave."

"Do you think they can sense the bears?" Mallory asked.

"Let's hope it is the bears and not something else that'll draw the attention of the bears so we've got too many things to fight at once," Ryan said.

Brodie held the weapon poison vial out to Danae. "Here. I have another one. You can put this on your arrows. There's eight doses."

"That's a good idea," Callum said. "Hand the other vial over. My bow does a lot more damage than your dagger."

"Then what am I meant to use?" Brodie demanded.

"You won't make as good a use of it as Danni and I would," Callum said.

Muttering under his breath, Brodie handed the weapon poison over to Callum. "I need better weapons too."

"Quiet," Ryan said softly. "I can hear something."

Mallory drew out her wand, slowly moving forward with the rest of her group. "Are you sure?"

Emica's ears became fox ears and she nodded. "I hear it too now." She glanced at Ryan. "You must have pretty good hearing."

"No. I can't hear it now. Just for a second I heard it. Whatever it is, it made a slightly louder sound for a second and has been quiet ever since."

"We need to find ways to hit the bears where they're vulnerable," Mallory said. "How do you make a bear raise its arms?"

"Tell them it's a holdup?" Ryan grinned.

Mallory rolled her eyes, slowly shaking her head. "That wasn't at all funny."

"You sure?" Ryan asked.

"I–" Mallory broke off. "I think I heard it that time."

Callum took out the brass spyglass. "As soon as someone spots it, let me know. It'll be good to know what we're up against before we attack."

"How hard can a bear be to kill?" Brodie asked. "Even leatherback ones. We've killed bears before and they weren't too bad."

"We stumbled across one a couple of years back," Jorgen said. "It took eight of us to bring it down."

"What level was it?" Callum asked.

"Eleven," Esben said. "That bear was really vicious. Worse than any normal bear I've ever come across."

"Maybe we should find another way to get the herbs. The hunter said there were three of them." Mallory's grip tightened on her wand, her gaze brushing across everything. Yet it didn't help. She didn't see anything. No bears and no other wildlife, which was in itself worrying. There were always creatures around. Even if it was only birds flying from tree to tree, pausing here and there to sing. "Where is everything? Where are the birds?"

"Every creature is wary of leatherback bears," Jorgen said.

"For good reason," Esben added.

"How bad was the-" Mallory broke off when a bear came running towards them out of a cluster of trees they'd been walking towards. It looked like she was about to find out how bad a fight was against a leatherback bear. The one coming towards them couldn't be anything else with its thick, hairless hide and sharp teeth that were well and truly visible with the way it snarled at them. She cast poison dart at the bear. It didn't slow in the slightest.

Callum put the brass spyglass away, readying his bow, first dipping an arrow in the weapon poison. "We better hope we only have to face one of them at a time. It's going to take a lot of effort to take them down with how much health it has."

"I'm almost afraid to ask." Mallory again cast poison dart at the bear, noticing that both Danae and Callum had fired arrows at it and Jorgen and Esben had become crystalline wolves and were now running towards the bear.

Emica rested her hand on her sword for a moment. "I think I have to agree with Mallory. I'm not sure I want to know." She turned into a fox and ran towards the bear, a few metres behind the wolves.

Brodie threw a dagger at the bear. "What's its stats?"

"It's level five and has sixty health," Callum said.

"It's going to take us forever to kill it." Mallory cast poison dart at the bear when Emica drew its attention, causing it to rise up above her, striking out at the kitsune.

Both Callum and Danae shot it in the vulnerable place under the limbs, close to the body. The bear roared, the sound echoed by three others.

Chapter Thirty-Four

Mallory again cast poison dart at the bear, trying not to think about how dangerous things were about to become. She should have added Emica, Jorgen and Esben to their party and told them to share their information so she'd know what their health was. They were the ones the bear was focused on.

Three other bears lumbered into sight as the first bear dropped to the ground, lying motionless. Callum took out the brass spyglass, checking out each of the bears that the travellers and Emica each attacked. "All have the same health as the first one. Sixty." Putting the brass spyglass away, he dipped an arrow in weapon poison before shooting the closest bear.

Mallory attacked each of the bears with poison dart, following that up by moving closer so she could heal each of those up close to the bears. She glanced at the dead body, wishing she had a better reanimate spell.

Hers only allowed her to reanimate the dead up to level three. When Emica was knocked to the ground, the bear about to swipe at her again, Mallory cast slow target, wishing it did more than slow the bear by ten percent.

The bear was slowed down enough that Emica was able to twist out of the way and come to her feet, still in fox form. She shook herself before darting in and attacking the bear again.

Mallory healed the kitsune twice, wishing she knew what Emica's health was and if she needed more.

"Mal!"

At Brodie's warning call, Mallory turned to see one of the other bears loping towards her, having knocked Esben to the ground. The crystalline wolf struggled to rise. She didn't have time to do anything other than throw herself out of the way.

The bear spun to face her, snarling, his sharp fangs showing.

Mallory stumbled to her feet, warily backing away as she cast poison dart at the bear. She wanted to heal Esben, but didn't dare take her gaze off the bear that was swatting at the arrow that had impaled it, the majority of its attention remaining on her.

When the bear began to move faster, she cast slow

target at it, wondering if she should level the spell up. Not that she knew what could be improved by doing that. She sympathised with Callum's desire to find out as much information as possible before making a decision about spending CAS points. It took so long to earn them and everything needed so many to completely level it up. Diving out of the way of the bear, she nearly ran into Esben, who was again on his feet. As she dodged out of the way, she healed him twice. A glance around the area showed that everyone was kept busy fighting the bears. Her only help against this one was Ryan with his hunting bow and Esben who didn't look so good.

Mallory tried to ignore the fear that settled in her stomach. Getting a horse at half price wouldn't be worth it if one of them lost a revive. The bear, that had been distracted by Esben again, turned from him and rose on hind legs, roaring as it faced her. She wished her shrink spell worked on wild creatures and not just domestic animals and some sentient races. She'd have to ask if there was a shrink spelt that worked on wild creatures. Right now, with the way the bear towered over her, she was the one who felt small.

Moving out of the way again, Mallory quickly went through her spells, trying to come up with another plan. Poison dart just wasn't powerful enough. She cast nightfall at the bear, wishing it would last longer than five seconds.

The bear roared, standing where it was to paw aimlessly at the air in front of it. While it remained blinded, Esben became human and drew out his stiletto, stabbing it in the eye. The bear roared again, striking out at Esben.

"Can you do that again?" Esben asked.

Mallory shook her head, backing away from the bear who seemed torn as to who to attack out of the two of them. "It has a sixty second cooldown. But I can make you invisible." She cast the spell as she spoke, grinning when the blood streamed out of the bear's other eye. Maybe none of them would have to lose a revive after all.

The bear roared, turning his head back and forth, fangs bared as it swiped in front of it, ambling awkwardly forward.

"Finish it off. I'll blind the other ones while I'm invisible," Esben said.

Brodie joined them, attacking the bear. "Why didn't you use nightfall on them sooner?"

Mallory didn't bother answering him, casting poison dart at the bear. The moment the sixty seconds were up, she glanced around the area to see if she needed to use nightfall, but none of the bears could now see. And there were only two alive. Then the bear near her fell to the ground and there was one. It was taken out within seconds. Relief rushed through her, making her feel momentarily shaky.

Brodie crouched by the bear, trying to use his stiletto on the hide. "That wasn't a bad lot of XP. But I don't think we're going to get much out of these bears. The hide is impossible to cut into properly."

Mallory checked Brodie's stats. "Brodie! Will you stop doing that? Finish off creatures. Stop attacking every single one for the XP." She moved closer to Esben, placing a hand on him so she could check his health, healing him until she ran out of mana.

Brodie shrugged. "It wasn't a problem. Everyone had it under control. It wasn't like I was doing much damage against them, anyway. Callum and Danae had the weapon poison."

Callum joined them, having collected the arrows and shared them around. "Hope you weren't wanting the weapon poison back. We used it all up. I gave the empty vial to Danae. She'll be able to use it, eventually. I also had to share out some of the spare arrows to replace the ones we lost. Four of them."

Ryan also joined them. "We've got three bear

canines. I don't think we're going to get much else, not without wasting too much time."

Mallory finished healing Esben before starting on Ryan. The day was moving on and Loral's mother remained in extreme pain. "Let's find the cave."

It didn't take long to find it and Mallory was working her way through healing everyone, still having Emica and Jorgen to heal. Brodie protested when she suggested they wait out the front until she'd finished. She also picked the handful of herbs out the front of the cave while waiting for her mana to regen, glancing over her shoulder at Brodie who was complaining. "I'm not having another person lose their revive." She put the herbs in Ryan's backpack.

"You can wait out here and I'll run in and find the herb," Brodie offered. "I'm hungry and this is taking too long. It's got to be after midday by now."

"Twelve thirty." Ryan returned the pocket watch to his belt pouch. "We'll wait until everyone is healed and all go in together." He looked pointedly at Brodie. "No need to go running into danger."

"I wasn't," Brodie muttered. "I'm starving and I've got nothing to eat. We need more jerky for me to carry in my belt pouch."

Fang made a soft bark of agreement.

"See," Brodie said. "Even Fang thinks that's a good idea."

Mallory finished healing Jorgen. "Okay. We can go in now." It wouldn't take long for her mana to regen.

"About time." Brodie took the lead.

Ryan drew him back. "We don't know what's in there."

"All the bears were out here." Brodie gestured towards the location where they'd taken out the bears.

"We don't know that for certain." Emica grinned. "Better be careful, goblin boy, that you don't become the meal."

"Should I cast magelight or will it be too bright?" Mallory asked.

"There's a spell called nightlight that gives off just enough light to see by," Danae said. "My father regularly stocks it and it isn't that expensive. Not compared to ones like magelight and tracking magelight."

"Cast the spell," Ryan said. "It'd be worse to go into the dark than to warn anything in there that we're coming."

"She could stay at the back of the party so that

the light doesn't go too far ahead of us," Jorgen suggested.

Chapter Thirty-Five

After a couple of minutes of discussion, it was decided that Mallory would go last, Esben bringing up the rear with her. Jorgen and Emica would take the lead with the rest of them in the middle of the group.

The cave angled gently downwards, the walls covered in moss, a steady drip running down the walls the further they went in. It was a single tunnel, meandering slowly downwards, no sharp turns, only slight bends. They were about five minutes into the cave when Jorgen and Emica came back towards them, Jorgen pressing a finger to his lips to warn them to be quiet.

Jorgen waited until they'd all gathered close before he spoke, keeping his voice low. "There's a bear ahead of us. It looks bigger than the ones we faced outside."

"The red lace fern is growing in the crevices and cracks of the wall behind it," Emica said.

Callum held the brass spyglass out, offering it first to Emica and then to Jorgen before holding it out at a point between the two of them. "The health might not be too bad."

Emica took the brass spyglass. "And unicorns are plentiful and easy to catch."

Mallory assumed from the tone Emica used that unicorns were anything but plentiful and easy to catch. "Did you want me to make you invisible?" When Emica nodded, Mallory cast the spell on her. She stared at the point where the kitsune had been, waiting for her to return. It wasn't until Emica pressed the brass spyglass into Callum's hand that she realised the kitsune was back. "Were you able to see?"

"It's level ten and has eighty-five health." Emica reappeared.

Mallory momentarily closed her eyes, drawing in a deep breath. "We can't take it on." They'd struggled with the ones that were sixty health.

"How are we meant to get the herbs?" Brodie asked.

"We sneak over and get them," Callum suggested.

"It'll have to be Emica, Jorgen or Esben," Ryan said. "We won't want to disturb it with the magelight."

"There are so many spells I need," Mallory said.

Ryan grinned. "There are so many things in general that we need."

"I can collect the herb," Jorgen offered. "Make me invisible and when I draw close, I'll use stealth."

"I can use stealth," Brodie said. "Why can't I go? I can use a night vision potion."

"No point wasting them," Ryan said.

Jorgen turned to Danae. "How many do you need?"

Danae shrugged. "I don't know. A half a dozen should be enough. Or a few extra since it's so hard to get. We'll dry them and keep them in the compact alchemist's station in case we need them again."

With a nod, Jorgen faced Mallory. "I'm ready."

She cast vanish I on him and listened for him to leave. There was only silence. In an effort to take her mind off what Jorgen was doing, Mallory turned to Danae. "Is there a shrink spell that can be used on wild creatures?"

Danae nodded. "Shrink II. It can only be used on non magical creatures. Shrink III can be used on magical creatures."

"Would I be able to use it on leatherback bears?" Mallory asked.

Danae laughed softly. "That would make fights so much easier."

"Would we be able to sell all the creatures Mal shrinks?" Brodie asked.

"Easily. People buy them for their miniature menageries," Emica said. "Especially in Shadhurst."

"Where would we get shrink II?" Brodie asked. "And how high a level mage would Mal need to use it?"

"It's a level four spell," Danae said. "By the time we reach a town where we might find one, Mallory will have a high enough level mage to cast it. Unless she stops alternating between the two classes and focuses on warrior instead."

Brodie looked worried. "You're not going to do that, are you?"

Mallory was half tempted to let him worry for a bit. Especially after all the worries he'd caused her lately. "I haven't changed my plans." She didn't bother telling him she was thinking of putting most of her attribute points into intelligence and wisdom for a while to increase her spell damage and mana regen. She didn't need him hassling her to keep doing it if she changed her mind.

"Good," Brodie stated. "Then we'll find shrink II

and buy a cage so we can shrink creatures and sell them."

Jorgen rejoined them, giving ten red lace fern to Ryan to put in his backpack. "Better get moving. The leatherback was waking as I was leaving. He wouldn't have heard me, but he may have caught my scent."

Ryan slung the backpack into place. "Keep the noise down then." He led the way.

Mallory followed Ryan, regularly glancing over her shoulder. All she could see was the rest of her party. When she saw Smudge looking over Callum's shoulder, one paw clutching at the makeshift sling to steady himself, she wished she could ask him what he was looking at.

Smudge made his soft warning cry, Fang joining in with a low growl.

Mallory didn't need to ask. Whatever Smudge was looking at, it was dangerous and as far as she knew, there was only one creature behind them. She lengthened her stride, trying to avoid making any noise. It was a little difficult with how fast she walked. She glanced over her shoulder again.

There was nothing behind them. Or at least nothing she could see. And yet the two companion animals continued to give warning cries. They stepped out of the cave, none of them slowing their pace. "A pity we didn't bring the horses." Mallory glanced over her shoulder. There was still nothing there.

"I could change form and run back to the camp and collect them," Emica offered.

"We should be right," Ryan said.

"Something with that much health probably has a crit attack of between twenty and thirty," Emica warned.

"I can go back with Emica and help her saddle the horses," Jorgen offered.

Mallory checked everyone's stats. Or at least the stats of those in her party. Their health was full. Not that it would help with an attack of twenty. Callum had the lowest health at thirty. Two crit hits and he'd be dead. "What if the two of you don't get back in time? How would we take on the bear with less help?" She slowed a little. "What are we doing?"

Ryan glanced over his shoulder at her. "What are you doing? Keep moving."

"If the bear is following us, we're leading it towards the village," Mallory said.

Ryan slowed too. "There are kids in Ransted."

Mallory nodded, slowing even further.

"We're going to take it on?" Esben asked.

"We can't lead it into Ransted. Or even to the

outlying farms." Callum slowed to a stop, turning to face the direction they'd come from.

Mallory did the same, those around her also joining her and Callum. "Is it still following us?"

Ryan shrugged. "The moment you see it, cast nightfall on it." He readied his hunting bow.

"I can change form and look around for it." Emica became a fox, dashing off through the trees before anyone could disagree.

"I can have a look too," Esben offered.

"Stay here," Ryan said. "One of us running into danger is more than enough for now."

As she glanced around the area, Mallory couldn't help thinking about Loral's mother. "Should some of us be collecting the rest of the herbs?"

"We'll stay together," Ryan said. "Once we deal with the bear, Emica, Jorgen and Esben can collect the horses and we'll get the rest of the herbs before returning to the village."

Emica came running towards them, changing from her fox form as she came to a stop. "He's coming this way. He spotted the ones we killed and he looks very angry."

Chapter Thirty-Six

Mallory took out her wand. "Are leatherback bears sentient?"

Danae readied her bow. "No. But they might have been its offspring. They live in family units until they're a few years old."

Jorgen and Esben drew stilettos as the bear burst through the trees, roaring at the sight of them. It loped towards them, heading for Ryan who was in the middle of the group.

Mallory cast nightfall and slow target followed by poison dart.

Jorgen darted forward, stabbing the bear in the eye, Esben doing the same to the other eye.

Blood streamed down the bear's face, not seeming to slow it in the least. It kept heading towards Ryan, roaring and shaking its head, swiping out at the two crystalline wolves as it lumbered past them.

Mallory was ready to heal Jorgen and Esben, but they avoided the attacks, well out of the way before the bear was past them. She again cast poison dart at the bear, not wanting to let her mana get too low in case she needed to heal someone.

Brodie darted in to use his stiletto while Emica attacked from the other side, jumping back from the paw that swiped at her. Callum, Danae and Ryan fired arrow after arrow at the bear.

Mallory drew in a sharp breath as the bear managed to hit Brodie. She checked his stats as she started to heal him, relieved he'd only lost fourteen health. His armour gave him enough defence that it blocked four damage. With how the bear had hardly struck him, she had to assume it was only a low attack. None of them could afford a crit. Finished healing Brodie, she backed away to the side, waiting for her mana to regen before she used any more.

Ryan dodged out of the way of an attack. "Lucky it can't see us. If it could, it probably would have taken us out by now. Or at least some of us."

Mallory didn't want to think about that possibility. She cast poison dart again.

The bear changed direction, spinning away from Ryan to lope towards Mallory.

The move was unexpected and she didn't have time

to get out of the way. The bear's attack knocked her onto the ground, pain exploding through her and the wand was knocked from her hand. She scrambled to reach it.

The bear rose above her, roaring as it came down towards her.

Mallory rolled in the direction of her wand, wishing she had more than one. Scooping it up, she didn't bother to rise to her feet, healing herself in case she was attacked again. That attack had taken twenty-two health points. She dreaded to think what a crit would take as that hadn't been a bad enough of an attack for it to be one.

Ryan drew the bear's attention, giving Mallory a chance to rise to her feet.

Before she could attack again, the bear was on the ground at Ryan's feet, Ryan having lost twenty-six health. She started to heal him, checking everyone else. "Is that it? Are there any more of them?" She scanned the area, seeing nothing dangerous, heart racing as she waited for an attack that didn't come. Nothing moved. Everything was silent.

Callum and Brodie both bent to check the bear for resources.

"Should I fetch the horses now?" Emica asked.

Mallory nodded, still healing Ryan, her heart

slowing to a more normal pace. That didn't stop her from scanning the area, keeping an eye out for anything else that might attack. "The three of you should go. It's not safe around here."

"We won't be long." Jorgen changed into his crystalline wolf form, Esben doing the same. Emica changed form also and the three of them took off, headed towards Milos' farm.

Callum and Brodie rose to their feet, Callum giving two bear canines to Ryan to put in the backpack before collecting arrows and needing to also share out ten of the spare arrows to replace those lost.

Callum finished putting arrows in his quiver. "We need to find a few archers to take out. At the rate we're going through arrows, we'll have to buy some."

"Where will we find archers?" Brodie asked.

Callum shrugged.

Brodie turned to Danae.

"No specific place. You just need to get lucky," Danae said.

"I need to keep putting points in luck," Brodie muttered.

Their walk back to Milos' farm was quiet and they arrived as Emica, Jorgen and Esben were about to bring the horses to them, having saddled them. They let Remora know what was happening and rode out to the pond. All they saw in the area was a rabbit that ran at the sight of them and a deer that froze for a moment before continuing to drink from the pond. The last two types of herbs were quickly picked, Brodie complaining that Jorgen shouldn't be picking them since he'd had the chance last time.

They called into Galna's along the way to Loral's, checking to see if she was there. She was finishing up with the fence and returned to the village with them, asking how their search for herbs was going.

"You can't believe how relieved I am," Loral said after they'd told her. "And it's good you cleared out that den of leatherback bears. It'll make the road to Estwater safer."

They were greeted at Loral's front door by one of her sons, a smile on his face as he rambled on about the blueberries they'd picked with Ninette.

When they reached the kitchen, where two baskets of blueberries sat on the table, Brodie's expression brightened. "I have a recipe for blueberry pancakes." His expression fell. "But I don't have milk, sugar or eggs. I've only got oil and flour."

"If you want to stay here with Ninette and my children and make enough pancakes for everyone, I have milk, sugar and eggs you can use," Loral offered.

"Well…" Brodie's voice trailed off as he looked between the basket of blueberries and Danae.

Danae looked wistfully at the basket of berries. "Pancakes sound good and none of us have had the midday meal yet."

Ryan took out his pocket watch. "No wonder I'm starving. It's a quarter to two."

"Okay. I'll make pancakes," Brodie said.

Loral turned to Malory and Danae. "We'll go to my mother's home if the rest want to wait here so we can keep the noise down for her."

Mallory nodded, making sure everyone was added to the party in case she didn't get the chance before the quest was completed. She took the backpack from Ryan, which contained the herbs.

They walked over to Loral's mother's house, entering the dim interior where Loral filled a pot with water and put it over the fire she lit. Once that was done, she went to check on her mother.

Danae added two red lace fern, two river moss and two golden lily bulbs to the pot when it began to gently bubble. By the time the herbal tea was ready, Brodie, along with the rest of their party and Loral's four children had arrived out the front with the blueberry pancakes. They waited outside rather than come inside and make too much noise, only Brodie coming to the door.

"We'll be out in a minute." Mallory took the cup of herbal tea from Danae.

"Don't take too long. The pancakes are quickly cooling down. They're best hot," Brodie said.

Mallory nodded, making her way to the bedroom where she sat on the edge of the bed and helped the elderly lady sit up so she could drink the tea. The heat in the woman's skin reduced as she drank the tea, although her face remained flushed. "How do you feel?"

The elderly woman tensed as Mallory spoke, relaxing before she'd finished speaking. "How can I thank you? That's the first time in months that sounds haven't caused my headache to worsen. Although headache seems such a mild term for the blinding pain sounds have caused."

Loral remained in the doorway. "You're feeling better?"

The elderly woman smiled. "I'll be on my feet in no time. Now where are those grandchildren of mine? I've missed them terribly."

Loral fetched her children, the four of them clambering onto the bed, the second youngest offering her grandmother a half eaten pancake.

Chapter Thirty-Seven

Mallory quietly left the room, leaving them to enjoy their reunion. She stepped outside, taking the pancakes her brother held out to her.

Danae was also outside. "I've put the first batch of herbal tea into a waterskin Loral gave me and have put a second batch on. I can stay here and keep an eye on it if you want to visit the hunter and see what he needs done."

"I'll come with you," Brodie offered.

In the end, only Ninette and Danae remained behind, the rest of them walking to the hunter's home, finishing up the rest of the pancakes Brodie had brought with him as they walked.

Brodie finished his mouthful. "There's more pancakes at Loral's house. I should have brought more of them with me."

The hunter opened the door on the first knock. "I was wondering when you'd get back."

Mallory stepped forward. "Are you ready for me to check your health?"

The hunter nodded.

She rested a hand on him. "You have a piece of arrow left inside you that keeps pressing on a nerve. I have surgical instruments, but I don't have anything to numb the pain so I can operate on you. You also have a rib that didn't mend right, if I was to try and heal it, it would break again and I can only do average rapid mend." She lowered her hand.

The hunter shrugged. "I can manage a few weeks off. And the pain isn't an issue. I have a bottle of lightning whisky inside. Half a bottle of that and you could probably cut off my leg and I wouldn't feel it."

"Who gets the other half a bottle?" Brodie asked.

Mallory sent her brother a pointed look. "Not you."

"Aww, but I want to try it," Brodie protested.

"It's not good to drink alone," the hunter said. "I could shout you a glass. And any of the rest of you who want one." He glanced at Mallory with a chuckle. "Other than the apothecary, of course."

"Surely there must be something better than alcohol to use," Mallory said.

"There is," the hunter said. "But I don't know

where you'd get any of it around here. It's not like we have an alchemist."

Mallory sighed. It was all very good being able to heal people, but it made things a lot harder when she didn't have the right tools or potions.

"We haven't settled on a price yet. We might want to do that before I get started on the whisky. I'm not going to be making a lot of sense once I down a few glasses of that," the hunter said.

"You don't need–"

Brodie interrupted Mallory. "What were you thinking of offering?"

Mallory left her brother to do the negotiating since he enjoyed it so much, nodding when they settled on five gold pieces. She would have protested if Brodie had made the price too high. After slipping the coins into her belt pouch, she turned to Ryan. "Can you find out what herbs Danae needs for the boneset tea? Between that and rapid mend, I can heal the rib by twenty percent."

Ryan grabbed Brodie by the arm when he protested, wanting to stay and have some whisky. "You can come with us too."

"I need at least one person to stay behind in case I need help," Mallory protested. "And I need my surgical instruments." She was going to have to start carrying them on her. As well as finding out what was used for pain.

"I can get your surgical instruments for you," Jorgen offered.

Jorgen returned first and helped Mallory perform the surgery once the hunter was suitably numb, having a glass of whisky with him. By the time everyone else returned, Danae also returning with a strong boneset tea, it was three in the afternoon and Brodie was complaining about how long everything was taking. Mallory had waited until then to use rapid mend on the badly set rib. She roused the hunter enough to allow him to drink the tea, worried about how he'd manage since she wasn't going to be in the area to come back and check how he was doing.

Mallory turned to Danae. "How often can he have the boneset tea?"

"Once a day. I made enough to leave him with eight doses. And enough herbs were found for me to make up another two lots of eight doses," Danae said. "Can you see if he has a waterskin to put the boneset tea in? I don't want to leave any of our waterskins behind."

"I'll look." Jorgen found an empty waterskin in the kitchen, and they left a note with instructions for the hunter.

Mallory checked on him once more, relieved he was doing well. The surgery had worked and the newly set bone was on the mend. "He should sleep all night and feel a lot better by morning. We can get on with finishing all our quests now. And the next time we're in a town, I want to see what we can do about buying a sedative or painkiller."

"What about the lightning whisky?" Brodie asked. "Don't I get to have any?"

Jorgen chuckled. "He said that if you asked again, you can have a glass."

"Cool." Brodie was across the room and pouring himself one in seconds. He took a large mouthful, coughing and spluttering after he'd swallowed it. "Whoa! That's strong."

Callum took the glass from him, also taking a mouthful, laughing when he coughed as badly as Brodie. "I think it'd take a bit to get used to it."

Mallory rolled her eyes when Ryan tried the whisky, handing it over to Danae when she asked if she could taste it. "I hope it's not so strong that none of you will be able to help me finish up the quests."

Danae held the nearly empty glass out to Mallory. "Did you want the last of it?"

Mallory shook her head. "I better not. Just in case someone else needs medical help." She'd hate it if they did and she wasn't able to do anything because she was tipsy. Or drunk.

Brodie took the glass from Danae, downing the last of the contents. He breathed in sharply, this time not coughing. "The second mouthful isn't as bad as the first. That first one felt like I was drinking lightning."

Danae led the way outside. "You are. The whisky is made with the help of a mage and they put a small amount of lightning in the drink during the process of making it."

"Cool." Brodie moved closer to Mallory as they walked towards Loral's house. "We need to find that spell for you when I learn how to make whisky. Not sure when I'll be able to do that since it takes so long to get CAS points."

Mallory found herself slowly shaking her head. "You're a worry, Brodie."

"No I'm not," Brodie protested.

Mallory would have argued the point with him, but they'd reached Loral's house and she came out to greet them, ushering them inside.

Loral didn't stop smiling. "I can't thank all of you enough for what you did to help my mother. She's well enough that the children are with her and she's reading them a story. They've missed that. She also had her first proper meal in ages."

"We were glad to help and fixing Galna's fence was all we needed," Mallory said.

"The ingredients to make the blueberry pancakes were good too," Brodie added.

"There are pancakes left if you want more." Loral gestured towards the table where a calico cloth covered a plate.

"Cool." Brodie was across the room in seconds and helping himself to the pancakes. "Anyone else want some?" He held up a pancake, laughing when Smudge stretched out a hand and made soft sounds and Fang sat at his feet looking wistfully up at him.

After the pancakes were shared around, Smudge and Fang getting some as well, and two dozen left on the plate for Loral and her children to have the next day, Loral asked, "You're happy then with what you've received for healing my mother?"

Mallory nodded. "We're even." She smiled when a notification appeared. "As I said already, we were happy to help."

"We should get moving and see if Galna is happy," Ryan said. "Especially if we want to get on the road today."

Loral walked them to the door. "You're welcome to call in if you're ever back in the area." She stopped at the front door. "Safe travels."

They bid her farewell, collecting the horses from across the road. As there weren't enough horses for all of them to ride, even two on a horse, Jorgen changed forms. He trotted alongside them while they returned to Galna's farm.

Chapter Thirty-Eight

Mallory checked the journal notification along the way, finding it was a quest notification like she'd assumed. *Sickly Relative: You provided Loral's mother with a cure and in return Loral repaired Galna's fence. You also earned five experience points each.* Mallory couldn't help smiling. Only another two experience points and she'd gain a character level.

"What are you smiling about?" Brodie asked.

"My stats," Mallory said.

Brodie didn't answer immediately. "That's good. Even if we only get two XP for finishing the next quest, you'll gain a level. Then you can use tracking magelight." He looked over at Danae. "And Danni gained a CAS point. So that's good too."

Mallory slowly shook her head. She shouldn't be surprised that her brother was focused on how her character levels would benefit him. "I'll only be able to use the spell if I put my character level in mage." She couldn't resist teasing him, even though she planned to do exactly that. Put the character level in mage.

"Aww, come on, Mal. You've got to put it in mage," Brodie protested. "You said you would."

She strung him along for a bit, finally telling him he'd find out soon enough. When they reached Galna's farm, Brodie was glaring at Mallory who was still smiling, Ryan and Callum also both amused by Brodie's comments.

Galna met them at the door of her house, smiling at the sight of them. "I can't thank you enough for convincing Loral to fix my fence today. I don't know how you managed it, but I'm extremely grateful."

Mallory dismounted, waiting till the rest of her party had also dismounted before she spoke. "Are you grateful enough that you'll sell hay to Jefnas at the price he wants to pay?"

Galna nodded. "It's the least I can do and it is a fair market price, when you don't take into account what he owes me for the apples. You can let him know we have a deal."

"Thank you." Mallory ignored the journal notification since she was still talking to Galna. "We'll let him know now."

Galna sighed heavily. "I assume he'll be over here the moment he hears." She sighed again. "At least I've been forewarned, I suppose."

After bidding her farewell, they again mounted the horses, Jorgen having remained in his crystalline wolf form, and headed down the road to Jefnas' farm. During the ride, Mallory checked her journal notification. She couldn't help smiling when she saw how many experience points she'd earned.

Broken Fence: Galna was happy with the repairs on her fence and in exchange will accept Jefnas' price for her hay. You also earned two experience points each.

Mallory's smile remained in place as she considered making her brother wait to find out what she'd do with her new character level. And with the way he kept glancing at her, she was certain he was impatiently waiting. Before she did anything with her class point, she decided what to do with her attribute points. She put one in constitution so it was now fifteen and two each in intelligence and wisdom bringing them both up to fourteen.

Her health was now forty-five, stamina seventy-five and mana seventy with a regen of sixty-four a minute with her new stats and her regen jewellery and armour. The two points she'd put into intelligence also meant her attack spells had forty-two percent more damage to their base stats. That meant her basic fireball attack, instead of being a low of three, normal of five and crit of seven, was now four, seven and nine respectively. Not quite what she was hoping for when she was thinking about getting better spells, but maybe it was a way to improve them. That and a better wand. Even though she had better attack stats now, at character level six, there was no new revive added to the five she had. There'd be no new ones until character level ten. She'd have to be more careful with them.

"Aww, come on, Mal. Are you just going to leave the point there?" Brodie demanded.

She laughed, having been caught up in looking at her stats and forgetting all about the class point. She put it into mage, looking over at her brother who rode beside Danae, Ninette behind him on Scorch and Emica behind Danae on Augusta. "Happy?"

"About time," Brodie muttered.

Reaching the front of Jefnas' house, Mallory swung down to the ground, wanting to tell everyone to hurry up. She couldn't wait to see Jefnas' reaction. The man had been certain they'd fail. She led the way to the barn, finding him in there and wondering if he ever left it during the day. Surely there were other things on the farm that needed his attention.

Jefnas faced them, crossing his arms over his chest and frowning as he looked them over. "You were gone awhile. Turn you down, did she?"

Mallory struggled not to smile. "Not at all. She just needed us to do a task for her."

Jefnas stared at them, his frown deepening. "She didn't turn you down?"

"She'll accept your deal," Danae said.

"And won't charge you for the apples," Mallory added.

Jefnas took a step back, uncrossing his arms and letting them fall to his sides. "She accepted the deal." He said the words slowly and carefully.

Mallory lost her battle against smiling. "Yep."

"I can go over there right now and she'll sell me hay at the price I offered her," Jefnas said.

"That's what she told us," Ryan said. "Do we have your agreement that you'll accept Arnnik's offer?"

"If Galna sells me hay, I'll head straight on over to Arnnik's place the moment I've loaded up my wagon and talk to him about continuing our usual deal with the stallion," Jefnas said.

This time, Mallory checked the notification to make sure the quest was completed. *In Need Of Hay: Jefnas agreed to visit Arnnik once he collects hay from Galna and talk to Arnnik about letting him use his stallion for breeding. You also earned two experience points each.* "Thank you." She couldn't help smiling when the only reply she got from Jefnas was his frown deepening again and something that sounded like a grunt. "We'll let Arnnik know to expect you."

They returned to the horses and headed back towards Arnnik's farm. Brodie grinned. "I was starting to think it'd take more than that to prove we'd completed his quest."

Danae laughed softly. "His expression made me want to laugh. I can't believe I managed not to."

Ryan chuckled. "You're not the only one who was tempted to laugh at his antics. I thought we might have to take him to Galna's before he believed us."

"We've only got one more quest to complete," Callum said.

"A pity two of them have been worth so little," Brodie muttered. "Especially with how long it's taken to do all of them. We're never going to get to Simria at this rate. What if we take too long to get all the way to Bard's Hollow near Buckneth and someone gets to the treasure before us?"

"Then we ask Goswin what other treasures we can go after," Ryan said.

Brodie's expression brightened. "I hadn't thought of that. He has tonnes of treasures in his books."

"There are always treasures that people want found," Emica said.

When they reached Arnnik's farm, the man came out to greet them. "Any luck?"

"Jefnas said he'll be over once he picks up hay from Galna," Mallory said.

"How on Inadon did you convince him?" Arnnik asked.

Danae laughed softly with a glance at Callum. "By not letting the old lady who swallowed the fly die."

"Well…" Arnnik's voice trailed off in confusion. He cleared his throat. "I guess you'll be wanting to look at the horse now." When they nodded, he took a step towards the barn, beckoning them to follow.

Chapter Thirty-Nine

They left the horses tied up near the front of the house before following him, Jorgen becoming human again. They waited outside the barn, where Arnnik pointed for them to stay, and he soon returned with a large horse. Like Bug, this mare was also a mixed draft of solid build, was eighteen hands high and a dark bay.

"Meet Sun Lily. She's just as sweet-natured as her sister," Arnnik said. "Fifty-five gold pieces. Half price like we agreed."

Danae was the first to go forward and check Sun Lily over. "She's a good looking horse."

Arnnik nodded in agreement. "It's why I was keen to breed a few more mares to Jefnas' stallion. All the offspring have come out nice like Sun Lily and her sister." He glanced in the direction of where the horses had been left, slowly shaking his head. "What

I can't understand is why you could saddle the poor horse with a name such as Bug."

"It's actually Moondancer," Mallory said. "The people who owned her before us realised she wasn't actually dancing under the moon, but chasing bugs.

"What a character," Arnnik said fondly. "Well, do we have a deal?"

Mallory glanced at each of her party, smiling when they either nodded or shrugged. She turned back to Arnnik. "We have a deal. Do you mind holding onto her while we collect the money?"

"Not at all. Rather sensible of you not to wander around the countryside with your pockets full of gold," Arnnik said. "How long do you think you'll be?"

"Long enough to hitch up the wagon we left at Milos' place and get back here," Ryan said.

"I'll see you within the hour then," Arnnik said.

When they were back on the horses and riding along the road, Jorgen once again a crystalline wolf, Brodie asked, "Will it really take that long? An hour?"

"If you start complaining you're hungry it will," Ryan said.

"Goblin boy is always hungry," Emica said.

Brodie glared at everyone when they laughed. "I'm not always hungry." He paused a moment. "But it has been ages since we've had anything to eat." He muttered under his breath when they laughed at him again. "It's not at all funny."

Back at Milos' place, he and Remora were sitting by the campfire, rising to their feet when all of them arrived. Remora moved closer to Bug, looking up at Mallory and Ryan. "Everything is as you left it."

Mallory swung down to the ground. "Thank you. We appreciate the two of you helping us."

"No, we're the ones who appreciate all you've done for us," Remora stated.

"We better get packed up and on the road before Brodie is trying to convince us to give him time to make something to eat." Ryan dismounted and led Bug over to the wagon.

It took them less than half an hour to finish packing, hitching the horses and saying their farewells to Remora and Milos. Mallory clambered onto the wagon and waved to the couple who watched them leave. Once they were out of sight, she turned to Ryan. "I know we said we'd leave around midday, but I'm glad we didn't. Loral's mum and the hunter needed help."

Ryan entwined his fingers with Mallory's. "Sticking around to help people who are sick or injured is different to running around doing unimportant quests."

"The unimportant quests led to an important one," Mallory pointed out.

Ryan chuckled. "I guess they did."

They arrived at Arnnik's farm at the same time as Jefnas. He wasn't impressed with having to wait for Arnnik to finish with them first. Mallory handed over the coins, a notification appearing in the corner of her vision, and Danae tied Sun Lily's reins to the back of the wagon. They said goodbye to the two men, ignoring Jefnas' frown, waiting until they were down the road before any of them spoke.

"What terrible luck," Emica said. "If we'd only been a bit quicker we wouldn't have had to put up with Jefnas again."

"I pity his neighbours," Esben said.

Danae, who was driving the wagon, glanced over her shoulder. "Are we heading straight for Lilica now?"

"How far is it to there?" Brodie asked.

"I'll have a look." Callum took out a map, glancing at Danae as he did so. "And yes, we're heading to Lilica."

"So much for leaving at midday." Brodie said. "What's the time now?"

Ryan checked the pocket watch. "A quarter to five."

While Callum calculated how long it would take them to get to Lilica, Brodie asking him endless questions, Mallory opened her journal to have a look at the notification. She was surprised to find they'd gained four reputation in Ransted and there were two quest notifications. She assumed Brodie hadn't as yet checked his journal.

Stud Fee Negotiations: Arnnik sold the mare to your party for half his asking price since you were able to convince Jefnas to agree to his terms. You also earned five experience points each.

Break The Curse: Your emissary broke the curse keeping Kyla of Velkden's great-grandmother in the form of a harp.

"I know who our emissary is," Mallory said.

Brodie looked up from the map. "Who?"

"Check your journal notification." While Mallory waited for Brodie to look, she removed all the extras from their party now they'd completed the last of the quests for the day.

"It's Jenet Grayrock?" Brodie asked.

"She must have done that other quest after seeing it in your journal," Callum said.

"I hope we get the XP for this one too when she finishes it," Brodie said.

"I wonder how she manages to complete them on our behalf," Danae said. "She's not even in our party."

"It's all to do with the wording when they complete the different steps of the quest," Emica said. "Some of the lords and ladies in Shadhurst pay adventurers to complete quests on their behalf."

"It feels a bit like cheating," Ryan said.

Callum shrugged. "It's smart to use the mechanics of things."

"Or abuse them, by the sounds of it," Ryan said.

Callum shrugged again. "There's always someone who will. It doesn't matter what world you're in. Or game." He returned to the map and calculating the distance to Lilica.

"Is anyone going to collect resources on the way to Lilica?" Esben asked.

"I need to," Brodie said. "I only need a few more XP to level Fang up." She was fast asleep beside him and he patted her on the head. She half opened her eyes to look up at him, going straight back to sleep.

Ryan grinned. "Mallory will be able to cast tracking magelight on us so we don't have to waste lantern oil."

Brodie's expression brightened. "I forgot all about that. Cast it on me now. I want to see what it's like."

Chapter Forty

After her brother's comment, Mallory gave Ryan a look. "Did you have to remind him?'

"You're welcome." Ryan's grin remained in place.

"Come on, Mal," Brodie begged.

"You can wait until it's time to gather resources." Mallory interrupted her brother when he started to speak. "Which will be after Callum figures out how long it'll take us to reach Lilica."

Callum looked up from the map. "Done. At this pace, it'll take us approximately five hours. But we wouldn't want to go too fast and wear the horses out."

"Is that it?" Ryan asked. "I was expecting it to take longer."

"I guess that will depend on if we run into any trouble," Callum said.

Ryan chuckled. "There is that."

"Are we going to gather resources now?" Brodie asked.

Since Esben was so close to gaining character level five, they let him go first, giving him ten minutes to gain the experience points he needed. It was more than enough and he ended up with thirty-three more experience points than he'd needed to level up.

In an effort to get everyone to character level four, Brodie went next since he was the one closest to reaching that level out of those who were below level four. His turn lasted three-quarters of an hour and included reaching character level four and arguing that there was enough time for him to gain a bit more experience points. His bit more took him just over halfway through his next CAS point. During his turn, Fang reached level four as well. The wolf cub gained twenty-five percent increased strength. Brodie put his class point in rogue and put one attribute point in each of strength, constitution, dexterity, charisma and luck. That took his health up to thirty-nine and his stamina to sixty-five. He could now use the skill sleight of hand and had gained another revive.

Ryan, Callum, Danae and Emica took turns next, swapping out every fifteen minutes. Ryan and Callum both had four turns while Danae and Emica only had three since about half an hour from Lilica the area was cleaned out.

Emica grinned. "It doesn't matter that I didn't get the chance to gather resources as many times as they did." She nodded towards Ryan and Callum. "I'm quicker at it than they are and now I only need three CAS points to gain my fifth one for level three. I'll gain that point when we reach Lilica."

"If we'd run into something to fight, we'd have all got a heap more XP," Brodie muttered.

"The tracking magelights probably scared everything off," Callum said.

"We got a lot of XP without needing to fight anything. I'm happy I only need another thirty-five XP to reach character level four," Danae said. "We also have plenty of resources to sell. And I'll be able to set some more aside for health tea and boneset tea."

Ryan grinned. "Better do that before Brodie sells them all on you."

"As if I would," Brodie protested.

Callum glanced at Emica, a brief smile appearing. "Ryan and I might gather resources more slowly than Emica and Danae, but not only am I just thirty-four XP off character level four, but Smudge is now level five and has a twenty-five percent increased agility.

Next level he'll gain an extra twenty-five percent attack damage."

"That'll be more useful to Fang than it will be to Smudge," Brodie said.

Smudge chattered up at Brodie, sounding like he scolded him.

Ryan chuckled. "Sounds like Smudge doesn't agree with you. I bet he'd do okay in a fight. Once he has revives. No point risking him when he can't revive."

Smudge scampered over to Ryan, leaning against him and patting Ryan's arm, making soft sounds of agreement. The sounds became those of contentment when Ryan patted him on the head.

"Why does Smudge get an agility bonus while Fang gets a strength one for level four?"

"They're different types of animals. The companion animal book did say it'd be strength or agility," Callum said.

"It depends on which stat the animal relies on the most," Danae said.

Ryan peered through the arch of canvas, the town ahead of them. "It'll be good to get to Lilica and have a break. Four and a half hours of walking and half an hour in the wagon has made for a really long day after all we've done. It'll also be nice to get a bit more XP for reaching a new place. Unlike the rest of you, I still have a tonne of XP before I reach character level four."

"A hundred and five isn't a tonne," Brodie argued.

Rather than joining the discussion between Brodie and Ryan over experience point gains and how many CAS points Ryan had spare, Mallory took out her notebook and wrote in it in case she didn't have time once they reached Lilica. It didn't take her long to write a few lines about their day and she was putting the notebook back in the chest as they arrived in Lilica.

Callum, who was studying the map of Ruby Isle, looked up from it. "It's only about an hour and a quarter to Simria from here. Jorgen and Esben can ask about The Nelly at the tavern and we can travel on to Simria in the morning so Danni can see her father." He gestured ahead of them. "The tavern is obviously still open and busy."

Jorgen glanced over his shoulder, still driving the wagon. "As long as we can find out that information from those still about at this hour, I'm happy with that plan."

There were murmurs of agreement from all of them and Jorgen pulled up just down the road from the tavern, no space available any closer. He and Esben headed towards the tavern, the rest remaining in the wagon. They didn't want to leave it unattended with how many people were still around, as well as the fact they were parked along the waterfront with several ships at the jetty that stretched away from the shore.

Emica turned to Brodie. "Have you heard from my father yet?"

Brodie shook his head. "I looked about half an hour ago."

"Can you look again?" Emica asked. "It's been awhile."

Brodie took the duplication paper out of his satchel. "It's the same."

"Can you send him a message?" Emica asked. She waited until Brodie got out the pen and ink before she spoke again. "Make sure you write the exact words I give you. It's important."

"Hurry then." Brodie held the pen above the paper. "Before I get ink splatters everywhere."

"Little Ivan lost in cave again. Search all fissures eventually."

Brodie looked up from the paper, having only written the first word. "That doesn't make sense."

"It will to my father," Emica said.

"What does it actually mean?" Callum asked.

"Lilica. Safe," Emica said.

Callum smiled. "You've used the first letter of each word to spell it out. Simple yet effective with the way you've been able to make actual sentences. Even though the sentences are abbreviated. After all, that's a logical thing to do with duplication paper."

Brodie finished writing the sentences, handing the paper over to Emica when she asked to look.

Emica handed the paper back. "Let me know if he replies."

"Anyone'd think I never check." Brodie muttered, returning the paper to his satchel.

"Sorry," Emica said. "It's just surprising I haven't heard from him."

"I'm sure he's just busy looking for the spy," Mallory assured her.

Chapter Forty-One

Before Emica could reply to Mallory's comment, Jorgen and Esben returned, Jorgen shaking his head when Ryan asked him if they'd had any luck.

Esben climbed in the back of the wagon. "We might need to go to Eridell. They could have headed straight there and not gone to another port on Ruby Isle."

Jorgen, once again in the driver's seat, urged the horses into a walk. "There's no point leaving before we check as many ports as possible."

"They could have gone to Shadhurst," Danae said. "A lot of ships tend to go there before they leave Ruby Isle."

"Would they have gone there if they're a dark forces ship?" Callum asked.

"They don't have it written all over their ship that they're from the dark forces," Emica said. "Sometimes my father doesn't learn about one coming to Shadhurst until after they've left. You could ask my father if he can find out anything about The Nelly."

Brodie took out the duplication paper. "Hey, he sent a reply. It's as weird as yours. He said, 'No rush. I'm sure Ivan will be safer where he is.' And putting together the first letters of the words gives nothing either."

Emica laughed. "He's referring to my comment. Not using codes. Things mustn't have changed. He doesn't want me to come home yet."

"Did you want to go home?" Mallory asked.

Emica shook her head. "Not yet."

Brodie returned the duplication paper to his satchel. "I sent him the message about The Nelly."

"Will we go to Eridell after we hear from Hisoki?" Esben asked Jorgen.

Jorgen shrugged. "I guess that depends on what we learn."

Ryan shifted towards the back of the wagon. "I'll gather resources. It's too cramped in here to stretch out my legs."

Mallory cast tracking magelight on him as he hopped out the back of the wagon, following him. The spell only lasted for five minutes and she needed to be within five metres of him to recast it.

"I'll help." Ninette joined them, everyone else other than Jorgen doing the same.

There were fewer resources along the way to Simria and they had to go further from the road to gather them. Ryan reached character level four and gained twenty-seven experience points of the next hundred and thirty-eight needed for a CAS point. He put his class point in warrior, which meant he was now able to use a longsword. When they pulled up just outside Simria, planning to camp on the beach, he swapped the cutlass on his right for the longsword they'd taken from the orc mage, and swapped the short sword that was on his left with the cutlass he'd taken from his right since it had higher stats.

Mallory put the firewood she'd gathered next to Brodie, adding it to the ones Ninette and Esben had gathered. "I wonder what time it is at the Adventurers Guild."

Shrugging, Brodie lit the campfire. He started to speak, stopping when Ryan joined them, looking at Ryan before he spoke. "Now you can put all those CAS points into longsword."

Ryan chuckled. "It bugs you when we have a heap of CAS points."

"They give you bonuses. Why wouldn't you use them?" Brodie asked.

"Because you don't know what's coming and what you might need down the track." Callum set the cook pot beside the fire, having half filled it with water.

"I'm not sure if I want to always use a longsword," Ryan said. "I've been looking over the weapons I'll be able to use at higher levels and battle axe looks pretty good. The only problem is that I can't use it until I reach level fourteen."

"If you plan to use the longsword until then, it's probably worth putting CAS points into it," Callum said. "Level fourteen warrior is a long way off."

After a moment, Ryan nodded. "Yeah. Probably." He was silent for nearly a minute. "Done. Level twenty-seven longsword. Only another three CAS points needed to max it out. And I've put two attribute points in each of strength and constitution and one in dexterity. That gives me forty-five health and seventy-five stamina."

Mallory was about to ask if they should visit the Adventurers Guild when Danae joined them at the campfire.

Danae held Augusta's reins. "My father will still be awake. I'm going to go home so I can talk to him about my plans. Giving him a chance to sleep on the information might help. He's going to want me to go straight to the Alchemy Academy."

"Did you want us to come with you?" Mallory asked.

Danae shook her head. "I'll be safe enough. Simria is only minutes away."

"What about dinner?" Brodie asked.

Danae smiled at him. "I'll have something to eat at my father's home. Thank you, though." She swung up into the saddle. "I'll be back early tomorrow morning."

Mallory watched Danae ride away. She guessed there was no point in going to the Adventurers Guild this evening. It'd have to wait until Danae was back with them. They were going to join as a group, so there was no point travelling there when they were missing one of the members of their party.

While they waited for Brodie to make dinner, they pitched the tents and spread out bedrolls, making sure everything was ready for them to retire the moment they'd eaten.

Mallory found herself nodding off over dinner, stumbling to bed to fall into a dreamless sleep. A sound woke her, very little light visible. She frowned. About to go back to sleep, the sound of a bark rang out in the early morning and she realised that was what had woken her. Grabbing her wand, Mallory glanced at Ryan who sat up on the bedroll next to hers, reaching for his longsword. There was another bark and she moved the tent flaps apart enough to peer outside. Not seeing anything due to the limited amount of light, Mallory cast beacon in the middle of the camp.

A rogue, who'd been creeping towards the wagon, froze. He ran towards the trees edging the beach, separating it from the road that led into Simria.

"Do you think that was the only one?" Mallory continued to peer through the tent flaps, Ryan having joined her.

"I don't know. I guess there's only one way to find out." Ryan pulled on his boots.

"What if there are more out there?" Mallory asked. "My beacon is going to highlight you just as well as any bandit that might try to sneak into our camp."

Ryan shrugged. He drew aside the left tent flap, slipping outside. He'd taken only a couple of steps before an arrow came out of the trees and struck him. He dived back inside the tent, looking up at Mallory with a grin from where he lay on the ground, having removed the arrow from his arm. "I guess that's your answer."

"We can't sit in here all morning. We don't want Danae walking into a trap when she returns." Mallory healed him, relieved to find he hadn't lost too much health.

"Make me invisible." Ryan sat up. "I'll sneak out the back. I can slip underneath the canvas of the tent and over to the trees."

"I'll cast vanish I on myself too." Mallory pulled on her boots, having taken them off before she went to sleep. "It's probably best not to risk my brother coming up with his own solution."

Ryan chuckled. "Good point."

As soon as her boots were on, Mallory cast vanish I on each of them. She waited until the canvas at the back of the tent was in place again before she slipped out underneath it. A glance around showed the area was clear. Or at least clear of anything she could see. It was always possible there was a mage with the rogue and archer. Or that they had invisibility potions.

Chapter Forty-Two

Mallory was nearly at the tent Brodie shared with Callum when she spotted an archer aiming at Ninette. The young warrior peered out the back of the wagon. Ninette took her guard duties seriously and tended to sleep in the wagon rather than sharing a tent with Emica and Danae. She'd chosen to remain in the wagon even though Danae was in Simria and there'd only be Emica in the tent.

Mallory cast poison dart at the archer, distracting him from his target long enough that Ninette was again out of sight. Mallory had to quickly recast vanish I on herself, continuing to move towards Brodie and Callum's tent. She slipped inside when she reached it, quickly speaking when Callum aimed his bow in her direction. "It's me."

Callum lowered his bow. "Sorry."

"How many are out there?" Brodie sat beside Fang,

an arm wrapped around her. He shushed her every time she growled. "We don't want them to know we're in here, girl."

Mallory shrugged. "There's at least two of them. An archer and a rogue. Ryan headed for the trees in an effort to find out."

"Make me invisible so I can help him take them out," Brodie said.

"So you can get some XP," Mallory corrected him.

"Not like I can do one without the other," Brodie protested.

"Do you and Ryan have a plan?" Callum asked. "Other than for him to go after them alone and get himself killed."

Mallory wanted to protest Callum's comment, but he was right. They didn't have much of a plan at all. "Any suggestions?"

"Cast vanish I on both the crystalline wolves. And on Emica too. The three of them can move faster than us when they're in their animal form. We also need to get Ninette out of the wagon. She's over there on her own," Callum said.

Mallory slowly nodded. "That sounds like a good start."

"What about me?" Brodie asked. "You're not planning on leaving me in here, are you?"

"I would have thought you'd be interested in getting everything sorted out as soon as possible so that Danae doesn't risk being attacked by them," Mallory said.

Brodie stared at her, mouth ajar.

Callum slowly shook his head. "Guess you didn't think of that."

"What are you still doing in here?" Brodie demanded. "Go make the others invisible."

Mallory cast vanish I on herself before slipping out underneath the back of the tent. If she'd had more mana, she would have cast the spell on Brodie, Fang, Callum and Smudge. Reaching Jorgen and Esben's tent, she spoke as she entered, having learned her lesson. "It's me."

"Do I take it you have a plan?" Jorgen asked.

"Of a fashion. I'll make both of you invisible, then do the same for Emica as well as get Ninette out of the wagon. The bandits attacking us are amongst the trees." Becoming visible, she cast the spell on both of them, her mana having regened enough.

"We'll see what we can do," Jorgen said.

Mallory watched as the tent flap opened and then fell closed again. An arrow pierced the canvas, flying past her and going out the other side. She sighed. That would need mending later. But at least it hadn't hit her. Worried about Ryan, she checked his stats. He'd obviously taken out one of the bandits as he'd gained some experience points. His health was fine though.

Casting vanish I on herself, she slipped through the tent flaps, stepping immediately to the right in the hope she wasn't shot by an arrow. None came for her and she hurried over to the wagon, which was on the way to Emica's tent, again calling out a warning before she clambered in the back and pressed herself against the floor of the wagon before she became visible.

"I tried to go after them, but there are two archers and they shoot at me every time I look over the edge," Ninette said.

"I saw one of them," Mallory said. "I'll make you invisible and you can head for the trees. Ryan, Jorgen and Esben are already over there fighting them."

Ninette nodded. "I'm ready."

Mallory cast vanish I on the young warrior, smiling as she heard her get out of the wagon. Ninette obviously wasn't as quiet as the travellers were. Seeing her mana had regened enough, she cast vanish I on herself and headed to the tent Emica was in. Again she called out a warning before she slipped inside.

"I was about to change forms and go after them."

Emica gestured towards the back of the tent, her ears those of a fox. "I was going out that way. I don't think any of them are in that direction. Or at least I couldn't hear them out that way."

"I'll make you invisible first," Mallory said. "Then it won't matter where they are."

Emica grinned. "Thanks. That's a really handy spell."

Mallory returned her grin, visible again herself, then cast the spell. She had to wait a few seconds before she could cast the spell on herself. The moment she did, she ran lightly back to Callum and Brodie, giving them a warning before she entered. As her mana regened enough to cast vanish on two at a time, she did so, using it on Callum and Smudge first.

Brodie waited until Callum had left before he spoke. "Have you seen if Danae is on her way back yet?"

"I've been busy getting everyone out of tents and the wagon." Mallory wished she could have told him something else with the worry she could hear in his tone. "I'm sure she won't be coming back this early. She'll probably have breakfast with her dad first."

"I wonder what they'll have for breakfast," Brodie said.

Mallory smiled. She should have known

mentioning food would help distract him. "You ready for me to cast the spell on the two of you?" She glanced at Fang as she spoke.

Brodie nodded.

Mallory cast the spell on them and waited twenty-four seconds for her mana to regen enough to cast it on herself again. While she waited, she checked everyone's stats. The seconds felt like they passed extremely slowly when she saw Ryan had lost eight health. She didn't know if it had been from a single attack or several. If it was a single attack, that meant another five attacks could take him out.

Casting vanish on herself, she ran towards the trees, searching for those of her party. She really needed the spell that would help her locate them. Although with how she was using up most of her mana casting vanish I she wouldn't have anything left to use another spell.

A mage wearing wire-rimmed glasses stepped out in front of Mallory, casting lightning at her.

Chapter Forty-Three

Pain arrowed through Mallory as she lost seven health and she automatically cast fireball at the mage, drawing in a sharp breath when the attack hit an invisible shield that was in front of him.

The mage laughed. "I can cast shield block all day. Your spells are useless against me."

Mallory drew her sword. "But can it block a weapon?" She attacked the mage, healing herself for two health. When the mage used lightning on her again, she healed herself twice more, the pain going the moment she used the spell on herself.

The mage laughed again. "That pathetic health spell of yours won't help you survive my attacks. Especially since mine heals me for all the damage you do each time with your sword."

She was tempted to try and grab the glasses off him. Then she realised it would be possible to do exactly that. She attacked again, not using any of her mana to heal herself when she was struck by his spell, casting vanish I on herself the moment she had enough mana. Darting forward, she grabbed the glasses off him, jumping back out of the way when he tried to snatch them back. Not wanting to risk the mage taking them from her by using the same trick, she folded the glasses and shoved them in her satchel.

"Show yourself." The mage did a slow turn on the spot.

Mallory attacked with her sword before her spell ran out, attacking again several times more. When she saw the mage slip a hand into his satchel, withdrawing it with dust on it, she figured out how he was able to cast so many spells one after the other. He had essence crystals. She needed his satchel.

Before Mallory could cast vanish I on herself again, Emica came out of the undergrowth, still in fox form, and attacked the mage. The mage spun to face Emica and Mallory used the distraction to cast vanish I on herself and sheathing her sword and wand, drew out her dagger. She cut through the strap of the satchel, pulling it away from the mage when he tried to grab hold of it. Sheathing her dagger as she backed away, taking out her wand to cast fireball at the mage, casting it until she ran out of mana.

Within minutes, the mage was sprawled on the ground, motionless. Emica gave Mallory a nod, remaining in fox form as she bounded away.

Looking around, Mallory saw no one. Nor could she hear any fighting. Was that it? Had they taken all of them out? Healing her health, she searched the mage before she went looking for the rest of her party. She'd found nothing on the mage and had presumably already taken all his valuables between the glasses and the satchel.

As soon as she had enough mana, Mallory repaired the cloth satchel and slung the strap over her head and shoulder so it sat securely across her chest. Not having any luck finding anyone, she stepped out of the trees and into their camp. No one attacked her and she made her way to the middle of the camp, scanning the area. She stopped in the middle of the camp, half expecting to be struck by an arrow. She tensed when she heard a noise. Spinning to face it, she drew in a shaky breath when she spotted Ryan coming out from amongst the trees, other members of her party doing the same.

Ryan reached her first. "Either we got all of them or the rest of them fled."

Callum joined them. "Or are hiding."

Mallory started to heal Ryan since he'd lost the

most health out of the two of them. "I was annoyed with being woken early, but after what I managed to get, I'm not in the slightest bit annoyed now."

"What did you get?" Brodie joined them at the same time as Ninette and Emica.

The kitsune changed forms, her ears remaining that of a fox. "Diplomat glasses." She turned to Mallory. "Nice move."

Mallory laughed. "He shouldn't have mocked me with how poorly I was doing against him." She drew out the glasses from her satchel as Jorgen and Esben arrived.

Callum took the glasses from her, trying them on and looking at each of them. "This is cool. Maybe I should consider putting my CAS points into diplomat so I can see more information about those we come across."

"Let me see." Brodie held out his hand. "I didn't get anything good from the warrior I attacked. "Only a gold coin."

Mallory couldn't help thinking about how exciting the drop of a gold coin had once been. They were obviously making progress. Not just in their stats.

Callum handed over the glasses. "I guess we don't really need to know much about those we attack other than their health."

"You just don't want to use your CAS points," Brodie muttered. He did a slow turn. "This is cool. Can I have them? Callum has the spyglass. I should get something."

Mallory held her hand out to her brother. "I'm keeping them. I was the one who took them from the mage."

"By trickery," Emica pointed out. "If he'd died with them on, you might not have been lucky enough to get them as a drop."

Brodie muttered under his breath.

Mallory smiled when she thought she caught the words 'not fair' in amongst his complaints.

"I'm going fishing." Brodie headed towards the wagon. "Might as well see if we can have something decent for breakfast. I'll put the coin in the chest."

"I'll help you, Brodie." Callum took several steps towards the wagon before turning back to Mallory. "I ended up getting five silver pieces. I'll put them in the chest too. I also gained three spare arrows after replacing the ones I lost."

Having finished healing Callum, Mallory nodded. Using the diplomat glasses, she looked at each of those around her, healing those who needed it. The glasses were going to make it a lot easier for her to keep track of who needed to be healed. Now if only she had a better healing spell. Maybe she needed to get one of those next.

"What's with the extra satchel," Ryan asked.

"I took it from the mage I stole the glasses from." Mallory sat by the fire, tipping the contents onto the sand. There were three small essence crystals and two potions, each with ten mana. Essence crystal dust was scattered across the sand. The crystals had thirty mana each. The mage wouldn't have run out of mana in a hurry. There was also a rag doll and a small drawstring bag.

"Nice haul," Ryan said.

Mallory looked up at him. "Do you know how many there were?"

Ryan shook his head. "Around six. But I couldn't say for certain. I know one of the ones I attacked vanished."

She checked everyone's stats. For once Brodie hadn't been able to get an attack in on all their enemies.

Emica joined them. "Here. I got a silver ring from the one I searched. I tried it on and it doesn't seem to have an enchantment. We might as well sell it."

Chapter Forty-Four

Mallory took the ring from Emica, also taking the seven silver pieces Jorgen gave her. "Thanks."

Jorgen pointed to the drawstring bag. "You might want to have a look inside that."

"Why?" She asked the question as she opened the bag, having slipped the ring and coins into her belt pouch. She frowned when she tipped out a vial of red liquid and a lock of hair.

"That's what I thought." Jorgen took the vial and lock of hair. He threw the hair into the fire, then poured the liquid in, the smell of burning hair and blood filling the air. "That mage was going to make a poppet. It wouldn't surprise me if the mage had been a member of the dark forces."

"I wonder if they all were." Mallory picked up the rag doll. "Are you certain it's not a poppet?"

Jorgen nodded. "I'll clean out the vial, then put it in the chest."

Mallory gathered up the items and rose to her feet. "I guess we should start packing the camp while Brodie and Callum catch our breakfast." She put the essence crystals, mana potions, drawstring bag and rag doll in the chest from Rodina before making her way to the tent and mending it with her spell.

By the time they'd packed the camp, putting away the tents and bedrolls, Callum and Brodie, along with Smudge's help, had caught ten fish. Brodie gave the companion animals a raw fish each before he finished cleaning the fish and cooking them, having to cook them in two lots.

They were finishing up their meal when Danae arrived. "You didn't keep any for me?" She smiled at Brodie, who blushed.

"Well, I… ah…" He scrambled to his feet. "I could catch another one."

Danae smiled at him. "I was only teasing. I had breakfast with my father. He bought sweet pastries from the bakery."

Brodie's expression brightened. "There's a bakery in Simria?"

"Don't even think about it," Mallory said when her brother turned towards her.

"But, Mal-"

Mallory cut him off. "No. You've just had breakfast." She faced Danae. "Lucky you didn't come back here too early." She told the half-elf about their morning, showing her the glasses when asked.

Danae returned the glasses. "That was really good thinking. My news is going to be unexciting in comparison. Although I do also have some bad news in that he doesn't have a copy of that spell I was telling you about. Nightlight. He sold a copy last week and hasn't received another one yet."

"What's your news?" Brodie asked.

Danae gestured towards the wagon where Bug and Sun Lily were hitched and ready to go. "I'll tell you on the way into Simria."

When the campfire was out and they were all in the wagon and on the way into Simria, Brodie asked, "What was your news?"

"I spent half the night talking to my father and again over breakfast this morning. He agreed I could keep Augusta if I promised to arrive at the academy before the date I'm due there and he gave me duplication paper. One to keep in touch with him and one lot to keep in touch with my mother." Danae turned to Brodie. "He also wants first look at all the items we have for sale."

Ryan chuckled. "You probably should have started with that news. I'm sure that's the part Brodie likes best."

"No, it's not," Brodie protested.

"What part do you like the best then?" Danae asked.

Brodie's cheeks reddened again. "Well… he's ahh… not going to keep you from travelling with us." Brodie glanced away as they reached Simria. "Where is your dad's shop?"

Mallory tried not to smile at her brother's discomfort, but it was impossible to keep one from forming. She checked her journal to make sure the notification was only for the location experience points. Seeing it was, she closed her journal and looked around at the town they were driving through. Ahead of them was the dock, shops and a tavern lining the waterfront.

Jorgen glanced at Danae. "Is your father's shop far from here, or should we get out and meet you there after we've asked around about The Nelly?"

"It isn't far. We're only several doors down from the tavern," Danae said. "Which made for some very noisy nights when ships that had been out at sea for a long time came to town." As they drew close, she pointed out a spot where Jorgen could park the wagon.

It wasn't until they were pulling up out the front of the shop, with a sign saying "General Goods', that Mallory realised Callum had gained a character level. She hopped down out of the wagon to stand beside him. "Why didn't you say anything about your character level?"

Callum smiled. "I was too busy being entertained by Brodie. If he ever asks Danni out, it'll probably only be by accident."

Mallory laughed, glancing over at Danae and Brodie who were heading inside the shop to let her father know they'd arrived. She quickly checked over Callum's new stats while they waited. He'd put his class point into archer and now had four revives. He would also be able to use enchanted slings and slingshot now. He had thirty-seven CAS points and had put one attribute point into each of strength, constitution and luck and two into dexterity. That had brought his health up to thirty-three and his stamina to fifty-five.

Danae and Brodie came out of the shop, a man following them. He was tall and broad shouldered and nothing like what she'd expected Danae's father to be like. Where his daughter was fair-haired, he was dark-haired and although they both had green eyes, his were a dark green while hers were a pale green.

Danae looked from her father to those gathered around outside. "This is my father, Henell." She gestured to each of them as she said their names, mentioning that Jorgen and Esben were enquiring about a ship at the dock.

Henell studied all of them before slowly nodding his head. "I've heard a great deal about all of you."

Mallory wasn't sure if that was a good or bad thing with the way Henell said it.

"Want me to show you what we have for sale?" Brodie asked.

Henell nodded. "I appreciate you letting me have first choice."

After going through what they were interested in selling, Henell wanted all the herbs and vegetables, the silver ring, packing crate that Brodie finally agreed to part with, the rag doll, the short bow, the two short swords that Ninette and Ryan no longer needed and the wand they'd got from the archers. When Brodie would have sold the two satchels, Mallory asked if those with them wanted one. Ninette and Esben wanted a satchel while Emica shook her head, saying she preferred to travel light.

Chapter Forty-Five

They returned inside the shop to talk prices and trading some items for what they needed rather than taking all the value in coins. Mallory smiled as she watched Brodie haggle with Henell, obviously in his element. In the end, Henell offered them fifty gold pieces and a further thirty gold worth of purchases. He also said he'd have Brodie's ring he wore assessed for enchantments, Brodie having forgotten to get it assessed when he'd sold the jewellery in Eastvale. Henell couldn't assess jewellery as he was ten levels below what was needed, but the jeweller several shops down the road did all such assessments for him in exchange for a permanent discount in his shop.

Mallory wandered around Henell's shop while Brodie visited the jeweller, taking with him a note from Henell. There was a variety of goods from weapons and armour all the way through to general goods and cooking supplies. She smiled when she heard Callum ask about coffee and Henell tell him he'd never heard of it. Before Mallory could decide on what they should buy, Brodie came racing inside the shop, grinning.

He held up his ring that he normally wore. "It's a rogue ring. Like we thought. It adds five seconds to rogue class skills." he turned to Emica. "I heard from your dad. He doesn't recall The Nelly ever having been in Shadhurst, but he'll check with the harbour master."

Emica nodded. "I'll find Jorgen and Esben and let them know." She headed outside.

Brodie glanced around the shop. "Has anyone chosen anything? We should stock up on food supplies. Things like flour that we rarely get as a drop or loot."

"There aren't any crafting ability books we don't already have," Callum said. "Or coffee."

"You've got heaps of coffee," Brodie said. "But we don't have much flour left."

"There isn't heaps," Callum said.

Brodie shrugged. "We'll get more. All we'll have to do is attack one of the dark forces villages down south."

Ryan grinned. "And gain a higher negative rep with them?"

Brodie picked up two calico bags of rolled oats, both a kilogram each. "I can make biscuits with this."

They helped Brodie pick out food supplies. Along with the two kilograms of rolled oats, they also put one kilogram of cornmeal, three kilograms of flour, two kilograms of pasta, four kilograms of rice, four kilograms of split peas, two kilograms of brown sugar, a dozen eggs, a split pea soup recipe and a forest stew recipe on the counter.

"How much is that so far?" Brodie asked.

"Four silver pieces," Henell, who'd been calculating the cost as they put things on the counter, said.

Callum looked up from the item he examined. "What's a cooling box?"

"It keeps things like milk, butter and meat cold enough they don't spoil too quickly," Henell said.

"Let me see." Brodie made his way over to Callum. "It's only two hundred and fifty gold pieces. We could have milk and butter with this. I'd be able to make lots of different types of food."

Mallory joined them, looking down at the small box that was about the size of a soft drink esky. It was twenty centimetres wide, twenty-eight centimetres long and twenty-five centimetres high. They wouldn't be able to store a lot in there, but there'd be plenty of room for milk and butter like Brodie wanted. "We don't have that much gold on us."

Brodie turned to Danae. "There's a bank here, isn't there?"

Danae shook her head before turning to her father. "What about the five leatherback bear canines? Are you interested in them now that we want a more expensive item?"

Henell beamed proudly at his daughter. "Are you sure you don't want to become a trader?"

Danae laughed softly. "I'm certain. Now what do you say?"

"I could offer you a hundred gold pieces for all five canines."

"Maybe there's some more things we can sell," Brodie said.

He went through all the items again and they decided to sell the spare leather backpack, two of the wooden buckets, the tall cane basket, a clay pot, the miner's helmet, two potions of swiftness, one of the lanterns, the light padded gambeson and one of the spare longbows. And, after a bit more haggling, Henell added a litre of milk and two hundred grams of butter to the trade.

Brodie grinned. "We have a cooling box."

"A little one," Ryan pointed out.

"That's all we need for now." Carrying the cooling box, Brodie started to step outside, stopping when someone tried to enter. "Kruth!"

"Brodie! What are you doing up this way?" Kruth looked past him. "What are all of you doing here?"

Brodie stepped back out of the way. "Henell is Danae's dad."

Kruth greeted all of them. "Your party is smaller now?"

Mallory shook her head. "Emica, Jorgen and Esben are at the docks while Ninette is out with the wagon."

"I need to take this out to the wagon." Brodie glanced at the cooling box he still held. "It's getting heavy."

"Let me take it out for you." Without waiting for a reply, Kruth took the cooling box from Brodie. He turned to Henell. "The wagoner sent me to let you know he's arrived."

"I'll be out in a minute," Henell said. "I need to bid my daughter farewell."

Chapter Forty-Six

Mallory followed Brodie and Kruth outside to the wagon, carrying some of the food supplies with her. Ryan and Callum followed, carrying the rest of them. She smiled as she listened to Kruth telling Brodie all of what he'd been up to since they'd last seen him. After they'd chatted for a bit, while putting the items away, Mallory said, "I need to visit the apothecary. Did you want to come with me, Brodie, or are you staying here?"

Kruth interrupted Brodie when he started to reply. "I need to get back to work. The wagoner will want me to help unload his things shortly." He clapped Brodie on the shoulder. "It was good to see you. I've missed all of you."

"We've missed you too," Brodie said.

Kruth looked over his shoulder when his name was called, turning back to them with a grin. "Better get back to work. The wagoner is a good boss so I wouldn't want to go upsetting him."

After they'd said goodbye to Kruth, and decided to leave the wagon where it was with Ninette to guard it, they walked down the road to the apothecary. Brodie kept glancing over his shoulder. "I can't believe we ran into Kruth like that. I thought we'd have to ask around at taverns for him."

"It was good to catch up with him," Callum agreed.

Mallory nodded. "And to see he's doing so well." She'd worried about him.

Before they could enter the apothecary shop, a man was propelled out the door and nearly into their path, stumbling on the crutches he used. He drew out an aged map, holding one of his crutches with his arm against his body, waving the map at the apothecary. "It's not a fake. We were there. It's all I have to pay you with."

The apothecary shook his head. "I'm not interested in going after any treasures. You want to be healed, pay in gold like everyone else." Turning away, the apothecary stepped inside and closed the door.

"What sort of treasure?" Brodie asked.

The man turned awkwardly to face them, trying to hold the map and use his crutches. "Are you interested in buying it? I'll sell it for the price I need to pay the apothecary to heal my leg."

"My sister is an apothecary." Brodie glanced at Mallory before he returned his attention to the man. "So, what sort of treasure is it?"

"You can heal broken bones?" The man addressed Mallory.

She nodded. "I can do average rapid mend. That'll only decrease your recovery time by ten percent every twelve hours. But we can make strong boneset tea, which will reduce your recovery time by ten percent once a day." Before she could say that it didn't matter what sort of treasure it was, that she'd heal him anyway, he spoke again.

"My partner is still there. I have to get back to her. She's only a mage. I have to assume she ran from the fight as I was able to respawn, but that doesn't mean she's safe. She's a long way from any village. I can't wait that long to go after her. I can sell the map to you though," the man offered. "If I'd had anything other than a location specific respawn, she wouldn't be out there on her own."

"It'd probably have been worse if you had respawned near her," Ryan said. "Being injured."

"Why don't you have any money?" Brodie asked.

"I put my backpack down to get the lockpicks out

when we came to a locked door in the dungeon. We were attacked before I could unlock the door." The man looked at each of them. "All I need is enough money to pay the apothecary. Are you interested or should I see what I can get for the map from a trader?"

Brodie turned to Mallory. "It's a treasure, Mal."

Mallory couldn't help smiling at Brodie's tone. "We're already on our way to find a treasure. But we-"

Brodie interrupted her. "You can never have too much treasure. Come on, Mal. Treasure."

"What about the drake's nest? You were worried about getting there in time," Mallory pointed out.

"It won't take us long," Brodie pleaded.

Ryan and Callum shared a grin, saying at the same time, "Side quest."

Mallory sighed, slowly shaking her head. "Okay, but you better not complain if we miss out on the drake eggs." She pointed a warning finger at Brodie.

"I'll run back to my father's house and make a batch of boneset tea," Danae said. "It won't take me long. I'll meet you there once you're finished at the apothecary." She hurried back the way they'd come.

"You'll heal me?" the man asked. "In exchange for the map?"

Mallory shook her head. "Not exactly."

"But-"

Ryan interrupted the man. "We'll heal you as much as possible and give you boneset tea so you can finish healing over the next few days, but in the meantime, we'll help you find your partner and get the two of you back to safety."

"You'll escort us home?" the man asked.

"Where is your home?" Brodie asked.

"Ursen."

Ryan chuckled. "Just where we needed to go." He glanced at the map. "So where is this dungeon?"

The man stared at Ryan, speechless for a moment. "It's south west of here. About an hour in from the coast and halfway between Simria and Ursen. If you're serious about helping us, the map seems like so little in exchange. If you do escort us home, even though it's not much, you're welcome to stay in our home whenever you're in Ursen and need a place to stay. It's a small cottage on the outskirts of Ursen. We own a farm south east of Ursen, but bandits took it over and neither of us are of a high enough level to take it back from them. We offered a reward, but no one seems interested in helping us get rid of them."

Mallory checked her journal notification, finding two quests rather than the single one she'd expected.

Escort To Ursen: A rogue and mage are in need of an escort to Ursen. They will allow you to stay in their home whenever you are in Ursen if you see them safely home.

Overrun By Bandits: A farm south east of Ursen is overrun by bandits. The owners have offered a reward to anyone interested in ridding them of the bandits.

"Why didn't it mention the map in the rewards?" Brodie asked.

"The map isn't a reward for escorting them home," Callum said. "That's for healing him."

Mallory glanced towards the apothecary shop behind her. "I'll go buy what I need and then we can collect everyone else and find the missing mage."

"I'll come with you." Brodie led the way inside the shop.

Mallory smiled as she followed her brother, not at all surprised he didn't want to miss out on bartering with the apothecary. Especially with how much he enjoyed it.

"Can I help you?" the apothecary asked.

"I need something for when I operate on people. Something so they don't feel any pain," Mallory said.

"You have two options." The apothecary led them to a shelf with neatly labelled potion vials. He picked up one of them, a lavender coloured liquid filling the vial. "Strong dull senses. It lasts for twenty minutes and the person who drinks it will feel no pain, or any other sensation for that matter, but they will be awake. It's forty gold pieces." He returned it to the shelf and picked up another vial, the liquid a silvery grey. "Sleep of the dead. The person who drinks this potion will be unconscious and unable to move or feel anything for ten minutes. It's thirty gold pieces."

Chapter Forty-Seven

Mallory sighed. She should have known they'd be expensive. "Do you have anything that isn't so costly."

"You can charge the cost of them to your patients," the apothecary suggested.

"The people I've been helping don't have that kind of money," Mallory said.

"What about a recipe for one of them that can be made as a herbal tea?" Brodie asked.

"Yes, that would be good." Mallory frowned. "Maybe. How long would a tea last?"

"Two minutes for a dull senses tea or five minutes for a strong dull senses tea," the apothecary said. "Fifty gold pieces for the recipe."

"Fifty!" Brodie exclaimed. "That's ridiculous."

The apothecary shrugged. "Take it or leave it. I'm not about to argue price with you. My prices are set."

They didn't have fifty gold pieces and there was no bank here. Not that she wanted to start taking money from their savings. "I have two antipoison potions." She took them from her satchel, willing to sell them since they had another two stored in the chest from Rodina.

"I can offer you twenty gold pieces for them," the apothecary said.

"I have three hours of a night vision potion." Mallory took the vial out of her satchel, holding it up.

"For the three potions I can offer you fifty gold pieces," the apothecary said.

Brodie took the vials from Mallory and held them out to the apothecary. "We'll take the recipe."

The apothecary took the vials from Brodie and returned to the counter. Taking out a book of recipes, the apothecary removed the one for dull senses tea and handed it over.

"Thank you." Mallory tucked the recipe into her satchel before returning outside.

"What did you end up buying?" Callum asked.

While Brodie told Callum and Ryan, Mallory turned to the rogue, placing her hands on him and doing average rapid mend.

Thanking her, the rogue handed over the map. Brodie took it before Mallory had the chance, slipping it into his belt pouch and grinning at her. She slowly shook her head, turning to Ryan. "Are we ready to return to Henell's shop?"

Once they were back at the shop, they saw that Emica, Jorgen and Esben were waiting in the wagon for them and they found Danae inside talking to her father. The tea was already brewed and Danae had talked her father into giving her a waterskin for it. Mallory handed over the recipe to Danae.

Henell gestured towards the recipe his daughter slipped inside her satchel after reading it over. "Danae told me you've been helping her with her apothecary skills."

Mallory nodded, not sure what to say in reply.

"I was worried, even after she assured me you truly do treat her as one of your party. I'm glad to see my worries are unfounded," Henell said.

Mallory smiled at him. "She is one of our party. She contributes as much as the rest of us."

Henell nodded before turning to his daughter and enveloping her in his arms. "Be careful and let me know when you reach Merrow and I'll send your belongings to you."

"I'll miss you." Danae returned his hug.

Henell stepped back, his hands resting on Danae's shoulders. "Keep me informed of where you are and how you are doing. You have the duplication paper, so make sure you use it. I'll expect to hear from you at least once a week."

"I'll use it. And I'll keep my mother informed too once I deliver the duplication paper to her."

Henell drew Danae in for another hug, kissing her on each cheek. "Don't go doing anything stupid. Like you did with Sidree. I'm surprised I'm not completely grey with some of the mischief the two of you used to get into."

Danae laughed softly. "We weren't that bad." She kissed both of his cheeks before stepping away from him, staring up at her father for a moment before she made her way to the exit.

Henell walked with Danae, standing in the doorway to watch her leave.

Mallory watched Danae, who was driving, wishing she knew what to say when Danae glanced back several times until her father was out of sight. He'd remained in the doorway the entire time. But the moment passed while she was still trying to figure out what to say and as they headed south, she poured a cup of boneset tea for the rogue while asking Jorgen about The Nelly.

Jorgen shook his head. "No one has heard of her."

He held out his hand to the rogue. "I'm Jorgen and this is my cousin Esben."

Ryan grinned. "Sorry. I should have introduced everyone to you earlier." He told the rogue all of their names.

The rogue shook hands with them. "Relmir and my partner is Sarnla."

The journey to the location on the map Relmir had given them was quiet, the area clear of resources so they couldn't even gather any along the way. Pulling up in front of the overgrown entrance to the dungeon, some vines having been pulled back to show the open, weathered timber doors, Relmir clambered awkwardly down from the wagon.

Mallory joined him, glancing back along the dirt track they'd followed to the dungeon. The way the trees pressed in on either side of it and how it was overgrown in most places had made it difficult to follow. "I never would have known that was anything other than an animal trail."

Relmir nodded, scanning the area. "Sarnla said something similar."

The rest of their group, except Ninette, who would remain with the wagon, joined them. Brodie moved close enough to the dungeon entrance to peer inside. "Do you think Sarnla went back in there?"

"I don't know," Relmir said.

"What if we call out to her?" Ryan asked. "There's enough of us that we should be able to deal with anything else that hears us."

Relmir drew in a deep breath. "Sarnla!" He waited a moment. "Sarnla!" He did a slow turn, scanning the area. "Sarnla!"

A woman in a mage robe stepped out from amongst the trees. "Are you trying to call all the creatures out of the dungeon?" She looked Relmir up and down. "What have you done to yourself now?"

Relmir laughed at her scolding tone. "I was obviously worried about you for no reason. Glad you're unharmed and your usual self."

Sarnla slowly shook her head, giving him one more look over before turning her attention to everyone else. "Who's with you?"

Relmir introduced all of them. "I gave them the map in exchange for a rapid mend and boneset tea."

"Does that mean we have to give them what we've already found in the dungeon?" Sarnla asked.

"No, only what's beyond the door we didn't get to open," Relmir said.

"What if we can't open it?" Brodie asked. "We don't even have lockpicks."

"If you can protect us, we can go with you to the door and I can unlock it for you," Relmir said.

"And give you the chance to collect your backpack," Sarnla said dryly.

Relmir moved towards the dungeon entrance, the process difficult on crutches with the uneven ground. "I would like my backpack back, if you can protect me." He glanced down at his crutches before glancing around the group. "I can't attack anything while on these."

Sarnla stood at Relmir's side. "We're never going to earn enough coins to hire mercenaries to take back our farm. The reward we've currently offered isn't getting any interest."

"What is the reward?" Brodie asked.

"Fifty gold pieces," Sarnla said.

Chapter Forty-Eight

Mallory checked her journal when a notification appeared. *Overrun By Bandits: The current reward for clearing out the farm south east of Ursen is fifty gold pieces.* She smiled. There was a good chance her brother would want to do that quest. Fifty gold pieces was more than they usually earned from a quest. She couldn't help wondering how bad the bandit problem was that no one was interested in collecting the reward.

Relmir looked over his shoulder. "Are you all ready to go in?"

Mallory cast magelight before joining Relmir at the dungeon entrance. "Will we need a map?"

"It's fairly straightforward," Sarnla said. "A main corridor, with rooms branching off it, that leads to a sharp corner. That part of the corridor leads to the door we were trying to unlock. It was the room next to that last room that the creatures came from. We should have opened it first instead of getting impatient and trying to open the last room."

Relmir entered the dungeon, moving to one side so everyone else could enter. "I doubt it would have made a difference. Whatever was in the end room might have come out if it heard us fighting the creatures in the last room."

Ryan led the way, glancing back at Relmir when he spoke. "What creatures? What will we need to face?"

"Carrion rats," Relmir said. "About twenty of them."

Mallory, who'd been glancing in an empty room to her right, nearly ran into Danae when she came to a halt. "Do I take it that's a problem?"

The half-elf nodded. "No wonder Relmir had to use a revive. I'm surprised Sarnla escaped."

Sarnla came to a stop when everyone else did. "I used an invisibility spell."

"What's the problem with them?" Ryan asked.

"Carrion rats swarm you," Danae said. "They don't spread out and attack everyone like most creatures do. They focus on a single person and all attack that one person."

"How bad can twenty rats be?" Brodie asked.

"Twenty rats the size of a large wolf," Danae said.

"Oh." Brodie took a step back, glancing towards the end of the corridor where it made a sharp turn.

"There are a lot of you," Relmir assured him. "If everyone focuses on a rat, it shouldn't take long to deal with all of them."

"What if Mallory casts vanish I on anyone they focus on?" Ryan asked.

"They don't need to see you to keep attacking you," Sarnla said. "The only reason that worked for me is because they were focused on Relmir when I went invisible."

"There's got to be some way of dealing with them," Ryan said.

"How fast are they?" Callum asked.

"It's possible to outrun them," Relmir said. "Do you have a plan?"

Callum didn't answer immediately. "Possibly. What if only one of us went down and caught their attention and the rest are in the rooms along the way, taking them out as whoever is bait runs along the corridor, following behind once the carrion rats are past the room they're hiding in?"

"Who'd be bait?" Brodie asked. "It better not be me."

"It'd have to be whoever has the highest stamina," Callum said. "Ryan has seventy-five."

"So do I," Mallory pointed out.

"Yes, but your spells are useful," Callum said.

Ryan grinned. "Should I feel insulted?"

Callum smiled at his brother. "I'll let you decide." He glanced around the group. "Anyone?"

They all shook their head or said 'no'. Ryan clapped his brother on the shoulder. "Thanks for volunteering me," he said dryly.

"You're welcome," Callum said.

"Who will be where?" Emica asked.

After some discussion, it was decided that Jorgen, Emica and Callum would go in the short hallway that was closest to the room with the carrion rats, Mallory would go in a room of the long corridor just before the sharp bend and the rest of them would be in the rooms along the long corridor with Brodie in the room closest to the exit. He'd protested since he wouldn't get as many experience points, but since his attacks were the lowest, his protests were ignored.

Mallory cast tracking magelight on Callum and Ryan before entering the room she was to wait in. Her grip tightened on her wand as she peered through the doorway, waiting for Ryan to appear. She heard him and the rats before she saw them, the sound of scampering and squealing proceeding them. The noises were regularly punctuated by a spine chilling shriek. She didn't know if the shriek was a common sound they made or if it was from being attacked. If it was from being attacked, then not enough of them were being targeted. Would Ryan's stamina last long enough for all the rats to be killed? She dreaded to think what would happen if it didn't. Obviously, Ryan would lose a revive, but who would the carrion rats go after next and how many of them would lose revives before they could be killed? All the thoughts ran through her head in a jumble, many of them simultaneously, the time feeling like it stretched out into hours, which was far longer than the actual minute it was.

Ryan came around the corner and Mallory prepared to cast poison dart at the rats. She held her breath as he ran past her, letting it out in a rush as she cast poison dart. She had time to cast it three times, having no idea which ones she attacked with the way they swarmed through the corridor. Before she could cast it a fourth time, they were past her and Jorgen, Callum and Emica were in her way.

Hurrying after everyone, Mallory cast fireball every chance she had. Rats fell as they progressed along the corridor, but not enough. She checked Ryan's stamina. He was a third of the way through it. They weren't a third of the way through the rats. Not if there'd been twenty of them. There had to be around fifteen left.

Another rat fell to the ground, trampled by the other ones as they scampered over it. Fourteen left.

Mallory cast fireball, keeping the journal up so she could watch Ryan's stamina decrease. His health was fine. None of the rats had managed to attack him. Not yet. Another rat was left behind.

As they travelled along the corridor, more joined the ones chasing the rats, unable to do much against the creatures due to how many were now in the way. As they went, Emica, Jorgen and Callum dropped back, running out of stamina. Callum continued to attack, shooting the rats from a distance.

Chapter Forty-Nine

Mallory tried to count the rats. There was approximately nine left. It would have been easier to count them if they didn't scamper all over the place in an effort to catch up to Ryan. She checked his stamina. Six left. The rats were going to get him. She checked her own stamina. She was halfway through it.

Fear exploded through her. What had they been thinking? The plan was looking worse by the second. They were all going to die and none of them would be able to respawn because the fight wouldn't be over. They wouldn't even have someone from their party to run to safety since they were leading the rats outside to where Ninette waited with the wagon.

Brodie dashed out from the last room, slicing at carrion rats, Fang joining him to attack the ones he attacked. The rats remained focused on Ryan, who had slowed a little so that now he was barely keeping ahead of them.

Running outside, the last of Ryan's stamina was used up and he staggered forward, one of the rats attacking him. Another did the same.

Mallory cast health I on Ryan as his health dropped. She cast it every three seconds. It wasn't enough.

Brodie threw himself on one of the rats that attacked Ryan, pinning it to the ground, using his stiletto on it. "It's working. I didn't know if it'd work. Tackle them to the ground."

Emica was the first to do as Brodie suggested, throwing herself on one of the rats. Soon all the rats were pinned, struggling to escape, and Mallory was finally able to make a difference to Ryan's health.

"You need a health potion." She took one out of her satchel and used weak increased healing to make the potion twice as effective.

Ryan had no sooner downed the contents, and dropped the vial back into Mallory's hand, when a rat escaped from Esben and attacked him. He was knocked to the ground.

After dropping the vial in her satchel, Mallory automatically cast health I on Ryan then wished she'd attacked the rat instead. Before she could do so, Ninette was at Ryan's side, attacking the rat. It lay sprawled out on the ground, Ryan beside it. Mallory healed him again, holding out a hand to help him up.

Ryan stared at her hand for a moment before taking it and getting to his feet. "Next time, how about we get someone else to come up with a plan. Anyone other than Callum."

"What about me?" Brodie asked. "How about I come up with the plan next time? I reckon I'd be good at it."

Ryan grinned. "Okay. Anyone other than Callum and Brodie."

When everyone laughed, Brodie muttered under his breath, claiming he'd have come up with a good plan.

Ninette sheathed her sword. "Was that it?" She glanced at the carrion rats strewn around the area. "Have you taken all of them out?"

"All those ones," Mallory said. "We need to find out what's behind the locked door." She kept healing Ryan, using the diplomat glasses to check the health of everyone else. No one else had lost any. She returned the glasses to her satchel.

While Ryan was being healed, they gathered resources from the carrion rats. They ended up with seven rat tails, four rat pelts, eleven rat tongues, thirty rat teeth, a rat heart and twenty-one claws. Brodie held up the heart like it was toxic and he might drop it at any second. "Do we need this?"

"They're extremely rare and used in alchemy," Danae said.

"They better not be used in anything like health potions," Brodie muttered. "I'm never having another one if they are."

Danae laughed softly. "I believe they're used in a type of poison. I'm just not sure exactly which one."

"That's okay then," Brodie said.

They left the resources at the wagon when they headed back inside to open the last room, Ninette again remaining behind to guard the wagon. Reaching the locked door, Sarnla picked up Relmir's backpack, holding one of his crutches while he unlocked the door. He left it closed, turning to face them once the lockpicks were away and he was again holding both crutches. "I don't know what's behind this door. Well, I believe we know what treasure is behind it, but other than that, anything could be in there. Are you sure you want to go inside?"

"What's in there?" Brodie asked.

"Thief's bane," Relmir said.

"What's that?" Brodie asked.

Relmir smiled, sharing a look with Sarnla. "If

you're planning on going in there, I wouldn't want to ruin the surprise."

Ryan glanced around the group. "Well? What does everyone think?"

"It's treasure," Brodie said, as if the words explained everything. "Beside, I gained a CAS point from all those kills and I didn't even get to attack all of them. There might be more of them in here to attack."

"I gained a CAS point too," Danae said. "Which took me up to character level four. I'll sort out my attribute points later."

Relmir had moved away from the door while they spoke, speaking in hushed tones to Sarnla. He nodded and looked up. "We'll wait out here. I can't be of use and Sarnla isn't that high a level. Neither of us can afford to lose another revive."

Mallory would have preferred that Sarnla join them. She had no idea what was behind the door, but another to fight at their side would probably help. In case she needed to use lightning trap, she added Emica, Jorgen and Esben to their party. "Is everyone ready?"

"Not quite." Callum set Smudge down next to Sarnla. "You stay here. I don't want anything to happen to you."

Brodie pointed at the floor beside Smudge. "You stay there too, Fang."

She whined in protest.

"I mean it," Brodie said. "Stay, girl."

"Now is everyone ready?" When they all nodded or agreed, Mallory tightened her grip on her wand, and taking a deep breath, she recast magelight and flung open the door. Entering the room, she stepped to the side, her mouth dropping open at the sight that greeted her.

"You have got to be kidding," Brodie muttered. "Not more rats."

Mallory finally managed to close her mouth, slowly shaking her head before she spoke. "That can't be a rat. Look at the size of it."

"You can admire it later," Ryan said. "Right now, those creatures it's feeding are looking at us."

"It's a carrion rat brood mother," Danae said. "And those little ones suckling are her offspring. They're half blind and don't attack in packs." She fired an arrow at one of them. It died instantly. "And luckily they don't have a lot of health. But we better get rid of them before she decides to attack because they will do some damage and there are enough of them it could become a problem."

Mallory attacked the hairless rats that shuffled

towards them, their noses twitching as their heads turned back and forth. For a moment she thought they were making headway and then the brood mother moved and many more offspring fell from her, tumbling away until they came to a stop and rose on unsteady legs. Mallory's gaze was drawn upwards to the brood mother's head. The creature towered over them. "We're dead."

Callum took out the brass spyglass. "Yep. We're dead."

Chapter Fifty

Mallory took the diplomat glasses out of her satchel and slipped them on. She instantly wished she hadn't. The carrion rat pups weren't so bad, with only ten health each. The only problem with them was that there was over fifty of the creatures. The main issue was the brood mother.

"Don't just stand there." Brodie attacked the rat pup that had reached him. "Do something."

"She's got two hundred and ten health." Mallory threw a fireball at the rat pups, needing to attack them twice to take them out. She jumped back out of the way of a pup, attacking it once, seeing it had already lost half its health before she'd attacked it. She assumed Brodie had got to it first. "You better not be focused on XP," she warned her brother.

The brood mother, having finished stretching, dropped down on all fours, the action causing a tremor to radiate out from her. She shrieked at them, her dark eyes momentarily fixed on each of them.

"Why do I feel like I've just been marked for death?" Ryan swung his sword at another carrion rat pup.

Callum aimed at the brood mother. "I have the same feeling." He shot her with an arrow, the same shriek filling the room. "Danae, help me with her. I don't think we should risk getting too close to her. With health that high she's sure to have a high attack too."

Mallory finished off the rat carrion pup that had been near her, turning her attention to the brood mother. Casting fireball, she nearly groaned when she saw how little damage the spell did. Three. A point below her lowest attack. "She has some kind of natural armour." She tried ice shard then lightning strike. Both did the same amount of damage. "My spells are hitting for a low of three instead of four." She tried poison dart and lightning trap as she backed away from the brood mother. When the creature swiped at her, she jumped back, almost tripping over one of the dead bodies.

"Our bows are doing far less damage than they should too." Callum returned the spyglass to the pouch. "Or at least Danni's is, so I assume mine will also be doing less damage."

Brodie darted in and attacked the brood mother, needing to run out of the way of her attack. "She's quick when she wants to be."

"You better not have attacked her only in an effort to gain the XP," Mallory warned her brother.

"I killed all the little ones that were after me." Brodie again attacked the brood mother.

The large creature rose on hind legs and tried to come down on top of Brodie. He barely managed to get out of the way, one of the claws raking across him, tremors radiating out through the dungeon floor beneath her.

Brodie moved closer to Mallory. "Can you heal me? Even with my armour, that was still eleven damage. With only twenty-five health left, it won't take her too many attacks to kill me."

Mallory healed Brodie twice, attacking the brood mother in between healing him.

Emica sheathed her sword. "That's the last of the pups. Time to focus on the mother." She shifted into fox form before leaping at the brood mother, attacking before darting away.

Mallory couldn't stop checking the brood mother's health, casting fireball as frequently as possible. It reduced a bit at a time, painfully slow. Yet each attack the creature made on them took large amounts of their health. Way more damage than any of them were doing with their attacks. "None of us could have faced her on our own."

Ryan attacked with his longsword, jumping back from the brood mother's attack, staggering from the tremors that were growing stronger with each attack. "I think you'd have to be a pretty high a level to take on something like this alone."

Mallory glanced around the room, taking note of everyone's health. She tried not to think about how close to losing a revive many of her party was. She healed Emica and Esben, who had the lowest health. At least she could heal shapeshifters regardless of what form they were in. Fear rushed through her when Ryan's health plummeted to four. Slipping her hand into her satchel, she grabbed the essence crystal that only had thirteen mana in it. The crystal crumbled into dust as soon as it was empty and she grabbed the other small essence crystal, using up the thirty mana in it to heal Ryan. She kept healing him until his health was full, focusing on healing rather than attacking. Her mana struggled to keep up and she thought wistfully of the essence crystals in the chest

Rodina had given them. Did she need to carry all of them around with her?

Ryan's health plummeted again and he staggered back from the brood mother's attack. "Why is she mostly focusing on me?"

"She's focusing on everyone who doesn't have a range attack." Mallory healed him again, waiting for her mana to regen to heal him for another two health. "Stay back and use your hunting bow until I can heal you some more."

"How much health does she have left?" Callum asked.

"Eighty-seven," Mallory said.

Emica was flung from the brood mother's back to lay crumpled on the floor near the wall. The brood mother turned to face her, raising up on hind legs.

Seeing Emica had one health left, Mallory rushed towards the kitsune, heart racing as she grabbed her by the front legs and dragged her out of the way of the brood mother's attack, healing her as she did. The brood mother came down near them, the impact of her movement knocking Mallory over. She looked up at the brood mother who rose up on hind legs, unable to move as she tried to catch the breath that had been knocked from her when she'd landed on the stone floor. The creature had forty-two health left. None of the party would be able to kill her before she could land on top of them.

Jorgen launched himself at the brood mother at the same time as Esben, the two crystalline wolves knocking her back a metre. It was enough that when she landed on all four paws she missed striking Mallory and Emica.

Mallory came to her feet, healing Emica enough that the kitsune could rise and dart out of the way of the next attack. Mallory dived to the side, lying sprawled on the floor. Before she could rise to her feet again, she saw the brood mother jumping towards her, claws outstretched. All she could do was roll out of the way, clutching her wand. Again she tried to get back on her feet. It was impossible. The brood mother leapt at her again, the tremors strong enough that Mallory thought she might have been knocked over if she had been on her feet.

Emica, Jorgen and Esben attacked the brood mother at the same time. The creature was knocked back, lying motionless on the floor. Emica stopped beside Mallory, becoming human, apart from her ears, and holding out a hand.

Chapter Fifty-One

Mallory checked the brood mother's health was at zero before she took the hand offered, rising to her feet, wincing at the pain it caused her. She healed Emica once before starting on healing herself. "Thank you."

Emica grinned. "No, thank you. I was sure I was about to lose a revive."

Letting go of Emica's hand, Mallory turned towards the brood mother. "That was much harder than I expected."

Ryan strode towards the creature. "Let's see what we get out of it."

Relmir came inside the room to stand by the door. "You killed it?"

Sarnla joined him. "I'm surprised you managed."

"It was close." Mallory alternated between healing everyone as they checked what they could get from the brood mother, having discovered that the pups yielded no drops.

Fang ran inside to sniff the brood mother, after checking Brodie was okay. Smudge scampered into the room too. He ran over to Callum and held up his paws until Callum scooped him up and returned him to the makeshift sling.

Relmir pointed to a dust and cobweb covered plinth that stood in the middle of the room against the far wall. "There. That's what we came here for."

Mallory moved closer to the plinth. She didn't realise what he was talking about until she stood on a crate not far from the plinth, having pushed it closer before she stood on it. On top of the plinth, in a hollowed part of the stone, was a large topaz. Picking it up, she dusted it against the leg of her trousers. Holding it up, she studied the large gem that rested on her palm. "What is it?"

"Fireball topaz," Sarnla said. "Can't you see the little explosions of fire in the golden brown of the gem? That's where it gets its name. It's a rare type of topaz."

Mallory turned it back and forth, watching the play of light on the gem, dashes of colour shooting around the room as the facets of the gem caught her magelight. "Yeah, I can. Like miniature fireworks caught in time."

"Is there anything in particular that's special about this one?" Callum patted Smudge who leaned forward out of the makeshift sling, his paw stretched towards the gem as he made soft sounds.

"That is the thief's bane. It was made by a jeweller in Shadhurst and stolen by a thief. He didn't have it long before it was stolen by another thief. This happened about half a dozen times and thieves began to think it was cursed and would bring bad luck to those who live beyond the law," Relmir said. "That's how it earned its name and collectors have been wanting it for a long time. Although I hear tell they only want it if it comes to them through honest means."

"How do you guarantee it's through honest means?" Callum asked.

Sarnla shrugged. "We don't know. We'd planned to worry about that problem after we got a hold of it." She smiled. "Looks like that's your problem now."

Ryan chuckled, stepping back from the brood mother. "Looks like it is." He turned to Mallory. "I managed to get the heart of the brood mother." It was large enough he held it in both hands.

Mallory made a face. "That's disgusting." She stepped off the crate, moving closer to Brodie so she could heal him.

"It's worth a lot of gold," Danae said.

"I hope so," Ryan said. "Because it was disgusting getting it."

"There are items in the crate you were standing on, Mallory," Callum said.

"Loot?" Brodie picked up the last of his throwing knives that had been stuck in the various creatures scattered around the floor.

Callum held up three scrolls and a small drawstring bag that crumbled and dropped gold coins across the floor. "Looks like it."

Brodie helped Callum collect the coins. "There are twenty-two gold pieces." He gave them to Mallory, who was still working on healing everyone.

"What are the scrolls?" Danae asked Callum.

Mallory glanced around the room. "How about we focus on getting out of here first? This room gives me the creeps." The body of the brood mother with all her dead pups scattered around her made her uncomfortable. She half expected the creature to respawn. And if that was possible, she didn't want to be anywhere near the dungeon when it happened.

It wasn't until they'd turned the wagon around and were on their way to Ursen, that Mallory had the chance to find out what they'd gained. As well as the heart of the brood mother, they'd also managed to get six teeth from her. When Callum opened up one of the scrolls, he laughed and handed it over to Mallory.

"What's so funny?" Brodie asked.

Mallory smiled. "I think we all need to put more points in luck."

"What is it?" Brodie demanded.

"A spell." Mallory held it out to her brother.

He took the scroll and looked at it. "You've got to be kidding. Polish brass. What kind of spell is that?"

"A utility one," Danae said.

"I don't know whether this one is better or worse." Callum handed the second scroll to Mallory.

She sighed. "I'd really hoped we'd get something decent." She glanced at the chest where she'd put thief's bane and taken out three of the small essence crystals and put them in her satchel. "Well, other than the fireball topaz."

"What's that one?" Brodie asked.

"Starlight shimmer." Mallory held the spell out to Brodie.

"That's not too bad." Brodie handed the spell back. "Can you cast it on Fang? She'd look awesome with fur that looks like it's been sprinkled with starlight."

Ryan peered over Mallory's shoulder at the spell. "Sounds like it makes you look like someone has thrown silver glitter at your hair or fur."

Chapter Fifty-Two

Mallory tucked the two spells into her satchel. She'd learn them later. "What is the third scroll?"

"Experience scroll. Although it would have been a lot better if the CAS point you gain wasn't in artist," Callum said.

"The two spells make more sense now," Danae said. "They'd be the type of spells you'd expect an artist to use if they'd also unlocked mage."

Brodie took the experience scroll off Callum. "When can we use it?"

"I'm not holding it this time," Mallory hurriedly said. She clearly remembered how crowded she'd been last time and there were a lot more of them now.

"We'll pull over and use it now," Ryan said. "We're going to need space for all of us to hold on to it."

It took them several minutes to all stand in a way that each of them could hold the scroll, including

Relmir and Sarnla. They all read off the words on the scroll, which vanished as soon as it was read.

"It's not fair that companion animals don't get XP from the scroll." Brodie clambered back into the wagon, patting Fang who curled up on his lap.

"I'm happy with it. The scroll took me up to character level seven," Jorgen said.

"It's going to take me forever to reach that level," Brodie muttered. "Why couldn't the CAS point have been in something more useful. Like brewer? Who needs the ability to create poor quality drawings on parchment?"

While Callum and Brodie debated which would have been the better crafting ability to have gained a CAS point in, Mallory took out her notebook and started on the day's entry. As soon as she finished writing in her notebook, she returned it to the chest, realising the conversation had moved on to one about when they'd return home.

Mallory turned to Relmir and Sarnla, who sat together in the back of the wagon. "If you were serious about letting us stay at your place, we could leave everything there and Ninette could look after it while we return home for a brief amount of time. Everyone else could go with us too if they wished."

"I don't mind looking after everything," Ninette said.

"Mallory could shrink the horses," Callum suggested. "It would make it easier to take care of them."

"I can't wait to see where you live," Danae said.

"What about the Adventurers Guild?" Brodie asked.

"We can join them when we return," Mallory said.

"There's also the other treasure we were going after," Brodie pointed out.

"You were the one who wanted to go after this one," Callum said.

"But what if we miss out on the other one?" Brodie argued.

Ryan shrugged. "There'll be more."

"We're going home, Brodie," Mallory said firmly. "Quit stalling."

"If everyone goes home with us, we'll lose heaps of money. We haven't been home for ages," Brodie pointed out. "You'd have to have everyone in our party so they can go back with us and then they'd be paid a share of the money we're owed too."

"We could go back first and then immediately return and collect them," Ryan said.

It took a few minutes to come up with a plan,

Danae also suggesting that she stay behind and be removed from the party so they could have the money that would normally be paid into her account. It was also decided that Jorgen and Esben would visit the docks while the rest of them sorted out everything that was being left behind, including giving Mallory time to shrink the horses.

Once everything was sorted, Mallory noticed that Danae had dealt with her new character level. She'd put one point in strength and two each in constitution and dexterity, taking her health up to thirty-nine and her stamina to sixty-five. She'd also put her class point in archer, which meant she'd now be able to use enchanted slings and slingshot. And she'd gained a revive. Mallory dreaded to think what they'd do once they all reached character level five and only gained a revive every five levels.

The journey into Ursen was quiet and they pulled up at a cottage on the outskirts, Mallory adding Ninette to the party, having left everyone else in it, before Relmir thanked them for escorting him and Sarnla home. Mallory read over the quest details. *Escort To Ursen: You escorted a rogue and mage home and were rewarded with the option for your party to stay in their home whenever you are in Ursen. You also earned twenty experience points each.*

Since the quest was completed, Mallory removed everyone from her party. It felt odd to remove Danae too. But she'd be adding the half-elf back in soon enough.

They set up camp behind the cottage, parking the wagon under a tree and making sure Ninette didn't need anything. Once the horses were shrunk, Ninette found a place under the tree where she fenced them in with a few pieces of firewood and put a bowl of water in their enclosure for them.

"That'll save on feed." Ryan stood by the enclosure, watching the horses eat the grass that looked extremely large in comparison.

Before Mallory could comment, Jorgen and Esben returned. They both looked dejected. "No one has heard of The Nelly here?"

"I almost wish they hadn't," Jorgen said.

"Someone has heard of it?" Ryan asked.

Jorgen nodded. "The ship was here not that long ago. One of the dock workers said they heard the crew talking about going home to Hethgar. But they didn't know when they were going there."

"Where's that?" Brodie asked.

"Hellfire," Esben said.

When a journal notification appeared in the corner of Mallory's vision she checked it, surprised to find it was a quest update. *Hunt For The Nelly: A dock worker in Ursen heard talk that The Nelly will eventually sail to Hethgar in Hellfire.*

"I don't know how we'll manage to get there, but we're going to need to level up and earn a lot of money," Jorgen said. "We don't want to be a low level in that area."

"Are you going back to our world with us?" Mallory asked. "We won't be gone too long."

Jorgen nodded. "If you don't mind, we'll stay with you for now and travel around Ruby Isle and level up some more."

"You can stay with us as long as you like," Mallory assured him.

"And you never know, we might be ready to go to Hellfire when you are," Ryan added.

"It'd be better travelling to a place like that with friends," Jorgen said. "It's not the safest of areas to be in."

Ryan grinned. "Callum will probably want help raiding a coffee plantation."

Esben returned Ryan's grin. "Sounds profitable."

"Are we ready to go home now?" Brodie asked.

"Before you do, can you see if my father has sent a message?" Emica asked.

Brodie had to get his satchel out of the wagon

before he could check, shaking his head. "Nothing." He put the satchel back in the wagon.

"And your mask," Mallory said. "You can't take that home with you."

"But we were told some simple bits of leather armour can go with us," Brodie protested.

"I don't think the mask is even close to being considered simple," Callum said.

After complaining about needing to remove it, Brodie left it in the chest.

"Everyone ready now?" Mallory asked.

"Yeah," Brodie muttered with a glance towards the wagon. "I suppose."

Everyone else nodded or agreed.

Chapter Fifty-Three

Mallory closed her eyes, mentally going over the words she needed to speak before they left, not wanting to get them wrong. Everything went black as soon as she spoke the words to take them home, sounds returning before sight. They stood at the kitchen table and it took her a few seconds to remember her mum had just left. Checking the message that came through on her phone, Mallory held it up. "We made a difference."

"A big difference if how much we were paid is anything to go by." Ryan looked up from his phone. "We were paid eight hundred and five dollars each."

"Cool," Brodie said.

"We've done twenty-two quests since last time we were home," Callum said. "Unless I've missed counting some of them." He frowned. "No, I think that's all."

Ryan chuckled. "No wonder it was so profitable this time. We also took out quite a few of the dark forces."

Another message came through and Mallory checked it, her heart sinking as she read it over. "I'm not sure if this is a problem."

"What's it say?" Brodie asked.

"Make an assessment appointment with headquarters." Mallory put her phone back on the table.

"I wonder if they'll be able to tell us how to meet the guardian who knows us," Brodie said. "The one who gave us that warning."

Ryan shrugged. "I doubt it, but who knows how these things work."

"I wonder how far into the future he is and what is coming," Callum said.

"Who cares," Brodie said. "We'll just spend more time on Inadon and it won't matter."

"It doesn't really help though." Mallory thought of needing to go to their father's place on the weekend. "As much time as we spend on Inadon, it doesn't change what we need to do here."

Brodie scowled at her. "It could. If you left me behind and didn't come back for me until after the weekend."

Ryan chuckled. "Nice try, Brodie. I bet the guardians wouldn't be impressed though." He turned to Mallory. "Are you going to call them and find out what they want?"

Mallory shook her head. "We can call them tomorrow. If we want to get everyone out of here before Mum returns, we better collect them so they can leave before we're caught with even more people in our house."

Ryan grinned. "I don't think exchange student will work for that many people."

Mallory smiled. "No, she'd probably think we were throwing a party." She looked at each of them. "Are you ready to return?" When they nodded, she put the disc back in and clicked yes. The world went black around them.

When they reappeared, Esben took a step back. "You were barely gone. I didn't expect you to be so quick."

"Is everyone ready to go with us?" Mallory added each of them to their party. When they nodded, she again thought over the words she needed to say before speaking them.

It was crowded around the table when they all arrived, Danae doing a slow turn, smiling as she did so. "I've been waiting forever to visit here."

"I'll show you our place," Brodie offered.

Mallory stepped in front of him when he started to move away from the table. "We don't have time. Ryan needs to take them to the place he rented. The last thing we need is to get in trouble even more then we already are."

"Aww, come on, Mal. Just a minute. It's not like it's that far away."

Mallory shook her head. "After school tomorrow."

Brodie was still protesting as Ryan and Callum ushered everyone out the door. He turned to Mallory when they were alone. "Do you think we'll be able to sneak everyone in here after school tomorrow?"

Mallory thought wistfully of her spell vanish I. "We can try."

"I wonder why the Guardians want us to ring. I thought we had six months before we're tested." Brodie started to head towards the kitchen. "You don't think we're in trouble, do you? Maybe they don't want us to join another guild."

"I don't know, but I doubt it has anything to do with wanting to join the Adventurers Guild. And what do you think you're doing?"

Brodie turned to face her. "Getting something to eat. I'm starving. We never had time for lunch."

"Shower first. Before Mum gets back and wants to know what we've been up to."

Brodie tried to argue, but Mallory kept interrupting him. Eventually he headed for the bathroom and Mallory was left alone by the table. She picked up her phone and stared at the message from the Guardians. Should she ring them now or wait until business hours? Putting her phone back in sleep mode, she took the disc with her when she headed to her bedroom. She'd call them in the morning. Before school. If it was some kind of problem, she'd rather not be kept up all night worrying about it.

Reaching her room, she paused in the doorway at the sound of an incoming message. She missed the ease of checking notifications on her journal. She smiled when she saw the message was from Ryan.

Arrived at our place. They're marvelling over the magic of electricity. Will go shopping soon and grab a few things. Good thing we were paid so much since I can't go hunting or gathering for food around here.

Mallory laughed at the image that came to mind after reading his second sentence. That of when they'd first arrived on Inadon and had marvelled over everything. It seemed strange that those from Inadon would feel the same way about her world. But she supposed there were a lot of differences.

Still thinking about Inadon and all the things she loved about it, Mallory put the disc away and gathered clothes for when it was her turn to shower. A bathroom was one of the few things she missed about her world, but soon that might not be an issue. Not with their plan to join the Adventurers Guild. And whatever might be in their future, both here and on Inadon, they'd face it together. The four of them, or five, depending on which world they were in.

Hearing her brother leave the bathroom, she headed for a shower, thinking about all the quests they still had to do and the progress they'd made this time. Soon they'd be ready to head to the mainland. She couldn't wait to find out what Eridell was like and in particular the town of Merrow. Would it be different to Ruby Isle? And if so, how different. A touch of sadness filled her as she thought of all the friends they'd made and the people they'd met, all of who they'd leave behind when they moved to Merrow. But there'd be new people to meet and hopefully new friends to make and they could always return to Ruby Isle and catch up with old friends.

A smile formed as she thought of the many people they now knew on Ruby Isle. Kruth, Roast, Danae's parents, the Buckneth wagoner and so many more. She couldn't wait to return to Inadon.

Final Stats

Character weight does not include any backpacks, satchels, their contents or items carried by livestock.

Mallory

Character Level: 6
Health: 45
Stamina: 75
Mana: 70
Weight: 5kg 863g/90kg

CAS XP: 141/159
Available CAS Points: 6
Available Class Points: 0
Level Progress: 6:1/10

Attributes

Strength: 9
Constitution: 15
Intelligence: 14
Wisdom: 14

Dexterity: 5
Charisma: 5
Luck: 6

Class

Mage: 3
Warrior: 3

Class Skills
None

Spells

Fireball: 0
Health I: 0
Poison Dart I: 0

(Expand For More Details)

Weapon and Armour Affinity

Wand: 1 (+1% damage)
Cloth Armour: 0
Short Sword: 0

(Expand For More Details)

Crafting

Alchemy: 1
Apothecary: 50
Wheelwright: 1

(Expand For More Details)

Reputation

Global: 0
Local Areas:
Ruby Isle
(Expand For More Details)

Buffs and Negative Stats

Necklace: doubles healing done
Silver bracelet: +1 mana every 15 secs
(Expand For More Details)

Available Revives 5

Mallory

Spells Expanded

*All attack spells have +43% damage to base attacks.

Level 0

Fireball: 0
Mana cost: 3
Cooldown: 2 seconds
Damage: low 3, normal 5, critical 7
Duration: Instant

Flame: 0
Mana cost: 5
Cooldown: 3 seconds
Damage: low 4, normal 6, critical 8
Damage Over Time: 4 every 2 seconds
Duration: Non-flammable materials 6 secs,
flammable materials until runs out of fuel

Ice Shard: 0
Mana cost: 3
Cooldown: 2 seconds
Damage: low 3, normal 5, critical 7
Duration: Instant

Lightning Strike: 0
Mana cost: 3
Cooldown: 2 seconds
Damage: low 3, normal 5, critical 7
Duration: Instant

Mend I: 0
Mana Cost: 17
Cooldown: 5 seconds
Area Of Effect: 1cm2
Duration: Instant

Level 1

Beacon: 0
Mana Cost: 15
Cooldown: 5 seconds
Area Of Effect: to be cast on a
solid surface
Duration: 10 mins

Health I: 0
Restores health to target
Mana Cost: 6
Cooldown: 3 seconds
Area Of Effect: +1HP to target within 2m
Duration: Instant

Poison Dart I: 0
Mana Cost: 6
Cooldown: 3 seconds
Damage: low 4, normal 6, crit 8
Damage Over Time: 5 every 3
seconds
Duration: 3 secs

Mallory

Spells Expanded 2

Level 2

Lightning Trap: 0
Mana Cost: 10
Cooldown: 5 seconds
Damage: 10
Duration: damage on contact

Nightfall: 0
Causes the target's vision to go black.
Mana Cost: 20
Cooldown: 60 seconds
Targets Effected: 1
Duration: 5 seconds
Range: 2 metres

Shrink I: 0
Mana Cost: 20
Cooldown: 10 seconds
Area Of Effect: cast on the object,
living creature or sentient being
the castor wishes to shrink
Duration: Permanent.

Shrink Reversal: 0
Returns an object, living creature or
sentient being, that has been shrunk,
back to normal size.
Mana Cost: 25
Cooldown: 30 seconds
Range: Touch
Duration: Permanent
Target: unenchanted objects and
creatures up to level 10
Quantity Effected: 1

Slow Target: 0
Slows target.
Mana Cost: 10
Cooldown: 30 seconds
Targets Effected: 1
Duration: 120 seconds
Range: 2 metres
Target Slowed: 10%

Vanish I: 0
Mana Cost: 25
Cooldown: 5 seconds
Area Of Effect: causes target, within
a 2m range, to vanish
Duration: 1 min

Water Manipulation: 0
Mana Cost: 12
Cooldown: 5 seconds
Area Of Effect: relocate up to five
litres of water up to a distance of
five metres
Duration: Instant

Mallory

Spells Expanded 3

Level 3

Magelight: 0
Mana Cost: 20
Cooldown: 10 seconds
Area Of Effect: creates a ball of light near caster
Duration: 15 mins

Spellbound Shield: 0
Mana Cost: 35
Cooldown: 120 seconds
Duration: 10 minutes
Size: Small
Target: Warrior
Defence: -2 damage

Teleportation Link I: 0
Mana Cost: 30
Cooldown: 1 minute
Initial Area Of Effect: Cast at a location the castor wishes to return to
Initial Duration: Instant
Delayed Area Of Effect: Recast to return to the initial location, transporting the castor, companion animal and gear worn or carried by the castor
Delayed Duration: 1 hour

Weak Reanimate: 0
Mana Cost: 20
Cooldown: 5 seconds
Area Of Effect: reanimate one of the dead level 3
Range: 2m
Duration: 1 min

Level 4

Tracking Magelight: 0
Creates a ball of white light that trails a fraction behind the target above head height
Mana Cost: 25
Cooldown: 20 seconds
Targets Effected: create a ball of light that follows 1 target
Duration: 5 minutes
Range: target within 5 metres
Target Type: sentient race

Mallory

Weapon and Armour Affinity Expanded

Dagger (and enchanted): 1 (+1% damage)
Wand (and enchanted): 1 (+1% damage)
Cloth Armour: 0
Unarmed: 0

Chain Mail Armour: 0
Short Sword (and enchanted): 0
Shield (and enchanted): 0
Dual Swords (and enchanted): 0

Crafting Expanded

Alchemy: 1
Apothecary: 50
Artist: 1
Bard: 0
Bartering: 0
Brewer: 0
Cooking: 0

Diplomacy: 0
Enchanting: 0
Fishing: 0
Glassblowing: 0
Hunting: 0
Husbandry: 0
Languages: 0

Mason: 0
Potter: 0
Sailing: 0
Scribe: 0
Sculptor: 0
Shipwright: 0

Smithing: 0
Thatcher: 0
Weaver: 0
Wheelwright: 1
Woodcutter: 0

Reputation Expanded

Ruby Isle:
Buckneth 22
Coastview 0
Cutthroat Harbour -17
Delten 2
Eastvale 1
Estwater 0
Jenlea 0

Donris Island:
Drohgolrik 0

Lilica 0
Longmeadow 0
Mer Point 10
Ransted 4
Seacoast 2
Simria 0
South Peak Mine 5
South Point 2

Surith 5
Valley Of Wandering Souls 10
Velkden 42
Wayholt 10
Wildebay 10
Wrentville 1

Mallory

Buffs And Negative Stats

Necklace: doubles healing done
Silver bracelet: +1 mana every 15 secs
Mage cloth armour hooded jacket: -1 dam when attacked, +1 mana every 5 secs
Gold ring: +1 mana every 10 secs
Gold ring, single jewel: +5 mana/1 min
Gold ring, single jewel: +5 mana/1 min
Silver bracelet, single jewel: +10 mana/1 min
Gold ring, blue jewel: +8 mana/1 min

Ryan

Character Level: 4
Health: 45
Stamina: 75
Mana: 20
Weight: 10kg 736g/150kg

CAS XP: 124/139
Available CAS Points: 0
Available Class Points: 0
Level Progress: 4:1/10

Attributes

Strength: 15
Constitution: 15
Intelligence: 5
Wisdom: 4

Dexterity: 8
Charisma: 5
Luck: 6

Class

Warrior: 4

Class Skills
None

Spells

None

Weapon and Armour Affinity

Chain Mail Armour: 0
Dual Swords (and enchanted): 0
Longsword: 27

(Expand For More Details)

Crafting

Artist: 1
Hunting: 10
Wheelwright: 1

(Expand For More Details)

Reputation

Global: 0
Local Areas:
Ruby Isle
(Expand For More Details)

Buffs and Negative Stats

None

Available Revives 5

Ryan

Weapon and Armour Affinity Expanded

Chain Mail Armour: 0
Short Sword (and enchanted): 1
Shield (and enchanted): 1

Dual Swords (and enchanted): 0
Longsword: 27

Crafting Expanded

Alchemy: 0
Apothecary: 0
Artist: 1
Bard: 0
Bartering: 0
Brewer: 0
Cooking: 0

Diplomacy: 0
Enchanting: 0
Fishing: 0
Glassblowing: 0
Hunting: 10
Husbandry: 0
Languages: 0

Mason: 0
Potter: 0
Sailing: 0
Scribe: 0
Sculptor: 0
Shipwright: 0

Smithing: 0
Thatcher: 0
Weaver: 0
Wheelwright: 1
Woodcutter: 0

Reputation Expanded

Ruby Isle:
Buckneth 22
Coastview 0
Cutthroat Harbour -17
Delten 2
Eastvale 1
Estwater 0
Jenlea 0

Donris Island:
Drohgolrik 0

Lilica 0
Longmeadow 0
Mer Point 10
Ransted 4
Seacoast 2
Simria 0
South Peak Mine 5
South Point 2

Surith 5
Valley Of Wandering Souls 10
Velkden 42
Wayholt 10
Wildebay 10
Wrentville 1

Brodie

Character Level: 4
Health: 39
Stamina: 65
Mana: 25
Weight: 6kg 859g/70kg

CAS XP: 66/140
Available CAS Points: 7
Available Class Points: 0
Level Progress: 4:2/10

Attributes

Strength: 7
Constitution: 13
Intelligence: 5
Wisdom: 5

Dexterity: 11
Charisma: 9
Luck: 8

Class

Rogue: 4

Class Skills
Stealth: 0 (30 seconds, 1 hr cooldown)
Sleight of hand: 0 (take low value
small object unnoticed, cooldown 6
hours)

Spells

None

Weapon and Armour Affinity

Stiletto (and enchanted): 1 (+1%
damage)
Throwing Knives (and enchanted): 2
(+2% damage)
Leather Armour: 0

Crafting

Bartering: 15
Cooking: 15
Wheelwright: 1

(Expand For More Details)

Reputation

Global: 0
Local Areas:
 Ruby Isle
(Expand For More Details)

Buffs and Negative Stats

None

Available Revives 2

Brodie

Crafting Expanded

Alchemy: 0
Apothecary: 0
Artist: 1
Bard: 0
Bartering: 15
Brewer: 0
Cooking: 15

Diplomacy: 0
Enchanting: 0
Fishing: 0
Glassblowing: 0
Hunting: 0
Husbandry: 0
Languages: 0

Mason: 0
Potter: 0
Sailing: 0
Scribe: 0
Sculptor: 0
Shipwright: 0

Smithing: 0
Thatcher: 0
Weaver: 0
Wheelwright: 1
Woodcutter: 0

Reputation Expanded

Ruby Isle:
Buckneth 22
Coastview 0
Cutthroat Harbour -17
Delten 2
Eastvale 1
Estwater 0
Jenlea 0

Donris Island:
Drohgolrik 0

Lilica 0
Longmeadow 0
Mer Point 10
Ransted 4
Seacoast 2
Simria 0
South Peak Mine 5
South Point 2

Surith 5
Valley Of Wandering Souls 10
Velkden 42
Wayholt 10
Wildebay 10
Wrentville 1

Callum

Character Level: 4
Health: 33
Stamina: 55
Mana: 25
Weight: 8kg 416g/90kg

CAS XP: 117/139
Available CAS Points: 37
Available Class Points: 0
Level Progress: 4:1/10

Attributes

Strength: 9
Constitution: 11
Intelligence: 5
Wisdom: 5

Dexterity: 14
Charisma: 5
Luck: 9

Class

Archer: 4

Class Skills
None

Spells

None

Weapon and Armour Affinity

Hunting Knife: 1 (+1% damage)
Studded Leather Armour: 0
Longbow: 0

(Expand For More Details)

Crafting

Artist: 1
Wheelwright: 1

(Expand For More Details)

Reputation

Global: 0
Local Areas:
Ruby Isle
(Expand For More Details)

Buffs and Negative Stats

Silver Ring: +2 damage to bow attacks

Available Revives 4

Callum

Weapon and Armour Affinity Expanded

Short Bow (and enchanted): 1 (+1% damage)
Hunting Knife: 1 (+1% damage)
Studded Leather Armour: 0

Sling (and enchanted): 0
Slingshot (and enchanted)
Enchanted Arrows
Longbow: 0

Crafting Expanded

Alchemy: 0
Apothecary: 0
Artist: 1
Bard: 0
Bartering: 0
Brewer: 0
Cooking: 0

Diplomacy: 0
Enchanting: 0
Fishing: 0
Glassblowing: 0
Hunting: 0
Husbandry: 0
Languages: 0

Mason: 0
Potter: 0
Sailing: 0
Scribe: 0
Sculptor: 0
Shipwright: 0

Smithing: 0
Thatcher: 0
Weaver: 0
Wheelwright: 1
Woodcutter: 0

Reputation Expanded

Ruby Isle:
Buckneth 22
Coastview 0
Cutthroat Harbour -17
Delten 2
Eastvale 1
Estwater 0
Jenlea 0

Donris Island:
Drohgolrik 0

Lilica 0
Longmeadow 0
Mer Point 10
Ransted 4
Seacoast 2
Simria 0
South Peak Mine 5
South Point 2

Surith 5
Valley Of Wandering Souls 10
Velkden 42
Wayholt 10
Wildebay 10
Wrentville 1

Danae

Character Level: 4
Health: 39
Stamina: 65
Mana: 25
Weight: 6kg 702g/80kg

CAS XP: 69/139
Available CAS Points: 20
Available Class Points: 0
Level Progress: 4:1/10

Attributes

Strength: 8
Constitution: 13
Intelligence: 5
Wisdom: 5

Dexterity: 14
Charisma: 5
Luck: 8

Class

Archer: 4

Class Skills
None

Spells

None

Weapon and Armour Affinity

Hunting Knife: 1 (+1% damage)
Studded Leather Armour: 0
Longbow: 0

(Expand For More Details)

Crafting

Alchemy: 9
Bartering: 1
Cooking: 1
Glassblowing: 5

(Expand For More Details)

Reputation

Global: 0
Local Areas:
Ruby Isle
(Expand For More Details)

Buffs and Negative Stats

None

Racial Bonus

Archer +10% damage
Mage capable of using spells
one level above class level

Available Revives 3

Danae

Weapon and Armour Affinity Expanded

Short Bow (and enchanted): 1 (+1% damage)
Hunting Knife: 1 (+1% damage)
Studded Leather Armour: 0
Sling (and enchanted): 0

Slingshot (and enchanted): 0
Enchanted Arrows: 0
Longbow: 0
Unarmed: 1 (+1% damage)

Crafting Expanded

Alchemy: 9
Apothecary: 0
Artist: 1
Bartering: 1
Brewer: 0
Clothier: 0
Cooking: 1

Diplomacy: 0
Enchanting: 0
Fishing: 0
Glassblowing: 5
Husbandry: 0
Languages: 0

Mason: 0
Potter: 0
Sailing: 0
Scribe: 0
Sculptor: 0
Shipwright: 0

Smithing: 0
Thatcher: 0
Weaver: 0
Wheelwright: 1
Woodcutter: 0

Reputation Expanded

Ruby Isle:
Buckneth 4
Coastview 0
Cutthroat Harbour -17
Delten 2
Eastvale 1
Estwater 0
Jenlea 0

Donris Island:
Drohgolrik 0

Lilica 0
Longmeadow 0
Mer Point 10
Ransted 4
Seacoast 2
Simria 22
South Peak Mine 5
South Point 2

Surith 5
Ursen 0
Valley Of Wandering Souls 10
Velkden 42
Wayholt 18
Wildebay 10
Wrentville 1

COMPANION ANIMALS' FINAL STATS

Smudge 8HP (Callum)

4288XP/5000XP

Level: 4

Items: None

Wearing: Jewelled bracelet (tiny colourful jewels creating a bright band).

Abilities: +25% movement speed, increased ability to forage or hunt for food, +25% increased agility.

Fang 6HP (Brodie)

4525XP/5000XP

Level: 4

Items: None

Wearing: Leather collar (made from belt) with revive ring tied to it (plain gold band)

Abilities: +25% movement speed, increased ability to forage or hunt for food, +25% increased strength.

Free Ebook

Subscribe to Avril's newsletter and receive a free ebook. This ebook is exclusive to those on her mailing list. To find out more about this offer visit:

www.avrilsabine.com/free-ebook

*

We value your privacy and will not sell, rent, exchange or loan your email address to third parties. Your information is confidential and you are under no obligation to remain on the mailing list and can unsubscribe at any time.

Acknowledgements

As always, many thanks to our usual crew. We appreciate your help.

To The Reader

If you enjoyed this book, why not consider leaving a review to help other readers discover it too? Reader engagement is one of the few ways that lets an author know readers want more books in a particular series or genre. So leave a review and tell friends, not only about this book but also about other ones you've enjoyed, so you can continue to enjoy books by your favourite authors for years to come.

Dreams are meant to be lived,

Avril, Storm and Rhys.

About The Authors

Avril is an Australian author who lives with her family on acreage in South East Queensland. She writes mostly young adult and children's speculative fiction, but has been known to dabble in other genres. She has been an avid gamer since she was ten, which was the year she discovered Dungeons & Dragons and was given a Commodore 64.

Storm has a wide range of interests from gaming and blacksmithing to cooking and sewing. It's not unusual to find him cooking at any hour of the day or night, particularly after a long gaming session.

Rhys loves books and gaming and has thoroughly enjoyed combining two of his favourite things. He has been running tabletop gaming sessions for the past few years and enjoys creating characters and doing in depth worldbuilding.

Guardians Of The Round Table Series

To learn more about this series visit:

www.avrilsabine.com/series/gotrt

Find maps, stats and details about the various books.

BOOKS AVAILABLE IN THE GUARDIANS OF THE ROUND TABLE SERIES

Book 1: Dexterity Fail

Book 2: Goblin Boots

Book 3: Singed Feathers

Book 4: Frog Mage

Book 5: Crystal Mine

Book 5: Crystal Mine

Book 6: Cursed Harp

Book 7: Treasure Seeker

BOOKS SET IN THE SAME WORLD AS THE GUARDIANS OF THE ROUND TABLE SERIES

Adventurers Guild Handbook (Lore Book)

Legend Of The Ancestral King (Lore Book)

Lost And Powerful: Myths Of Misplaced Staves (Lore Book)

Titles By Avril Sabine

Stories about strong characters and characters who discover their strengths.

SERIES

Assassins Of The Dead- Young Adult Fantasy/ Paranormal

Book 1: Dark Blade

Book 2: Dragon Touched

Book 3: Society Against Vampires

Book 4: King's Request

Dragon Blood- Young Adult Urban Fantasy (with elements of romance)

(5 book series)

Book 1: Pliethin

Book 2: Wyvern

Book 3: Surety

Book 4: Knight

Book 5: Mage

Dragon Mage- Young Adult Urban Fantasy (with elements of romance)

(Series two of Dragon Blood series)

Book 1: Promise

Dragon Blood Chronicles- Young Adult Urban Fantasy (with elements of romance)

(Companion stand alone series to Dragon Blood)

Book 1: Oath

Book 2: Betrayed

Guardians Of The Round Table- Young Adult Fantasy LitRPG

(Co-written with Storm and Rhys Petersen)

Book 1: Dexterity Fail

Book 2: Goblin Boots

Book 3: Singed Feathers

Book 4: Frog Mage

Book 5: Crystal Mine

Book 6: Cursed Harp

Book 7: Treasure Seeker

Rosie's Rangers- Young Adult Western Steampunk

(6 book series)

Book 1: Justice

Book 2: Vengeance

Book 3: Treachery

Book 4: Accused

Book 5: Wanted

Book 6: Corruption

Mark Of Kings- Children's Fantasy

(Upper middle grade/preteen)

(4 book series)

Book 1: The Arena

Book 2: The Island

Book 3: The Assassin

Book 4: The King

STAND ALONE SERIES

Demon Hunters- Young Adult Urban Fantasy/ Horror (with elements of romance)

Book 1: Blood Sacrifice

Book 2: Retribution

Book 3: Tainted

Book 4: Premonition

Book 5: Cursed

Book 6: Feud

Book 7: Extrication

Plea Of The Damned- Young Adult Urban Fantasy/Paranormal

(6 book series)

Book 1: Forgive Me Lucy

Book 2: Forgive Me Aiden

Book 3: Forgive Me Jena

Book 4: Forgive Me Kobe

Book 5: Forgive Me Marti

Book 6: Forgive Me Dawson

***Realms Of The Fae- Young Adult Urban Fantasy
(with elements of romance)***

The Sword (short story in Like A Girl Anthology)

Heart Of Stone

Book 1: A Debt Owed

Book 2: Marked By The Hunt

Book 3: The Magic Collector

Book 4: An Unexpected Betrayal

Book 5: Imprisoned By Iron

Fairytales Retold (Short Stories)

Snow-White And Rose-Red

The Twelve Brothers

The Light Princess

Beauty And The Beast

Sleeping Beauty

Aschenputtel

The Golden Bird

The Frog Prince

The Death Of Koshchei The Deathless

Myths And Legends Retold (Short Stories)

Ion, Son Of Apollo

Sir Gawain And The Maid With The Narrow Sleeves

Princess Ilse, The Giant's Daughter

YOUNG ADULT NOVELS

Young Adult Fantasy (with elements of romance)

Elf Sight

Earth Bound

Young Adult Urban Fantasy

Stone Warrior (with elements of romance)

The Jungle Inside

Young Adult Contemporary (with elements of romance)

Through Your Eyes

The Ugly Stepsister

Perfect Little Princess

Young Adult Contemporary/Paranormal

Whispers In The Dark (with elements of romance and same sex relationships)

Over Too Soon (with elements of romance)

Young Adult Sci-Fi

Experiment X-One-Six (Urban Sci-Fi/Superheroes)

An Endless Dawn (Post Apocalyptic Sci-Fi)

CHILDREN'S BOOKS

Dragon Lord (Preteen/early teens) (Fantasy)

The Irish Wizard (Upper middle grade) (Urban Fantasy)

SHORT STORIES

Urban Fantasy

Eternally Late

Dealings With Joe

Glimpses (short story in That Moment When Anthology)

Contemporary

The Brat Next Door

Fantasy LitRPG

(Set in the same world as Guardians Of The Round Table Series)

Tales Of Inadon 1: The Disc (Co-written with Storm and Rhys Petersen) (short story in Game On! Anthology)

Post Apocalyptic Sci-Fi

Compulsive Directive

NONFICTION

A Year Of Weekly Writing Exercises (Creative Writing)

Cooking For Families With Allergies (Cooking) (Co-written with Storm Petersen)

Tell Me A Story, Grandma (Memoir)

For the most up to date details on available titles visit:

www.avrilsabine.com/books/bibliography

Disclaimer

This is a work of fiction. Names, characters, businesses, places, events and incidents are either the products of the author's imagination or used in a fictitious manner. Any resemblance to actual persons, living or dead, or actual events is purely coincidental. The opinions expressed or beliefs held are those of the characters and should not be assumed to be the opinions or beliefs of the author.

www.ingramcontent.com/pod-product-compliance
Lightning Source LLC
Chambersburg PA
CBHW030953190726
48285CB00004BB/1317